Dreaming the Enemy

David Metzenthen

Dreaming the Enemy

ALLEN&UNWIN
SYDNEY • MELBOURNE • AUCKLAND • LONDON

This project is supported by the Victorian Government
through Creative Victoria.

First published by Allen & Unwin in 2016

Allen & Unwin
83 Alexander Street
Crows Nest NSW 2065
Australia
Phone: (61 2) 8425 0100
Email: info@allenandunwin.com
Web: www.allenandunwin.com

Allen & Unwin – UK
Ormond House, 26–27 Boswell Street,
London WC1N 3JZ, UK
Phone: +44 (0) 20 8785 5995
Email: info@murdochbooks.co.uk
Web: www.murdochbooks.co.uk

A Cataloguing-in-Publication entry is available from the
National Library of Australia: www.trove.nla.gov.au. A catalogue record for
this book is available from the British Library.

ISBN (AUS) 978 1 76011 225 7
ISBN (UK) 978 1 74336 874 9

Teachers' notes available from www.allenandunwin.com

Cover and text design by Bruno Herfst
Cover images by Larry Burrows/Getty and williammpark/Shutterstock
Set in 10.75pt FreightText Pro by Midland Typesetters, Australia
Printed in Australia by McPherson's Printing Group

10 9 8 7 6 5 4 3 2 1

In memory of Hamish William O'Donnell,
a young man of pictures, words, music, love.

My friends have been the trees, the sun, the stars.
My relatives are the grass, the fish, the birds,
the ants...

—an Australian Vietnam War veteran's
words on life after combat

'Charlie' was a common name given to Vietnamese enemy forces in the Vietnam War by Australian troops.

SLR is the abbreviation for Self Loading Rifle, an assault weapon carried by Australian soldiers in Vietnam. M16 is the name of an American-made assault rifle also carried by Australian soldiers in Vietnam. The AK-47 was an assault rifle carried by many North Vietnamese fighters.

One

They'd played Samurai all summer holidays, Johnny remembered, like the show on TV. Long sticks for swords. Short sticks for star knives. And that Aboriginal kid, David, who was staying at someone's house for a month, played the game harder than anybody else. Jesus, that old Davey-boy was fierce; Johnny almost smiled. And he'd always insisted on being Shintaro, the good guy.

Johnny looked across the dull green water of the inlet and let his thoughts wander. It was always Shintaro and Tombei against the marauding forces of the evil Iga Ninja. So Johnny had to settle for being a bad guy that January. And maybe he still was, he decided, although Vietnam was nothin' like Japan and Australia was nothin' like either of them.

Looking back on days of fighting without hurting anybody, Johnny felt something collapse. How had he gone from a kid holding out a hanky to a fallen warrior to someone casually tossing grenades down an enemy bunker? How had he gone from a kid swinging a stick as a Samurai sword, the star of a flickering home movie, to a nineteen-year-old digger on ambush, prepared to shoot someone in the side of the head?

At school, teachers said Johnny Shoebridge's stories lacked imagination. Now he seemed to have too much of the bloody stuff. He could call up everything, anything, anyone, and anywhere from here and over there at any time. There was the spray of freckles on Jillian Goldsborough's bare back. There was the sick crunch of a black scorpion under a jungle boot. There was the severed brown hand found after a firefight. There was the smack of a bullet hitting a jaw. Johnny could recall *everything*; even shit he hadn't truly seen or done.

Johnny Shoebridge had perfect recall of one million chopped-up moments, real and imagined. His memory could take him up the narrowest jungle track. His mind could follow any bullet fired, any soldier seen, leaf touched, sound heard, word spoken, smell smelled, or wound inflicted. So it was hard to see a country kid, with a shoe-brown Sherrin footy tucked under one arm, making any sort of a comeback after a year patrolling in the Vietnamese scrub.

Yet here he was trying to do just that. Johnny Shoebridge was sitting on a rock by an inlet in southern New South Wales, trying to fix his head. A single bird call, like a spoon striking metal, came across the water. This, Johnny decided, was a signal that it was time for a smoke. So he lit a Marlboro, smoked it, and felt a little bit better for just a few minutes.

The opposite shore pressed itself on his eyes. Not a soul to be seen. White sand. Hot rock. Dry bush. Silver driftwood. Here might be a good place, he reckoned, to make some kind of a stand. Yes, he would be like the Lone Ranger, without Lex and Barry, or any of the other boys. And yes, it would have to be without the assistance of Brother Rifle, because he was no longer a soldier in any way, shape, or form – except in the dark pressing reaches of his mind.

But them was the breaks.

Two

The surface of the grey laminex kitchen table reminded Johnny of an aerial photograph of a U.S. airstrike. It was amazing how quickly, he thought, bombs turned the skin of the earth into a lunar landscape. He sat back, looked up at the white plastic light fitting, and knew that there was an awful lot of stuff that he wished he didn't know. Johnny's mum, April, sat across the table, her hands loosely linked as if she was considering saying grace, or perhaps offering up a small prayer to help the conversation along.

'Go away for a couple of weeks, John.' Carefully April poured tea from a yellow pot into a yellow cup. She looked up. 'Don says take the shop ute. Visit Viv. Or drive to the coast. Think things through.' Now April Collins advanced a hand towards Johnny's knuckles and made gentle contact. 'Give yourself some time before you see Jilly again, don't you think? Things'll get better. Let some stuff settle.'

Things get better? Settle? Jesus. If only he thought they

ever would or could. Johnny gave his mum a smile because she was trying hard.

'Yeah, I might take off for a while.' He reclaimed his hand. 'Good if I did, I guess.'

April Shoebridge sipped tea with sudden enthusiasm, put her cup down smartly.

'I think so.' She nodded, as if she was sure they were onto a winner. 'You can work things out, John. It'll all come right in the end. Back to normal. You'll see. You'll be right.'

Johnny considered that highly unlikely but the advice was better than anything he could come up with, so he chose to take it.

'I will,' he said. 'Clear me head.' *Of landmines*, he was tempted to add, but figured he'd spooked the old girl enough with his sitting in the backyard, smoking and talking to the little black ants that he admired a lot.

'Hullo there, boys.' Johnny would watch them running here, there, and everywhere. 'What are yers up to today? Out and about? Keepin' busy?'

Great little fellers, the ants, Johnny thought, wishing he was one and could do ant things, think ant thoughts, and that would be that. But he wasn't an ant. So he'd take the ute, give his sister a miss, and head to the coast – with the few hundred bucks his mother had pushed across the table as if she was paying to see his poker cards.

A day later Johnny said goodbye to Cam, his fat, simple mate who traipsed around Taralia, shoes on the wrong feet, in a happy world of his own. Then, driving slowly, Johnny shook loose the small dry town as he juddered out over the railway line, leaving its bare hills and struggling sheep farms to finish off a hard summer without him.

'Gimme air.' Johnny spoke to the shotgun-blasted population sign. 'Or somethin'.' He accelerated, thinking at least he was going forwards, hopefully not into an ambush as he'd been there, done that, and had not enjoyed it one little bloody bit.

Three

Green men spread out in green bush. Silently each rifle-man swivelled through the heavy heat, independent but chain-linked. The hush in the heavy undergrowth was like unexpressed hate. Look. Listen. Smell.

Wait out.

Nothing.

All clear.

Move on.

Johnny looked around, up, sideways, down, and inwards. There was nothing he recognised in this place, not even himself. He was now fair and square in the middle of the Asian killing fields. His past was flying away at a million miles an hour. His future was one step away.

Or less.

Johnny heard that single bright bird call – *tonk!* – come across the calm green inlet. Yes, he was listening to the bush and looking at the water but he was thinking about Lex and Barry, wondering where they were at this moment. Somewhere? Nowhere? Everywhere?

He rubbed out his cigarette and buried the butt. Ask the Vietnamese where the boys were, he thought. It was Charlie who wrote the book on the spirits of the dead. Civilian or soldier, friend or foe, Charlie had the lowdown on the life hereafter; never forget them, was basically it. Offer them what you could. Give them what you had. Visit their soul place. Stay tuned to Radio Deceased.

I will, Johnny thought, scanning the beach, his heart keeping time, insisting on slow searching for camouflaged humans hiding in the bleached dunes or the low patchy scrub. Was that the bottomless black hole of a rifle muzzle? A square of green cloth? A trip wire? Did that leaf twitch or twig snap? No, there were only five grey gulls loitering at the waterline because this was February, Australia, 1973, and Johnny knew he shouldn't have a worry in the world.

Wrong.

'Jesus,' he murmured, his eyes narrowing, jaw tightening. 'Where'd she come from?'

A girl wearing a white dress sat in the low grassy dunes looking at the water, hands locked around her knees. Shoey appreciated her stillness, her slender bare arms and brown legs, but he wondered *how* he'd missed her because he had not missed much over there. Johnny Shoebridge had walked point as good as anyone. Still, it was a terrible mistake because he held the lives of all the boys in his hands. Or he had once. Now he pretty much held nothing but a pack of smokes and a few lost souls.

Settle down, Lex said, looking at him from under a wide, pale brow, his hair the colour of dry grass. *Those lovely days in the jungle have gone, feller. Relax. You're not dead. You're just a country-and-western lunatic trying to get your shit together. Buy a Cat Stevens record, man. Get on the peace train.*

Yeah, get a grip, Barry added. *You're home and hosed in the land of the living. Maybe a 'roo or two loose in the top paddock, bud, but eh, the beer's cold and the fight's fuckin' over. Move on.*

'I wish I could,' Johnny murmured, but he knew the fight wasn't over, he wasn't home and hosed, and he was not even close to getting his act together.

Right now a newsreel was running in his head starring himself, Andrew Lexington, Barry Grainger, and thirty of the other Delta Company boys. Out they scrambled from hovering Hueys like green seeds from steel pods, shit-scared as they hit the deck in a landing zone so hot it smoked. Weapons up, pounded by down force, loaded like donkeys, they scanned the waving bush as more choppers dropped in and more diggers scrambled out.

'It is *over*.' Johnny looked at waves breaking white at the mouth of the inlet. 'It is finished. It is done.' Except

9

that memories with the weight of a lake were flooding the deepest valleys of his mind. 'Oh, Jesus. *Now* what?'

The girl had seen him. So Johnny raised a hand, impressed he'd been able to do that. I am not the enemy, he thought. Anymore. Or among the enemy. Nor am I a ghost. Although I do know quite a few, brown and white, it has to be said.

Four

Johnny had first glimpsed that skinny, quick Main Force enemy fighter in a battle in the Suoi Chau Pha valley. He hadn't had time to kill the guy as the young bastard in black sprinted between rice paddies while American Cobra gunships tore the village apart. But he'd had too much time to ever forget him. So Johnny gave him a name and a life because they'd crossed paths more than once in the war, and now it seemed they would cross paths always.

Johnny called the fighter Khan. He was tall for a Vietnamese and perhaps older than the other two guerrillas he ran with. All were soldiers who'd most likely trekked south for months down the Ho Chi Minh Trail to join the fierce D555 battalion. This battalion, living deep in the caves of the haunted Long Hai Hills south of Nui Dat, had the sworn duty of removing Johnny Shoebridge's Royal Australian Regiment from the very ground they stood on.

Johnny fired five times at the fast-moving Khan, dirt and water spitting up around the Viet Cong's knees. Then incredibly the skinny bastard stopped, turned, levelled his weapon, a weapon with a bayonet, and aimed. Johnny threw himself sideways as half a dozen bullets chopped yellow chunks from the trees around him.

'Faaaark!'

Johnny fired again but with true VC flair the fighters disappeared into the bamboo as smoke and fire bloomed over thatched roofs, people and animals died, and the volume of the battle doubled – as did Johnny's fear.

That morning his fear was so great it felt as if he was lying naked between screaming sawmill blades. Things flashed from the tree line. Metal whipped by his face. Greasy black clouds billowed and through them the Cobras dived, flex guns roaring, rockets ripping, the enemy dead accumulating to wash carelessly in crazed waves as muddy geysers rose and fell across the flooded rice paddy.

That was the first time Johnny and Khan had tried to kill each other. Now the Viet Cong fighter wandered Shoey's mind at will, rising from cover, a wraith with an AK-47, only to slip silently back into the jungle of twisted dreams and a faulty imagination. So Johnny had to live with the enemy he'd dubbed, Vietnamese-style, Older Brother, as compared to the two younger fighters he'd seen that morning.

In this way Khan had taken Johnny prisoner, and Johnny knew that if he didn't somehow neutralise the ghostly enemy, he'd remain a prisoner of war for the rest of his life, possibly even after.

'Jesus *Christ.*' Folding his arms, Johnny figured he had a fair idea what Lex might say about the situation – if he wasn't dead.

I suggest you smoke plenty of dope, Johnny-boy. Lex would make his I'm-really-serious-about-this face and nod his beachside blond head. *Move to Byron, wear a sarong, live up a tree. Pretty soon you won't remember a thing. Take Barry with you. He'd love to be a vegetarian.*

Barry, if he also wasn't dead, would nail Lex with his bushman's stare honed and hardened under twenty searing country summers.

You hippy poofter long-haired dole-bludging uni wanker.

And Johnny would have laughed; even now he might have smiled if he could remember how.

You can never go back. Shoey had heard that said a lot but it was bullshit. He couldn't stop going back. That was the problem. There was nothing that could be unseen or undone, but that did not stop him revisiting the battlefields again and again. And everything from the simple to the brutal was there to be relived.

The touch of a ponytail of a dead female fighter was seared like a brand on his brain. The afternoon Lex tie-dyed Barry's army shirt pink was there. As was the evening Barry machinegunned Lex's bamboo flute, the morning they saved a pup from a Vietnamese butcher, the cool click and cold glint of new ammo, the dark grace of an oiled weapon, the long shot that hit a distant head, the frightful scream from a deep black valley that no one was ever going to investigate. It was the complete catalogue of chaos, carnage, and beauty, every moment perfectly preserved then pinned on the page like rare, dead insects, most poisonous, a few perfect.

And when Cam Pyke, Johnny's Simple Simon mate from Taralia, asked him what the war was like, Johnny's answer was weightless.

'Terrible, mate.' He'd dropped a hand on the big boy's shoulder. 'You don't wanna know, Cam. Bloody awful.'

'Guns and things, Johnny?' Cam had looked at him hopefully. 'Jets? Bombs? Noisy?'

'Too noisy.' Johnny had evaded everything by offering the kid a chocolate Paddle Pop and a pack of Juicy Fruit chewing gum. 'Deafening.'

Maybe, Johnny thought, to be born thick might just be a blessing.

The girl in white walked in Johnny's direction. Don't panic, he told himself. Light a smoke. Pretend you're normal and she'll be on her way in two shakes of a lamb's tail. Briefly she disappeared behind a boatshed then reappeared. Hands held low, she picked her way along the rocky path, lean-limbed, skin coloured dark by the sun. Now she was close, too close, Johnny thought, but there was nothing he could do about that. Spotting him, she pulled up, crossing her arms.

'Gidday,' Johnny said. 'How yer goin'?'

A spray of gum leaves framed her like an old-fashioned photograph.

'All right,' she said, without feeling. 'You?'

Johnny lit a cigarette. Let smoke out in a tight grey stream.

'Yeah, fine. Nice place.' It sounded wrong, the words grinding like shovelled stones. 'Spot on.'

The girl held worn pink thongs against a plain dress that wasn't new, looked cheap, and had a couple of dirty lines on it as if she'd leant against a wire fence. Johnny was aware of his army shirt, the only shirt he wore that didn't feel like it belonged to a kid who'd passed away years ago.

'I seen you drive down.' She smiled, a flash of teeth, maybe one missing. 'Y'in the army? Yer shirt 'n' hair 'n' that. Yer look like it.'

Johnny choked on words. Images leapt out of the fiery pit; of a bad battle, the worst battle, the boys fighting for their lives, and losing.

'I was, yeah,' he said. 'But I'm out now.'

He felt she looked at him as if he was a decent but unknown dog: had decided he was not dangerous, to her, anyhow. She tucked dark hair back with thin, supple-looking fingers.

'I sit there sometimes, too.' Surprising him, she sat a couple of yards away on a flat rock, eyes on the green water, assessing it. 'The tide's turned. Sharks come in on it. And rays. Big black ones. Dolphins, too.'

Johnny looked at the inlet. He could see the water moving as a whole, inland. Sharks and stingrays. Jesus. If only they were all he had to deal with. It was peculiar, he thought, that what worried him now had no heartbeat, did not sleep, did not breathe, but existed only in his head. The too-real had become the unreal. The dead had re-joined the living. The survivors became the casualties. And those three young VC fighters whom he'd fought tracked him endlessly, led by Khan – a trio of ghosts that had locked onto him as he'd once locked onto them, with no mercy in mind.

'Jesus, sharks.' Johnny tried to sound concerned. 'Gee.'

The girl told him her name was Carly, she didn't have a job, and she lived up the river. She knocked back the smoke he offered.

'Sometimes I work for Malcolm.' She pointed where the strip of riverside bush gave way to hilly green paddocks. 'Whatever needs doin'. He owns all that land up there. So what d'you do now?' She glanced at him. 'If you don't mind me askin'.'

Johnny liked her simple way of talking. Straightforward. No bullshit. He judged that she had grown up in a poor family

16

in a hard place. A girl who spent more time in a paddock or packing shed than in front of a mirror.

'I'm recoverin'.' He took a drag, managed a weak grin, like adding sugar to bad coffee. 'From Vietnam. I hope.'

She nodded. 'Right.'

Her hands were lithe and veined. Thin gold rings pierced her ears. She wasn't flat-chested but wore no bra, as if she'd put on her clothes without a thought, as if she neither expected nor cared about running into anyone.

'You went there?' She looked at him with eyes that were more silver than blue. He couldn't imagine her going to school or reading a book. There was something wild about her, as if she was connected to this place but not the people. 'That war.'

'I did.' The size of the experience was like a tidal wave sweeping through a slum. Total chaos. 'Not much chop.' He exhaled. 'Really. At all.'

'I bet.' She dropped a small white shell into the water. 'I seen it on TV. Horrible. Swamps. Fires. Them little guys. The helicopters an' jets.'

Her tone held him. He looked at her for more than a moment. What could she see? What did she know? There was a thoughtful stillness to her, even in this place of bright sunshine and clean water that pushed Vietnam further back into its own endless maze of shadows and fear.

'I thought the beach might help.' He wondered if she might be someone he could tell a little of the truth to.

'A few waves and some blue sky. A bit of peace and quiet. Some drinking. A fair bit of that.' He found a laugh, a poor one.

'The beach helps me.' She tossed another tiny shell, the size of a fingernail, into the water. 'But I ain't been where you been.'

He wanted to tell her that she mightn't have seen what he'd seen or done what he'd done, but she was soothing him bit by bit as if he was a shocked horse. He took a risk.

'Is there a place I can stay around here?'

She looked over Johnny's head, up the open slope then back again, to him and the water gently nudging the sand.

'Malcolm's got an old fishin' hut a bit along the river. He'd let yer use it, I reckon. It's rough, but.'

Johnny nodded. 'No problem. How do I find him?'

'I'll show ya.' She stood, dropped her thongs, and slipped her feet into them. 'We can walk. Over the hill. Not far. Five minutes.'

Johnny could see a farm gate that opened into a lumpy paddock. No house in sight. He also saw, as he stood, she had a short fixed-blade hunting knife in her pocket. Weapon or tool, he didn't care. He was sure she had her reasons.

The farm was like an odd little country village, Shoey thought. Large machinery sheds and two cottages were sited at a respectful distance around a low white homestead. The galvanised-iron roofs were a flaking cherry red.

'How many people live here?' Johnny surveyed the place: old and worn but grand and strange.

'One.' Carly shrugged, opened another gate, let Johnny through. 'Malcolm's family got it all a real long time ago.'

A long valley widened behind the homestead. Like a painting on a butcher's wall, Johnny thought; cattle grazing in the blue shadows of white gums and camel-humped hills. He climbed steps to stand with Carly under vines that released an old-fashioned fruity smell that he didn't like. Through a window he could see an upright piano and paintings in gold frames. A dog yapped.

'Freddy.' Carly stared at her feet. 'Malcolm's home.'

A sausage dog appeared, followed by a man who Johnny reckoned had to be six foot six. His face was long and craggy, his shoulders were broad and straight, but he looked worn-out and stiff rather than strong.

'Afternoon.' The farmer stepped out onto the veranda.

Johnny waited for him to say more but he didn't.

'Hi, Malcolm.' Carly brushed away the webs of silence by introducing Johnny. In ten seconds she outlined his story.

'I'll pay,' Shoey said. 'I'm from the bush. I won't burn it down.' It stuck in his guts to have to justify himself to anyone.

'Not necessary.' Malcolm took a step back. 'Just give it a sweep. Carly will get you a broom. There might also be a lantern in the tractor shed.' He nodded. 'I'll see you later.'

And he was gone, followed by Freddy who waddled import-
antly away, as if he also was six foot six.

It struck Johnny as bizarre that a country where one
person could own so much would bother to declare war on a
country where men owned so little. Then it struck him: that
was the reason.

Five

When Shoey's number was drawn from a barrel by a Test cricketer on TV, he didn't know what to say. All he could do was watch as his mum leant forward, hid her face, and cried. For the moment, Donald, Shoey's stepfather, sat unmoving, his combed hair catching yellow lamplight. A newspaper was draped over his knees like a blanket.

'The mongrels.' Then Donald got up awkwardly, as if there was someone he wanted to argue with. He glared at the TV. 'The *bastards*. I'm really sorry, John.' He went over and put an arm around Johnny's mother, spoke to her bowed head. 'It'll work out, April. He might not end up going, anyway. It's not always straightforward.'

'Well, this'll be interesting.' Johnny sat back, arms crossed, thinking, *I am in the bloody army. They bloody got me;* which would be somewhat of a change from Donald's furniture shop, where he'd spent the last year pretending to care about three-seater lounges and tartan recliner-rockers.

Johnny took in a big breath that did not seem big enough. 'Well, holy hell. There you go then.' He figured there was nothing much to add, although he knew there would be at a later date.

There'd be plenty.

The next day, as hot as the one before, Johnny walked through the backstreets of Taralia towards the cemetery. Brown grass held on grimly and small houses brooded behind pulled blinds. He felt as if he was being cooked under a magnifying glass.

Johnny thought about his dad. Les had been a bloke born for work and grateful for it. He would have seen Johnny's call-up as something serious that the country required; not good but no argument given. Les would've taken Johnny to the Woolpack Hotel, found a quiet corner, and lifted a pot of Carlton in his direction.

Cheers, mate. They would've have clicked rims. *Proud of ya, son. Look after yourself. You'll be right.*

And that would've been that.

Johnny navigated rows of graves until he stood in front of a headstone the dull grey of new track ballast. That, at least, would've pleased Les, he thought. A railway man to the last.

Johnny, standing in the middle of a grim sea of memorials, looked around. It was unbelievable that he could be ordered to join the army, no questions asked or answered.

How could people he didn't know, people out of sight and reach, have such power? At some level, it had to be wrong.

Who was he going to fight anyway?

Yeah, the Viet Cong, he knew that much. Seen them on TV. Little fellers in black shorts, nooses around their necks, hands tied behind their backs as they were hauled out of marshes at gunpoint. To Johnny they didn't look much but he got the feeling there was a calculated deadliness to them, viperous, cruel, and ugly. If he ended up in those rice paddies, it was going to be a nightmare; he would have to kill those people, him, Johnny Shoebridge, with his own hands. Or get killed. In that one moment, knowing this, that it was real, he was changed forever.

Johnny looked at his hands; they were square-palmed, tanned, and strong from storeroom work and season after season of footy and cricket. What they were capable of he had no idea, but he had the feeling one day he'd find out. Kneeling, he touched the grey marble bed with two fingers, registering the heat of the sun stored in the stone.

'I'll see yer, Les.' The grave was unyielding. So he spoke to the dry brown hills that ringed the town. 'Soon.' Or as soon as might be humanly possible.

He and Jilly sat in the ute at the Taralia lookout. Below, the town was mapped by a scatter of lights that faded out along the train line. The football ground was lit up like a landing pad, the Tigers' pre-season well underway. Next to it the trotting track glowed like a spaceship. This spelled out, Johnny figured, what the town rated important. He felt he'd been separated out, like a sheep for export.

Jilly Goldsborough looked at him steadily. Her blue eyes were bracketed by curly hair the colour of varnished pine. Her fingertips, pink-nailed and neat, sought each other out.

'So what about us, Johnny? When you leave.'

Two days ago he'd paused at the gilt-edged window of James Scott Jewellers. Engagement rings in heart-shaped beds of blue velvet reminded him of sideshow prizes, a bit too glittery to be true. He'd walked on, his future changed by people in Canberra, a place he'd seen on TV that looked like a laboratory complex.

'I'll go away—' He laughed softly, his eyes on the town surrounded by darkness. 'Then I'll come back. That's the theory.'

'And we'll pick up just where we left off?' Jilly posed the question like she posed all her questions; quietly confident she had some idea about the answer. 'All set to go. Maybe?'

She'd done better at school than he had. Not that she mentioned it or either of them cared; it just wasn't important in the overall scheme of things. The two had paired up as if directed by a dancing teacher. It had seemed inevitable then but it didn't seem like that now. A wild card had been dealt and Johnny had picked it up.

Jilly looked down on the straight wide streets where hardly a car moved, every family in every house in for the evening. 'Well, we might,' she added, answering her own question. 'I hope.'

Taralia, Johnny knew, was a place as solid as the Commonwealth Savings Bank. Here folks liked wool, wheat, footy, cricket, T-bone steak, Carlton Draught, Peters Ice Cream, the news, and the weather. And they expected weddings after engagements and no backing out.

'Good as I can do, kid. At this point.' Johnny felt too much was being asked of him by too many people. And there was the knowledge conferred upon him by his country, not to be shared with civilians, as unfathomable as space, that he had been designated as a killer. 'I'm not lying.'

Jilly studied him. 'You never do.' She squeezed his hand, hard, as if it was half-punishment. 'I love you anyway, Johnny. And always.'

Anyway or *any* way? Always or *all* ways? These were questions that could not be answered – not at this time. Maybe later, maybe a couple of years down the track, when he might know what sort of a person he had become.

'I love you, too.' And that was the truth, as far as Johnny Shoebridge could see that Saturday night. 'I promise.'

Six

Johnny sat on the army bus next to a lanky bloke who'd folded sharp elbows and bony knees into the window seat. The guy wore white jeans, no socks, brown desert boots, and looked out of the window, Johnny reckoned, as if he was checking for chicks on a school excursion. But there weren't going to be too many girls out here. Melbourne had dropped way back as the old coach laboured up the Hume Highway.

'Never thought I'd be doing this.' The guy forked long fingers through wavy blond hair. 'Not in a million years. The army. Far out, they wouldn't even let me bring my stick. Brand new. Trigger Brothers. Bummer, eh? Good waves in Asia. So Captain Goodvibes tells me in *Tracks*.'

Johnny guessed the feller was talking about surfing. He looked like a surfer. Well, he didn't look like a country boy. And he didn't sound like one, either. Clipped his words then dispensed them neatly and effortlessly. Never been within a hundred miles of Taralia High, Johnny thought. Or had an old man who only spoke about the weather, work, beer, and football.

'Where ya from?' Johnny figured he might as well ask, since they had a couple of years together to get through.

The guy didn't look at Johnny, as if he'd worked him out, trusted him already.

'Black Rock. Melbourne. Bayside. You?'

'The bush, mate.' Johnny felt rough and ready but proud enough. 'Taralia, mate. Past Ballarat. Home of the mighty Tigers. Who haven't won a flag for forty years.'

'Good stuff.' The boy put out a wide, flat hand. 'Andrew Lexington. Call me Lex.'

They shook hands. Johnny named himself, noting that Lex wore bright knotted cord bracelets, and a leopard-spotted cowrie shell on a leather necklace. That shit'd be gone in a flash, he thought, as well as the long hair and the bloody ridiculous no-socks bit.

'When we finish with this crap,' Lex continued, 'which I cannot fucking believe, you and me are going surfing, Johnny-boy. It's gunna be one long hot summer of sex, sand, Southern Comfort, peroxide, and reckless Kombi-driving.'

To Johnny that seemed like a great idea although he'd never been surfing, had only ever seen a Kombi on TV, and hated Southern Comfort like poison. He could at least picture a beach without too much difficulty: long and empty at sunset, breaking waves, a warm wind blowing in his face and tickling his stomach, the army-thing fading like the spreading rings of a skipped stone until there was nothing to see but smooth water.

'I'm in.' Johnny nodded with conviction. 'Bloody oath. We'll drive to Darwin. Make five grand on the prawn trawlers. Then do it all again.'

The bus crawled into the Puckapunyal Army Camp as if it was going to die there. When it stopped among blue wooden buildings the boys jumped up, cheered, and smacked on the seats. This stopped as soon as a big man in uniform stepped aboard – a big man who shouted at them non-stop for the next three months. Then it was on to Cobungra for jungle warfare training, and a ship that sailed from Sydney. Johnny could hardly believe any of it.

'It's embarrassing, Shoebridge,' Lex said, staring at his beer on the bar, on the Friday night before they sailed for Vietnam. 'How shit I am at the piano but how good I am with a rifle.' He drank, adam's apple sliding, put down the empty glass. 'My mother teaches music. She'd be appalled.'

'I'm not.' Johnny folded up shirt sleeves on arms that were bigger and stronger than they'd ever been. 'I'm bloody rapt. You keep it up.'

Lex looked thoughtful. 'Yeah, I suppose flattening the little bastards with a saxophone was never going to be practical. Looks like we're gunna have to shoot them after all.'

Johnny sipped Sydney beer. 'All going well.' For two, maybe three seconds, in the shallow lines on Lex's face and the strange, changing light in his eyes, Johnny understood the complexity and seriousness of what they were being sent to do. 'All goin' well.'

'Can't get my head around it,' Lex said suddenly, rearing back, as if from the very idea. He looked at Johnny. 'Me? Us? You? Shooting people? Shooting them *dead*? Jesus Christ.' Lex pulled his chin in. 'It's fuckin' crazy.'

Johnny knew a wildfire about to start when he saw one.

'Yeah, but that's the story, mate.' He fixed the tall boy next to him with a stare and held him to it. 'It's us or them, Lexy. It's you and me and the boys. We'll be right. Gotta be done. Only forwards. Yeah? Together. The boys.'

Lex looked away, not to break contact with Johnny but perhaps to align himself truly, make the change, accept finally Johnny's pact then lock it in.

'Yeah, I know,' he said finally, staring into space where the unfathomable lurked. 'I know.'

'We do.' Johnny held up two fingers to the barman, handed over a fiver, nodded his thanks. 'We look after each other, mate. We get home.' He tapped Lex's glass with his own, felt as if he was shoring up a framework, hammering props in to support the ceiling of a dark and dangerous mine. 'We do what it takes.'

Lex hunched his shoulders, shivered, picked up his beer, and raised it.

'And if that includes giving them money or drugs to fuck off, so be it.'

Johnny laughed. They were on their way. Already gone. Never to return to this place and even if they did, nothing would ever be the same.

Seven

For a while Johnny and Carly sat in silence on the steps of Malcolm's hut. There was a feeling to the place like the minutes before sleep, a feeling that took Johnny to a phantom village in the Red River Delta, a part of Vietnam, way up north, where he'd never been.

This dreamed-up village was home to the three fighters who had tracked him for a year and tracked him now. He could see skinny Khan and the two others, one hardly more than a kid, the other hard-muscled and square-faced as the trio walked in the cool evening by a wide river, passing through sighing stands of bamboo.

'We will go,' said Khan. 'We will fight. We will win. And we will come home.'

Shoey could see that the boys stood secure in the loop of Khan's words. He also knew the enemy fighters felt the power and pull of the land because it was theirs – and Johnny had never felt it over there, because it wasn't his. And that made a whole world of difference.

Tomorrow, the northern troops would begin the long march down the Ho Chi Minh Trail to join the war. They would trek onwards until the distance travelled, and time passed, would probably be too great for news of them to ever return. And then they truly would have united with their comrades in the south – because that was how, Johnny knew, the North Vietnamese thought, fought, and won.

The single bright birdcall from across the inlet dragged him back to the present. Carly was looking at him. He shrugged, letting out a breath that felt like an admission of guilt.

'I drift off.' This was no great explanation. 'I see things.' He managed a laugh. 'War movies. Long ones. Bad ones. Shockers. They just roll on and on.' He lit a cigarette, all he could think to do. 'My head's stuffed. Fair dinkum. I thought doing the shit was difficult. Well, forgettin' it's twice as hard.'

Carly sat with her elbows on her knees and her chin on her hands. She looked across the water, where shadows darkened below a wall of sheer rock.

'Yeah, you think stuff's gone just because it's over.' She said each word carefully. 'Then you find out it's not over at all. It stays with yer. For a long time and in a lotta ways. I don't know much but I do know that.'

Johnny knew when someone was talking from experience.

'Hit the nail on the head there, boss,' he said. 'Things happen. You do 'em or they happen to yer. Or yer just there. And boy, they stick like glue.'

'It's always people.' Carly looked over the water. 'Always people.'

Johnny Shoebridge could not argue with that.

Eight

Johnny was at a loss for what to do next, so he stayed on the step drinking beers. He'd watched Carly leave, then he'd watched another Vietnamese village rise from the still, black surface of the inlet. This village, sited deep among palm trees and spiked bamboo fences, exuded the silent menace of a set trap. And the harder he searched the place the less he could see; every space and surface created a mosaic of foreignness that deflected his senses until all he saw was a blur of leafy colours in a haze of humidity.

What Johnny could picture, though, were the muzzles of weapons and black eyes searching for white foreheads to put bullets into. He clearly sensed the enemy and the electrifying hatred that short-circuited into a blinding flash of recognition that he was *also* the enemy – which is why those invisible men wanted to kill *him*, and that was the truth. Anger struck, like the concussion of the bombs that soon after had blown that distant village to bits.

I was *sent* there!

It was *not* my idea to kill those people or change their lives.

With that thought, Johnny managed to punch a way through to clear air. Thank God he was here in a place of gumtrees, clean sand, and open country where a stranger was allowed to pass. Here there was no enemy. Here there was no razor-edged monster grass, no strangler vine, no silky bamboo that looked so beautiful but was only ever useful, in one hundred ways, to the Viet Cong.

'You're safe, buddy-boy.' Johnny was getting used to talking to himself. 'As houses.' He blew out a breath, lit a smoke and tried to think of Jilly, but she was too far away in too many ways to help.

So Johnny thought of Carly, a girl with cheap clothes, lank hair, and a punched-out tooth. A girl with something terrible locked down inside that allowed her to see there was something terrible locked down in him. Yes, the wounded understood each other. Yes, sorrow did take comfort in company. No, he didn't think either of them had quite given up, and that was what counted. Johnny realised he was thankful he had met her.

It was that uninvited skinny Viet Cong bastard, Khan, who insisted Johnny take up his story. Was it guilt, Johnny wondered? Was it punishment? Was it a soldier's unfinished business that never could be finished? Was it a death sentence commuted to life imprisonment? Or was it a way out? That perhaps he and Khan might somehow fight, or find their way, to an end of things? Because at the moment Johnny Shoebridge was ten thousand light years away from such a point, if it existed.

Johnny felt strongly that this soldier from North Vietnam had survived the war. So he let Khan go home, and become a fisherman, because that's what a lot of North Vietnamese did. And now he could see him fishing in a pond with three slender bamboo rods angled against a blue sky. Johnny also saw that the young man now had only one arm, which didn't make the fishing any easier. But he seemed to be getting along with it okay, so Johnny let the feller he called Khan fish on.

'Maybe I don't wish you luck, sport,' Johnny murmured, looking at the inlet, seeing the water was still, the tide not yet turned. 'But I would if you'd give me some peace and bloody quiet.'

In a bucket beside Khan, Johnny saw a few slender fish faced in the same direction, like desperate soldiers under attack. So where, he wondered, were Khan's two mates? The young one, whom he'd decided to call Trung, and the tough, square-headed one he'd named Thang?

Johnny figured they were dead. Perhaps they'd copped it in an ambush, or when Shoey's boys had taken on D555 in the big night battles for an Australian fire base out in the boonies, where the slaughter was a horror show of two parts that left no one unharmed.

He saw his old enemy Khan wore a faded green bush fighting hat as he fished. Perhaps he treasured it like Johnny treasured his army shirts? Maybe Khan felt this hat was symbolic of his time on the Trail, a reminder of the lives of his best friends, and their year of fighting from the Long Hai Hills with D555. But now you're a fisherman, Johnny decided, which is a pretty sweet occupation for a killer.

Perhaps I won't go down that road, he thought, being a killer myself. Perhaps we'll look in another direction for the moment. So he let Khan's attention wander to a path where a young woman, dressed in black, walked so lightly that she did not raise even the smallest puffs of dust. Elegantly she passed although she carried a full basket of vegetables and a hoe.

The girl's face was hidden under a traditional woven reed hat but Shoey knew she would be graceful and lovely. Khan waved but the girl did not wave back. Stick to the fishing, Johnny advised his old enemy. You're not doing so good with the ladies, sport – or anything or anyone else, for that matter.

'And neither am I.' Johnny opened another can, sipped cold Carlton. 'It seems.' Maybe, he figured, if he simply allowed the war to wind and unwind in his head, it would eventually reach its own conclusion because as surely as things started they had to end. Surely. 'So,' he said, looking into the starred blackness. 'Let the dogs out.'

Nine

Balloons floated on the wake of the ship like red bubbles on the bright blue sea. A regular soldier whose name was Barry Grainger picked up an M6o machinegun from the steel deck. A long, fully-loaded ammunition belt hung from the black weapon, each brass bullet as long as a cigarette.

'He's strong, that guy.' Lex stood with a boot up on the rail, watching the shooting drill as if he was waiting his turn to throw the javelin at after-school athletics. 'Like a bloody Mack truck. Says about as much. Look at him. Got a tatt for every day of the year. Plays the violin though, John. And sings very nicely, too, I believe. Welsh coal-mining songs. Lovely.'

'He's funny,' Johnny said. 'He cracks me up.'

'Really?' Lex lowered his eyebrows. 'That bastard? How can you tell?'

Johnny laughed. 'Just is, mate. Check him out. Man of steel.'

Barry, his short thick arms badged with tattoos of a tiger and an eagle, brought the big automatic weapon up, aimed, and fired. The sound punched Shoey's guts as empty brass cartridges scattered over the deck like golden hail. In fountains of white the balloons disappeared. Barry lowered the gun and the boys clapped as blue smoke cleared. The smell of gunpowder was like a fiery stain in the hot salty air. The shots seemed to echo endlessly over the ocean.

'Bloody *Bazza*.' Lex looked impressed, nodded with deep satisfaction. 'We definitely need to be mates with him, Shoebridge. You shout the cat a few beers. That'll work.'

Barry Grainger knelt, cleared the machinegun, and left it resting on its bipod. For a moment he talked to Captain McCrae, an ex-rugby league player from Sydney, before rejoining the boys as they stood holding their weapons.

'Good job, Baz,' Lex said. 'Johnny said he'll shout you a few beers. We need you and that machinegun in our section, because if the going gets tough, probably be best if you sort it out. And I don't mean by popping balloons. I mean by assisting the little brown jungle people to piss off as far away from us as possible.'

Barry, expressionless, moved to the rail, leant on his elbows, looked out to sea and spat.

'Well,' he said. 'We'll see.'

Johnny grinned. The bloke was a force of one.

Khan, Trung, and Thang crouched by their tiny fire. A wisp of smoke rose into Johnny's consciousness, unfurling another primitive scroll for him to interpret. Around the trio other men cooked rice or set about slinging hammocks under plastic. The troops from the north had been on the Trail for two months, marching and training. Khan knew he had never been so fit or so thin. He was always hungry but he was used to that.

Already they had buried seven people, their graves hastily dug and blessed beside the track. The equipment and possessions of the dead comrades were distributed among those who marched on. Khan now had an almost-new AK-47 assault rifle with a rare Russian AKM bayonet. Thang also had an AK but Trung carried an old M1 carbine repaired with nylon cord. Still, Khan thought, it was a good weapon in the hands of a committed fighter. He would not put his nose in front of it!

From aluminium bowls the three young men ate sticky rice, Khan looking across the fire, through the smoke.

'Enjoy, comrades,' he said. 'Each grain of rice equals, as they say, one drop of the enemy's blood.'

If only the B-52s had got them then, Johnny thought. If only the Yanks had managed to drop a string of thousand-pound bombs on the whole camp, things might be a whole lot different. But the bombs had missed, like they mostly did, and the Main Force men marched on.

Johnny and Barry stood at the rail, shirts off. Around them the wind flowed like warm water. Somehow, even though Johnny was a conscript and Barry had volunteered, they sensed something right and reliable about each other. In training, Shoey had learned about Vietnam, its people, and the enemy they were being sent to fight. He got the feeling that Barry would simply kill anybody he was ordered to.

'So, Baz, why'd you join up?' Johnny flicked a cigarette butt over the side, watched it tumble away.

Barry rested easily on the rail. He looked at the sea, as far as Johnny could see, without interest. Maybe, Johnny decided, he didn't even see it.

'To get paid,' he said, 'to shoot shit.'

Johnny accepted this. 'Yeah, well, that seems to be the name of the game.'

Barry offered Johnny a Winfield Red. They lit up, turned back to the empty ocean that was a bright azure blue. It looked bottomless, Johnny thought, as unknown as space.

'You are,' Barry said, and took a slow drag, 'on the money.' He looked at Shoey, and for the first and last time Johnny remembered, he grinned.

Ten

Malcolm's one-room hut was certainly simple. Its roof was tin, the floor bare boards, the door and walls painted a faded mossy green. Three of the four windows were broken but Johnny didn't care; there were no corners he couldn't see into and no entry points he could not cover. It was almost as if he was out in the open.

He could think more clearly here than in a house; was able to exercise all his senses, decipher every noise, reassure himself that he was safe for the moment. This place, the hut and the land around it, suited his animal instincts and gut reactions. Somehow the gumtrees, the water, grass, and sky, comforted him. No threat here. Nothing buried or hidden or hanging overhead. No unknown sounds, movements, or threats. Just the reliable presence of the Australian bush. Even so, if he'd had his rifle with a full twenty-shot magazine slotted home, he would've felt a whole lot better. That thing, his SLR, he grieved for like he grieved for the boys.

Shoey glanced into the hut's dark interior. There'd be spiders in the rafters and a snake under the floor but they wouldn't bother him. After the Asian creepy-crawlies he'd lived with – scorpions, leeches, chomper ants, jungle spiders, and tree snakes – Aussie pests, including vandals, seemed downright friendly.

Using three matches, Johnny eventually got the kero lantern lit. Then he swept the joint out properly, finishing at the steps. Glancing up, he saw a shooting star turn into a screaming Phantom jet that hit the enemy's tree line, leaving his mind as scarred as the smoking earth.

What was it like, Johnny wondered, to be where the Phantoms, the B-52s, the Cobras, and that incredible gunship, Spooky, unleashed? How could anyone survive the storms of bullets, bombs, Splintex, rockets, napalm, and white phosphorous? What did you think as you stumbled away, ears and eyes bleeding? Did you ever return to being the person you were? There was no way.

The bastard Khan would know this because he had been with D555, an enemy battalion hit with everything the Aussies and the Yanks had. Yet they'd emerged from the white boulders of the Long Hai Hills like enraged ants, to keep on coming, and were coming still. It seemed there was no way that Johnny could stop them, or this Khan-feller, in particular. Well, there had to be a way because if there wasn't, Johnny Shoebridge knew that sooner rather than later he'd hit the wall big-time, and that'd be that.

Johnny could see that Khan listened to the rain, the one-armed man watching it stream from the eaves of his tiny room. In a small fireplace rice and vegetables simmered in a pot. In front of photos of Thang and Trung josh sticks burned. He saw too that Khan had also placed cigarettes and fruit on a plate. What would he be thinking, Johnny wondered, the returned fighter, the crippled old mongrel, Khan?

Johnny knew he would be thinking about the war. Perhaps Khan would be hoping for something that might calm the madly running mind and heal the fractured soul of a returned soldier. Perhaps he might imagine that when darkness fell, it was like the cleanest and softest of bandages being gently draped across the entire country of Vietnam – because Khan was a man born of that place and of those people, the place that had given him life and still did, and that was what he had fought for.

Each night Khan hoped the wounds in the land and people would heal a little more. Each night he hoped the dead would sleep more soundly. And each night he hoped the war would withdraw like a beaten dragon.

Other nights, Khan, like Johnny Shoebridge, was simply overpowered by the war. The dead had lain in their hundreds of thousands on roads, in fields, and in jungles. They had floated down rivers, been buried in bunkers, and blown into trees. There were so many wandering spirits Khan felt the country would be haunted forever.

He looked at Thang and Trung smiling from the past. On a bad night, the shrine seemed empty of spirit, hope, and goodness. Khan wondered if the fighting, although honourable, had been too horrible for the dead or the living to ever recover from. Sometimes he felt he was nothing but an empty shell, perhaps that of a cicada; something that looked ancient and alive but had died long ago. Sometimes, on a similar note, Johnny felt like a scarecrow; frightening to a few, disregarded by most, left stuck in a field by a quiet dirt road, forgotten by just about everyone, even the farmer who'd put it there.

Neither he nor Khan had been able to speak of the two battles for the Australian fire base they'd fought in. It was enough to have lived through them. The experience was far too much to ever be forgotten. If only, Khan thought, he'd lost his memory instead of his right arm. But that would have been worse because he was the keeper of the memories of the boys and all other dead comrades. He was the custodian of their agony, bravery, and service to the country and people.

Same here, mate, Johnny thought, same here; except it didn't seem his country or his people were grateful at all. Embarrassed and disgusted was more like it. Johnny, looking over Khan's shoulder, saw his enemy had taken the tiny photo of a girl from a square of silk and studied it intently. Maybe this girl, whoever she was, might somehow offer comfort to the ex-guerrilla? It was not impossible, Johnny decided, if she understood that battles fought never ended, and wounds suffered never completely healed.

'Sister Phuong,' Khan whispered. 'Where did you go?'

Johnny guessed Phuong was a village girl who had also gone south to fight. He'd seen a few of these female Charlie guerrillas. Three he'd helped bury, which had loosened another handful of screws in his head. So this Phuong might also have disappeared into the meat grinder that was the war because it chewed up men, women, children, animals, and trees equally.

Khan contemplated Phuong's flawless skin and the depth of her gaze. Johnny saw she was not overly beautiful. Instead he judged her intelligent and thoughtful, attributes that he and Khan might agree were of more value than looks and style. For a minute the thin Vietnamese man looked out at the rain that would be swelling the rivers, following age-old patterns, laying down liquid rhythms, and he imagined Phuong's spirit as a swallow flickering over the water with other swallows on an endless flight. Then he carefully put the photograph away in its silk wrapping, lay down, and slept.

Johnny didn't rest. He was patrolling, unable to stop until the boys had reached their objective marked X on a map that did not exist. So he kept drinking and thinking, too scared to sleep, knowing he'd dream of friends and enemies circling in the jungle in the pouring rain, both sides seeking an opportunity to bury the other. And when that opportunity came, they would take it.

Eleven

At the first step Shoey took out through the wire, he felt his personality slide away until it locked down in a new place. He was ready and able to kill and knew it. His SLR was loaded. He wore two heavy belts of M60 ammo around his neck and hand grenades in his webbing. Two platoons from Delta Company were now in Indian Country, heading for a village where Viet Cong forces had reportedly been moving at night.

For a while the soldiers walked behind a column of armoured personnel carriers, then diverged into a plantation of rubber trees. Here, shadows tiger-striped the ground and the air was a dense block of humidity. Birds called but the brooding heat, hot as blood, stifled the place.

Slowly the boys patrolled, green men with black weapons, index fingers curled around trigger guards. Johnny could see Lex with his M16, Barry with his M60, every bloke ready to fire, knowing their role in the defensive perimeter if and when they made contact. What he did not know was how he would react if he had to shoot to kill; what he did know was that it would be unforgivable if he didn't.

Johnny felt totally exposed. A fearful, crawling sensation pulled at his skin and played tricks with his vision. Each second was a self-contained moment. Every sound, sight, and smell was examined. Walls of vegetation imprinted themselves on his eyes, were examined then replaced, re-examined then put by.

At any second he knew he might hear the fast rapping of an AK or the bass-blasting of a heavy machinegun. But so far there was nothing but the muted sound of his combat boots, birds, the damp brushing of his wet shirt, and the see-sawing of his breathing.

'The good news, JS,' Lex whispered, 'is that there's only three hundred days to go. And that includes Cup Day and Moomba. Put it in your diary, Shoebridge. I'd hate us to miss the plane. You know how time flies when you're having fun.'

Johnny didn't think time was flying; it had stopped just about dead.

When Johnny patrolled, for seconds on end, he was able to watch himself from above – this duality was uncanny but not unexpected. Detection of the enemy was so critical to the patrol that it was only natural he put himself in the picture, as if his spirit worked in tandem with his earth-bound self. And now, sitting on the steps of Malcolm's hut, he could imagine himself hovering over a village where Khan's D555 patrol, commanded by a captain Johnny decided to call Van, worked at securing supplies for the battalion.

In a granary, Khan, Thang, and Trung shovelled rice into bags. Behind them their weapons leant against the wall. Other men were taking essentials from the houses; essentials that Captain Van had assured his soldiers would be paid for. Secretly, Khan thought this might not be true, but said nothing. The southerners owed support to the northern battalions, and it was a small local boy on a bicycle who informed Captain Van that Australian soldiers were approaching the hamlet from the south.

Shoey saw, from above, that the D555 men were organising to leave. Outnumbered by his own Delta patrol, they'd wait for a better opportunity to engage the Australians. Gathering what had been collected, the North Vietnamese assembled quickly in the village square. There, Captain Van pointed a Browning handgun at the impassive village head man, made the sign for silence, then ordered his men out.

'Everywhere,' Van whispered to Khan, 'and everything, is war.'

True enough, Johnny thought. For you guys.

Johnny's captain, Dan McCrae, had been ordered to search the same village.

'More of a meet and greet,' the big man said. 'Take nothing. Break nothing. Put shit back. But shoot to kill, if you have to.'

'Well, that's fine,' Lex whispered to Johnny. 'But since these people all look pretty much the same, it's not that easy. No drivers' licenses, either, John. Or house numbers. It's a mess.' He shrugged. 'What d'you reckon? Knock over anyone over four feet tall?'

Shoey felt like a giant as he and Lex searched houses for tunnels, weapons, or a cache of anything intended for the Viet Cong. Pots of water sat over smoky fires and tea in delicate cups sat on low tables. He saw his face, strange and unsettling, in a couple of tiny mirrors. There was the spicy smell of cooking and the perplexing odour of people who lived differently. The families looked at him with shining eyes and said nothing. Johnny felt ignorance following him like a dog.

'Not a skerrick, Shoebridge.' Lex stood tall and lean in a narrow doorway, M16 comfortably cradled. 'Surprisingly. So shall we burn the joint?' He pointed to a thin mattress. 'Or catch forty winks? Or, if we get Barry, we could do a couple of Bee Gees numbers. The local folks might like that. It'd go a long way to explain our culture and dance moves. And what they're missing out on in the Melbourne nightclub scene.'

Johnny and Lex left the house. It would not be burned, today, anyway. Tactics changed minute by minute. Objectives, like the enemy, were impossible to pin down. Progress, like victory, was impossible to ascertain. Searching the village was like wading through a swamp. The instant the Australians moved on, the water swirled back even muddier than before.

Everywhere the sun blazed, throwing the darkest of shadows. And in the still, steamy air between the houses, unidentified things passed fleetingly at the sides of Johnny's eyes. At night, he could imagine this place being purely Vietnamese. Friend and foe would pass, merge, or murder as they had done for centuries. He felt like an alien fallen onto a strange earth.

'I'm tossing up between looking cruel and menacing—' Lex turned to Johnny, pulling a mad-eyed face, as they passed a gaggle of silent children, 'or trying out the old Zig and Zag clown routine. Perhaps you could teach them the recorder, Shoe? Kids love that thing. The whole program been a great success at state schools right throughout Victoria.'

'I'm stickin' with the boy scouts.' Johnny lifted his rifle. 'Be prepared.'

The boys took up defensive positions around the square as Captain McCrae spoke with the village chief. By a stone wall Johnny saw Barry had sited his M60 to fire across a vegetable garden and adjacent rice paddy. In the hot blue sky, a long way off, there was a triple silver flash. Then the jets were gone and the thunder rolled.

Johnny saw that Khan's patrol had evaded the Aussies and was now safely bunkered down in the Long Hais. The food liberated from the village had been stored and the men rested. They'd had to fight their way back, he noted – perhaps against Johnny's own Delta boys – because some of the men were wounded and one was missing.

'The Australians are tall,' Khan told Thang and Trung as they cooked rice. 'They walk carefully and love beer.' He grinned and spread his thin arms. 'The Americans are even bigger and noisier and they will never run out of bombs—' Khan nodded slowly. 'But we will never run out of fighters, so we will win. There is no question.'

You've got that right, Johnny thought. Not bad work for a bloke from the backblocks – not good news for the blokes from Down Under, though, at all, really. And that was both a fact and an understatement.

The Australian patrol left the village and filtered back into the bush. Johnny ploughed on, doing his best to stay sharp. Barry, he knew, was on point, machinegun welded to his hip as he led the way like an explorer in a country he did not like. Johnny, on the other hand, had decided to try to *like* the countryside. He figured that it would open itself up more to him if he embraced it. So far he was not succeeding. Every millimetre of it threatened.

'We'll eat.' Captain McCrae spoke quietly. 'Take five, eh? Then we'll get goin' and won't stop for a while. Set your perimeter, blokes. Chop chop.'

The patrol settled down, rations heated up over burning C-4 explosive. At four points, fire teams guarded the perimeter.

'Just like cadets.' Lex spooned lumpy brown stew from a dixie. 'Shit food. No girls. Sitting around with a bunch of homos. Did you bring your knitting, Barry? That scarf was coming along nicely. I don't know how you do it.'

'You're a disgrace.' Barry lit a smoke. His face, camouflaged with green and black greasepaint, only strengthened Shoey's idea that the guy was receding into the jungle for the purposes of more efficient killing. 'You are a uni poofter and a dirty hippy. Maybe a bloody commie. Certainly a bastard.'

Johnny forked up a small brown cube of what he guessed was meat.

'So what are you actually doin' at uni, Lex?' he asked. 'Arts?' Johnny didn't exactly know what *Arts* was, or were, but he'd heard Jilly mention it often enough to put the word out there.

'Of course I'm doing *Arts*, Shoebridge.' Lex shrugged. 'What else is there?' He gestured left and right. 'Just *look* where it's got me. And on the subject of general knowledge, and although this might come as a surprise to both of you country boys, did you know that Vietnam is not in Queensland? Anyway, John—' Lex raised a hand. 'Throw me one of your government-issued, taxpayer-subsidised smokes. I gave my last one to a little brown bloke who said he was minding a box of grenades for a friend.'

Johnny tossed over a cigarette and thought about Jilly. A sense of pride expanded. She was settled in Melbourne, also at uni, studying to be a teacher. He doubted she'd march against the war. Well, he bloody hoped she wouldn't. For luck, he touched the letter he carried that outlined her efforts to find a room to rent in Carlton, and her part-time job selling flowers. Her handwriting was large and loopy, leaving no space to read anything between the lines. Looking at it only served to widen the gulf between home and here.

Johnny thought about their last evening together. She'd waited for him at her house, sitting on the front steps at sunset, wearing a dress of pale blue and black lace undies. He wished she would write to him about that instead of netball, the Italians and Greeks in Carlton, and how mad Melbourne was.

The letters he wrote were short. This was mostly because he figured he hadn't done much. The unspoken message from blokes who'd been in the jungle for a while was loud and clear: just wait, mate, because you'll see it and you'll do it, and if you survive you won't be able to talk about it, either.

'Vietnam's not in Tasmania, either, Barry,' Lex added. 'If that was going to be your second guess.'

Twelve

At some time in the early evening Johnny threw his swag inside the fishing hut then went back to the step with another beer. The quiet of the inlet, pitch-perfect, and the colour of the water, pitch-black, had weight and substance. The air smelled of eucalyptus, salt, and seaweed. The upstream reaches he could make out were charcoal-smudged and overhung with trees, seeming to hint that the past was really not so long gone. In all this, Johnny could sense the beauty but his despair had fought it to a standstill.

He'd spent months wanting to be alone. Now part of his head needed people like oxygen. If Lex and Barry could have just wandered out of the dark, to sit and drink, he would've been fine for the rest of his frigging life.

He'd accepted the loss of other blokes; good blokes, *great* blokes, blokes he'd helped wrap in rubberised sheets for their last helicopter ride out of the bush – but he'd gone over the edge with Lex and Barry, and doubted he was ever coming back as anything but damaged goods.

He had, from where he didn't know, amassed a dose of fury that glowed like molten metal in the crucible of his mind. This anger had so little to do with the Viet Cong it was laughable. Yes, those little brown bastards fought sly, hard, and dirty. But they had real faces and real hearts that beat in their chests. The people he was looking for had neither.

He could picture them, though, up there in Canberra; old men in grey suits around a table in a beige government building, setting him up for the longest fall of his life. Then they'd done the vanishing act. Gone without so much as a *sorry about how that went, boys, but thanks for giving it a shot.*

Shoey looked into the gathering dusk. He'd been sold down the river, all right. He and the boys had fought the fight as fair and well as they could, yet now everyone was saying the whole thing was rigged, rooted, and wrong – although he didn't care too much about losing, if they had. The politicians would have to live with that little hiccup while he would have to live with the lost lives of the boys.

'My bloody *head* hurts.' He ran a rough hand across the bristles that stuck out of his scalp like nails. '*Jesus Christ!*'

He'd lost his best mates, and their families, girlfriends, favourite pubs, bloody dogs, and futures had lost them. They were so gone, the boys, that layers of pain just kept stacking themselves on top of each other like cold sheets of plasterboard. And Johnny was now stuck, because to leave the boys behind was to see them dudded twice.

Suddenly, on the far shore in the black bush, he saw flickering lights. Automatically he lifted his weapon but he had no weapon. Next moment he found himself sliding like a snake for a log, waiting for the flat crashing of Claymore mines, the body-punching of M60s, the flames of thirty fire-arms barking back and forth in the blackness. But there was only pressure in his head, panic in his chest, and a fiery burn on his forearm where he'd lain on his smoke.

He listened. Nothing. Not a bloody *thing*.

The lights moved steadily on up the inlet then turned jerkily towards the water. Bloody fishermen. Now Johnny could hear them talking and made himself laugh; fair dinkum, just a couple of bloody fishermen with rods, bait, beers, smokes, and one stupid Eveready torch between them.

He got up, brushed himself down then sat on the log. The hut stood behind him like a big rock. His arm stung, his head pounded but he smiled into the night.

'You're safe, sport,' he murmured. 'You're safe.'

He could see the moon, not white and not yellow but bright, sailing through the spread fingers of high branches. Watching it, he realised with a surge of joy that he was not hiding in the bush, it was the bush that was *hiding* him.

Johnny could feel the goodness of the place. Trees stood their ground like team mates. All stars, including the Southern

Cross, were present and correct, and a soft sea breeze brought him the tender calls of night birds as they reassured each other that all was well – this suddenly counting for nothing as tears blew from his eyes and a wave of sorrow held him down until he struggled to the surface and sat blinking, half-stunned. What could he do for Lex and Barry now?

That was the question.

'Have a smoke, for a start.' He lit up, took a drag, and wondered where the one-armed Khan was, and what he was doing. Even the enemy had a right to be heard. Especially since the bastard wasn't *personally* or *technically* his enemy anymore, because someone somewhere had signed a piece of paper and everything, supposedly, was all over red rover.

Well, far fuckin' out, Johnny thought; if that was all it took, perhaps they should've got round to it a little bit sooner.

Johnny found Khan staggering alone down a night road. He could see the one-armed fisherman held a bottle and a badly rolled cigarette flipped on his bottom lip. Pissed, Johnny figured. Look at the bloody drongo. About to fall in the river, if he's not careful.

'You're smashed, boyo.' Johnny might have said this out loud, he wasn't sure. 'Ya sad mongrel.'

Anyway, spoken or not, Khan replied that he was drunk

and went on and on about being a one-winged, brown-backed beetle who had returned from a torturous journey and yet felt he still was on the Trail.

You're home, pal, Johnny counselled. Be thankful.

Khan looked around, inhaling the moist agricultural air. The welcome of the earth was like a feather bed. The country acknowledged him as a simple saviour, as much a part of the natural world as the bough of a banyan tree, or a grove of bamboo that had sheltered him a hundred times.

'We go on, the both of us,' Khan muttered. 'The country and me. It's a miracle that I was spared, that I am here, alive.'

You wouldn't be, Johnny thought, if I'd had another second to get a decent sight on your head – unless, as Johnny had also considered, you actually were a ghost that could not be killed by bullets or bombs – or your gods stepped in to decide your fate. Or you just got really, really lucky.

Johnny was aware that parts of North Vietnam were relatively untouched by the fighting. The people weren't but the earth was. To the south of the country and the west, the land had been so badly tortured it writhed like a harpooned whale. To return home to a place virtually whole, as Khan's village appeared to be, was indeed a great thing.

The returned fighter scratched the stump of his right arm with his knuckles. Perhaps, Johnny thought, Khan might be thinking of the battles for Fire Base Leslie? Because it must have felt like the sky had fallen on the North Vietnamese forces as the place exploded and the air turned into fire and steel. The shouting and screaming were God-awful. The recoil of Shoey's rifle had felt like the heartbeat of a monster. Same went for Khan firing his AK. Torn faces and broken skulls. People turned inside-out and the world upside-down.

'We withdrew,' Khan said. 'Beaten but not defeated. And in the end, we drove you out.'

True enough, Johnny agreed, but we gave you a fair bit to think about before you did. And vice-versa, he had to admit.

It was obvious to Johnny that Khan loved the country he had fought so hard for. It only made sense, being a man of the land; perhaps a rice farmer before the war, like so many of the enemy. It was also obvious that Khan lusted after that good-looking girl whom Johnny named Lien, but it was the plain one, Phuong, the one who was missing in action, a sister-in-arms, that the returned Main Force fighter truly loved.

It was every soldier's dream that dead and missing comrades might return. Yet, until this happened, memory, powerful memory, was all that remained.

'It would be,' Khan muttered, looking at the stars, 'a heavenly thing to see Phuong.'

Johnny downed half a can. You could always go look for her, sport, he thought. Perhaps, one in a million, she's not dead. Head back down south. Why don't you? Do the honourable thing – because if neither of us stops searching, we both might find what we are looking for – whatever that is.

A future, maybe.

Thirteen

Shoey, up to his guts in brown water, held his rifle high as the patrol waded through a swamp. The place was dotted with tiny islands of tall grass that he would've loved to shoot the shit out of, but as this was not possible, he and the boys waded on, closing in on a line of tangled bush.

Suddenly an image of Taralia's main street popped up, Johnny conjuring craggy farmers, plump ladies, parked utes, and the town clock's stiff black hands. There was the Corner Hotel, and Nigel Stuart Menswear, a spray of grandpa shirts and Levi's in the front window – and there was he, Private JA Shoebridge, reflected in that window, green sleeves rolled, finger on the trigger guard of his SLR.

Get back in the swamp, you bloody idiot!

Johnny ploughed on, staring at the tree line, mud sucking at his boots.

'Shark!' Lex hissed. 'I swear. A fricken mako!'

The boys laughed and Johnny grinned, shaking his head.

'Oi.' Captain McCrae pointed. 'Save it, eh?'

The idea, Johnny knew, was to push the VC who'd been in the village towards two other Australian patrols. This silent, slow-motion pursuit was like brushing aside a hundred sets of curtains, not knowing what was behind any of them.

Was he about to trip a wire attached to a grenade?

Were machineguns two seconds away from cutting him in half?

Was a sniper aiming to blow his head off?

Were the boys about to walk into a killing field of mines? Be speared with bamboo stakes? Shredded by mortars? Surrounded and butchered? Johnny could not cancel anything out. It felt like he existed from one heartbeat to the next, his life as fragile as an egg.

He waded on, watched Barry working forward with a face set like iron, M60 held as if carrying that weapon was his life's purpose. And Johnny knew, as they closed in on the trees and the enemy, that's exactly what it was. Catching Baz's eye, Johnny gave him the thumbs-up, a simple sign that meant everything.

Khan, Trung, and Thang were running now. Each was bent low under heavy packs of rice as they splashed along an irrigation ditch. A scout had reported to Captain Van that an

Australian patrol was coming up behind. Van nodded. More trouble. He was also aware of two other enemy forces to the north-east. So the D555 fighters, inexperienced reinforcements, ran as if tied to the wrist of the man in front.

Khan prayed there were no mines in the ditch. There was always some local village lunatic who might have sown a few without telling anybody. He could imagine a thousand red-hot steel balls blasting into the faces and chests of the men. Down they would go, like dropped coals.

Van brought up a hand and the men stopped. Unsteadily they stood, heaving for breath. Khan listened, imagining time suspended. He could hear a fine, insistent buzzing. Yep, thought Johnny, that spells trouble for you, boys: little trouble now, big trouble very soon after.

'There it is, Captain.' Tien, the youngest fighter, pointed. 'Eleven o'clock. Spotter plane.'

Khan could see it, black as a gnat, coming directly towards the patrol. It was a Cessna Bird Dog, searching, capable of calling down all sorts of destruction on the fighters' heads. A tightrope of tension strung itself across Khan's guts; this was a truly bad sign. Captain Van, standing silent, watched the plane for ten seconds before ordering packs to be stowed under groundsheets and dirt and all men to lie face-down in the thick beds of tall reeds.

'Be careful with your weapons.' His voice was calm but edged. 'Keep them clean and dry.'

The boys stacked their packs. Groundsheets were

smeared with mud and weapons placed carefully on the bank. Then the men crawled into the reed beds and bellied down to wait. The droning of the plane nagged at Khan like a broken tooth. Closer it came, a foreign insect invading the airspace of the people.

'Faces down! Arms in!'

The fighters took a breath and eleven heads went under. Khan savoured the temporary coolness, the loss of noise, and an easing of the tension in his neck. He imagined himself swimming to an underwater cave where he would rest in dim silence. After a while he began to see fine silver particles floating before his eyes like stars but he did not lift his head to breathe.

'If anyone moves,' Captain Van shouted, 'I shoot.'

Khan listened as the sound of the aircraft faded pleasantly away. Going, going, gone, he thought. At last. On Van's order the fighters stood, knees and chests caked with mud. Some grinned and others coughed. Everybody was relieved. To Khan, it was as if the gods had granted them a chance to live and breathe. Then the firing began.

Hearing sudden, massed gunfire, Shoey brought his weapon up. The contact was perhaps, he reckoned, a kilometre away to the north-east. For the fiftieth time that morning he checked his rifle.

'Ours,' Barry said, the first word Johnny had heard from him since breakfast.

'Theirs,' said Captain McCrae as the chat-chat-chat of AK47s answered, and a 30-calibre light machinegun joined in.

'Skip, it's Sunray Three.' Young Pete, the radioman, held out the green handpiece to Captain McCrae, who stood in the swamp like a bollard a ship could be tied to. 'Engaged approx ten Main Force fighters,' Pete added. 'Wants us up there A-sap.'

Captain McCrae took the handset as Shoey searched the open farming land. Three muffled booms hammered the air. In the distance white smoke rose then drifted like clouds of vague thought.

'Nine hundred metres, nor-nor-east, Skip,' someone said calmly. 'White smoke.'

Captain McCrae looked, listened, said a few words then signed off.

'We go fast,' he said. 'We go carefully. They might double back. Although they're more likely to go east, towards the hills. Gunships are on the way. Let's move. Keep your eyes skinned.'

Shoey, with Lex and Barry, made for the bank.

'*Dry* land,' Lex said. 'I wonder if any of it's for sale? We could set up a dim-sim factory.' He looked at Barry. 'Or a dance studio, Baz? I think you'd be a hit. They might not have heard of country and western this far out, but you'd soon have them up on their feet and dreaming of Tamworth.'

Barry mouthed two words, and as usual, Johnny laughed.

The patrol, in two staggered columns, jogged towards the sound of fire and smoke. Shoey felt fear fade and excitement kick in. The siren had sounded. Game on. Waiting was worse. Or, at least, it felt worse. Through the bush he got a clear view up the ditch but saw no sign of Charlie.

'There!' someone shouted. 'Breakin' to the right! Seven, eight hundred metres!'

Shoey could see figures in the distance. The *bloody* enemy! They were out of rifle range and running, in combat greens, heavily loaded. It was surprising how small they were, their progress marked by bobbing green hats. Two M60s opened up, streams of red tracer streaking out in beautiful low arcs, the sound of the weapons claiming the place.

Captain McCrae spoke to a private called Billy.

'Throw yellow smoke, mate. Bushrangers incoming sixty seconds.'

Billy, the most tattooed bloke Shoey had ever seen, pulled a grenade from his webbing. Popping the pin, he casually lobbed it a few metres downwind. In seconds, mustard yellow smoke belched, indicating to the gunships where the Australians were.

'Best to get that right!' Lex shouted at Johnny, as the M60s hammered. 'I'd hate to get shot by a fuckin' Collingwood supporter!'

Shoey could no longer see the VC. Like a troupe of actors exiting a stage, they'd disappeared into thick bush. The machineguns now silent, Johnny heard the ominous hard thwacking of attack helicopters. In they came, low and fast, sinister-looking green grasshopper twins, lethally armed.

Suddenly they were overhead and turning. The sound was fearsome and rising, loaded with menace. Then they opened fire, rockets streaking, door guns blazing.

A bolt of fear almost lifted Khan from the ground. Johnny saw this in a dream-like sequence distilled from reality and experience. Bullets zipped past the Main Force fighter's head and then came the sound of the weapons. Nothing was clear. The North Vietnamese soldiers milled, the air full of noise and movement, confusion reigning until Captain Van pointed up the ditch.

'Go! Stay low! Go! Go! Go!'

Khan saw three of his comrades stop and return fire, spraying a patch of smoking scrub. He too fired, emptying a magazine into the trees, reloading as he ran. Something heavy smacked into his pack and in front of him a comrade went down as if pole-axed. Two fighters stooped to drag the man by the arms, a line of scraggly vegetation partially screening them from the enemy.

Khan turned to fire at a figure who'd popped up to hurl a grenade. Then the soldier was gone and Khan was running, his pack losing weight as rice streamed from a long rip.

Ignoring it, he took his turn to drag the wounded Noc, the weight of his comrade enormous. There was a slack feeling in the man's joints, as if his spirit had regretfully stepped aside, to wait for silence to return so it could commence its private journey away from the living soldiers and the battle.

Captain Van yelled constantly, encouraging, directing, and ordering his men to cover their retreat with disciplined gunfire. Now, hearing the helicopters, he ordered Khan and Thang, who held Noc, to leave him.

'Lay him on the bank. Let's go.'

The fighters obeyed, knowing this was wrong but unavoidable. On they ran as the helicopters unleashed a storm of rockets and machinegun fire. Dirt, reeds, and spray flew. Fear gave Khan desperate speed. With his comrades, he sprinted for the shimmering bush that seemed so far away he felt like howling.

Shoey's patrol followed the trail of spent cartridges, crushed reeds, spilled rice, and blood. Ahead the Bushrangers hammered the scrub with rockets and M60 door guns. Johnny saw a flock of black birds fly from the burning trees; human souls, he thought, getting the hell outta there.

'This'd make a good commercial.' Lex watched the action, nodding with obvious satisfaction. He held up an index finger. 'No, not for Cherry Ripes, Johnson. Or for Asian holidays. I mean for the army. *Our* army. You'd need to spell that out. You wouldn't want people joining the wrong side. That'd be disastrous.'

Shoey grinned. 'You fuckin' clown.' As the men in front went to their knees, scanning the ground over open sights, he and Lex did the same. 'See anything?'

Lex strained to look. 'Well, I spy with my little—'

'There's a Charlie here, skip,' someone called back. 'Brown bread.'

To one side of the ditch Shoey could see a body, a couple of the boys checking it for booby traps. Gingerly they lifted the wet green shirt, poking around in the webbing before tying parachute cord to the ankles. Then it was dragged backwards, leaving a bloody smear in the grass. There was no grenade under it.

'Search it. Bury it.' Captain McCrae turned to the soldiers behind him. 'Johnny and Lex, dig. Gary and Ant, give 'em a hand. Don't get too carried away. We're gunna link up with the other boys then search the woods as soon as the choppers have finished.'

Shoey and Lex downed packs. Quickly they freed their entrenching tools and started to dig. The smell of the ditch reminded Johnny of a stagnant summer creek back home. Behind him the dead Viet Cong, a small man about Johnny's age, eyes half-shut, exerted the presence of a stranger kept against his will but only faintly.

'Jesus. Hot,' said Ant, a wide-shouldered rifleman with red-brown hair. 'Dunno how these bastards can live 'ere.' He wiped his forehead with a brown forearm. 'Another minute and that'll do.'

Johnny dug, feeling as if he was hollowing out a small space in his mind to store this moment. He was hardly thinking about it now. Survival was uppermost in his thoughts. But he knew he would think about it at length one day.

The grave was filled in, the body so quickly gone that Shoey felt there was something like a magic trick about it; now you see him, now you don't. Ten minutes ago the guy was alive and running, with the enemy – *an* enemy. Now he was somewhere else, Johnny thought, or nowhere else. Whatever, he was gone and not coming back.

'Ashes to ashes.' Lex, holding his water bottle, looked at the turned brown earth. 'Dust to dust. *Guinness Book of Records.* World's fastest funeral. Thank you, linesmen. Thank you, ball boys. Who's for a G and T?'

'Let's go!' Captain McCrae lifted a heavy arm. 'Move!'

Johnny imagined how Khan would feel as the Main Force fighter sprinted for the bunkers. He bet the Vietnamese soldier was praying like hell he'd get to cover before the door gunners got a sight on his back. It must have felt like whole countries of foreigners were after him.

Ahead, Khan could see Captain Van calmly controlling lines of men as they waited to drop down into the tunnels.

'Safetys on!' Captain Van yelled. 'Check weapons. No accidents!'

Khan checked his AK was on Safe then clicked off the bayonet and sheathed it as he waited for Trung to disappear into the square hole. He followed, dropping into the dark chamber, making room for the men following. Other tunnels led away from the main bunker, two leading up to crawling trenches cut into the surface. Quickly the patrol spread, the soldiers knowing that fighting and winning was all about damage minimisation.

Khan, Thang, and Trung were directed to a tunnel that led to the north. The air was moist and hot, the three making for a dot of white light forty metres away. Below ground the sound of the helicopters was muted but powerful, the shockwaves of the rockets knocking down clods the size of pumpkins. Khan felt fear as never before. It filled him so suddenly he felt he might explode.

'Stay calm, boys!' Thang hissed. 'Breathe deep! And crawl!'

The men crawled through tunnels deep in Johnny's head. Overhead the sound of the gunships was like a thunderstorm fallen to earth, Khan expecting the ceiling to collapse with a life-ending *whump* – but it held, and in a minute he was looking out of a slit of silver like a view to heaven. When the helicopters left they were to bolt before the Australian patrols followed up.

'Scatter in threes,' Captain Van said. 'Meet at the Cracked

Boulders. We don't have the numbers to fight.' He smiled in the steamy gloom. 'Good luck, men. We are doing well. Be proud.'

The fighters waited, jammed together, heavy packs and weapons making everything awkward and dangerous. Captain Van moved among the boys, encouraging each with hardly more than the use of names. He patted Trung's bulging rucksack.

'We support ourselves!' Van nodded keenly. 'With the help of the people we *help* the people. And when these damn helicopters leave, so will we!'

Khan listened to machineguns and the wild smacking of helicopter blades. As rockets shook the forest, he prayed to the gods that no jets were zeroing in. He could picture them streaking over the country, slim like silver pencils, loaded with bombs and napalm, roaring at him from another world, intent on destruction. 'Run fast, men,' Captain Van said. 'Pray hard! And go!'

You'd better, Johnny agreed, because we knew there could be anything in those tunnels ranging from a thousand weapons to a hospital, so we were always gunna blow 'em in or up just like the big bad wolf, except with high explosive.

Fourteen

Johnny woke early, the dim light of dawn easing through the broken windows of Malcolm's hut. The air, cool and salty, smelling of peppermint, delivered him into the day with a soft landing. Putting aside a dream of patrolling alone along a narrow path between tall walls of bamboo, Johnny pulled on a pair of black and yellow Taralia footy shorts, and picked his way barefoot down to the water.

The sight of the mottled trunks of gumtrees and the glassy surface of the inlet was calming. Here, without people rubbing against him, he could think. No, better still, and this qualified easily as the thought for the day, he might be able to *not* think.

'No chance,' he muttered. 'At all.'

Johnny looked at water that was a clear, heavy green. It soothed with depth and volume. I've gotta swim, he thought. Stuff the sharks. And in he went, hands joined as if in prayer, opening his eyes to a blurred seascape that shelved away into liquid darkness. Down he kicked, into a coldness that pinpointed his scars as if they were his weakness.

But that wasn't right. His scars were like armour.

Later, sitting on a rock, drying off in the sun, Johnny found himself following the one-armed Khan through the tiny streets of an unnamed northern village. It was early morning, Johnny noted, and Khan was also making for the water.

'Good plan,' Johnny murmured. 'Good plan.'

Khan looked at a simple thatched house, Johnny deciding that would be where the stunning girl, Lien, lived. And lo and behold, there she was at a window, arms lifted, bare golden back visible as she dressed. At the sight of her, Johnny and Khan both took a good solid hit to the heart.

I know exactly what you're thinking, Khan, Johnny decided. On this subject, sport, I can read you like a book.

Khan's feet slowed but he forced himself go on. Eyes *forward*, he thought. But, oh, the loveliness of her! It filled his heart and head with a wild blurring, an awareness of everything fabulous that the world might bring to a person. But this blissful vision was underscored by loss. He felt keenly that the past was slipping further away and he was going with it. Khan knew, even though he was not yet twenty-four, that already he was as old as the hills and only getting older. No young women for him; not anymore.

'*So* lovely!' Khan shook his head, imagining. What could be more delightful than that girl? Nothing, nobody, surely?

You're forgetting someone, Johnny suggested. Aren't ya, mate? What about the other one? Phuong, the plain one. The special one. The fighter. The courageous one. Concentrate on her, champ, because this chick, Lien, will just bring you pain. What you need now is someone who thinks like you, knows what you know, has seen and done what you have seen and done – and might still be able to talk about it.

Khan walked on, Johnny seeing that he'd arrived at the jetty. Perhaps the veteran had his fish caged here, to be fattened in the forward-thinking Vietnamese way. And this is how it turned out to be, but there was an unexpected hitch.

Khan saw that someone stood on the jetty. A young man peered into the water, perhaps considering helping himself to what had taken the one-armed fisherman so many days to catch. It was the long-haired village layabout, Son, a so-called trader who carried a reputation as a bad communist. He was also extremely lucky, Khan thought, to be living in such a remote village that so far he'd escaped the attention of party officials.

Probably the kind of bloke, Johnny mused, who sold cars, fridges, or double beds on every second corner of every Australian town. This Son was nothing more than a *salesman*; meaning there was nothing wrong with what he did from one point of view and everything wrong with it from another. In a nutshell, Johnny wondered if half a dozen countries hadn't gone to war over the right and wrong way to sell a fridge – which guaranteed that this meeting between good communist Khan and bad communist Son would certainly be interesting.

Khan announced himself as he walked onto the jetty, Son looking up, open-faced and empty-handed, apart from a cigarette that smelled sweet on the early-morning air.

'You know, brother Son,' Khan said quietly, 'even though I have only one arm, I carried my AK home from the south. I should've handed it in when the war was over, but I couldn't. It's funny, isn't it?'

Johnny grinned and Son smiled, his black ponytail stark against a crisp, clean white shirt. He took a gold pack of cigarettes from a pocket.

'I won't tell anyone, brother Khan. Smoke?'

Khan saw there were three cigarettes left. He took one. Son flipped a brass lighter. For a while they stood smoking and Khan found it quite pleasant standing in the early morning with Son, although they had never been friends. He didn't trust Son. But he did feel he had a certain understanding of the world that others didn't. Johnny could see that, too; the bloke was a chancer, as old Les would've said. A Flash Harry, a professional punter, an unknown quantity – a guy who had somehow managed to dodge the call-up to go on his own merry way, like many blokes on all sides of the ditch.

Which was how the cookie crumbled, Johnny decided; if you could live with that, so be it. And this feller, Son, appeared to live with it quite easily, a man who plied the waterways alone and out of sight, doing business.

'I would not steal your fish, Khan,' Son said. 'Can you imagine me walking through the village with my pockets full of flapping fins and tails? It's just not me.' He smiled again. 'I prefer them cooked. By someone else.'

These two could end up as friends, Johnny thought. Maybe not yet, but when a bloke got back from a war, you needed as many *real* friends as you could get. Even if they might not be the type of person you would've hung round with before you left. He thought of Carly. Yes, if someone understood something about you, even just a little bit, it would be a serious mistake not to call them a friend.

'I saw sister Lien on my way down here.' Khan wanted to change the subject. He was also in need of sharing his feelings. These days he barely spoke to anyone, being the only veteran who had returned. 'She has everything, that girl. It kills me just to look at her. She is a true beauty. But she makes me feel *ancient.*'

Son smoked languidly. Leaning against a post, he looked across the river to the paddy fields that had, as yet, no colour. Johnny knew guys like him were hard to pin down. He also knew they were not to be underestimated.

'I've been out walking with her,' Son said calmly. 'Lien is a captive to her looks. If she doesn't give herself to someone soon, she'll have nothing left to give. Those breasts are like flowers in a vase, Khan. They will wilt. But they are in full bloom now.'

Khan laughed. 'Son, you should be a poet.'

Son put a hand on Khan's wrist. 'Well, if not a poet, an optimist and maybe a realist. It's been good to talk. We will talk again. See you, Khan. If you need anything, just ask.'

See? Maybe the bastard is all right, Johnny mused. Not everybody in this world has to be the same, think the same, or do the same things. Yet so far Johnny had only heard Son talk; it was action that made all the difference

Khan held up the cigarette. 'Thanks for the smoke.' The ex-soldier looked into Son's face. 'Yes, we will talk again. I look forward to it.'

Son walked off the jetty. Khan and Johnny watched him go. Among the wreckage in my head, Khan thought, in between the tons of shattered equipment, broken bodies, open ribcages, discarded bandages, splintered trees, burnt animals, and poisoned streams I still have a little place for a sneaky, funny man like that. And that is good. The war has not turned me into a policeman of every other person's life.

Khan knelt to unlatch the trapdoor of his biggest pen. Below, fish darted this way and that, heading to the surface then diving down. In the water, Johnny saw Khan's face reflected, wobbling.

'Get big and fat, boys.' Khan dropped in a ball of food scraps. 'That's the idea.'

Johnny, sitting on his rock by the inlet, lit a Marlboro. The smoke given to Khan by Son was a nice gesture, he decided. Small things, good and bad, were important. They added up, especially when you drifted like a boat in a storm. Or in Khan's case, Johnny guessed, when you'd been patched up in some rough underground jungle workshop, and sent home carrying the chaos with you – because it would have been impossible to leave it in the south like a destroyed weapon or an amputated arm.

Johnny wondered if Khan had seen the pile of North Vietnamese bodies the Aussies buried with Brutus, the bulldozer, after the first fire base attack. Perhaps Khan had been near the napalm strikes? Or where three hundred tons of bombs had been dropped from fifty thousand feet by the Stratofortresses? Perhaps he had endured Spooky's incredible onslaught from the sky? Whatever, everybody suffered, not that he cared much about Charlie's suffering, but the bastards were human. And they didn't start the fight, he didn't think.

Johnny watched Khan grind his cigarette out but the ex-soldier did not drop the butt into the water.

'You have had enough damage done to you, old man.' Johnny felt that this is what Khan had said, addressing the waterway that eased its way slowly on beneath his bare feet. 'I am not about to add to it.'

Johnny continued to watch as the first rays of warmth pierced the watery depths of Khan's imaginary river. It was a good thing to do, wait for sunlight, and look after the country and its people. Johnny and Khan were agreed on that. After all, supposedly it was what they had fought for.

Shoey walked along the inlet's edge to the beach, wearing only jeans and sunglasses, and carrying only his smokes. A few big rocks, like beached whales, were being washed by waves lit by bright morning light. No one was around. He could see along the misty coast for miles.

Sitting in the dunes, he lit up, and rested on an elbow. The amount of space around him stretched his mind. Everything was close in Vietnam. The country pressed from all sides, even when they'd been out in the open. Then it was worse. It was as if the sky was about to fall on his head, those fat foreign clouds towering. *Citadels*, Lex had called them. *Castles. Fortresses. Strongholds.* Or, as he had once added for Johnny's benefit, *Big bastards, Johnny. You know, larger than normal. Size twenty. The opposite to little.* In Vietnam, even the sky was against the Aussies.

Johnny could see himself, a rifleman in green in an extended line of riflemen in green. Armed foreigners crossing a foreign landscape. It was something to be proud of, though, he reckoned. The stuff those Viet Cong had done to their own people was unbelievable. He flicked ash. Heads on stakes and kids buried alive. True stories.

It wasn't hard to want to kill the bastards. All you had to do was flip the switch.

Good luck with ever trying to flip it back again.

Looking along the beach, he saw a girl walking, holding her thongs, and knew it was Carly. Same white dress. Same lank brown hair. Same hard life. He got up, drawn to her and her history, her understanding and suffering.

Strange days.

They stayed in the dunes to escape the wind, letting it get on with the job of blowing sand to the south in stinging sprays.

'Do you want to work, Johnny?' Carly lined up, with coarse-looking fingers, spiky brown banksia cones that reminded Johnny of old hand grenades. 'You know, now, around here?'

Work? Jesus Christ. Shoey knew he wasn't up to much as far as work went. Those gears, all four forward, were pretty much rusted solid. He'd concentrated so hard for every second of every minute of every day for a year that he could hardly concentrate on anything anymore. It was as if he was slow in the head, like Cam, his lumbering mate from Taralia. It scared him. And it was another thing that made him angry.

'Well, maybe.' He looked at her. 'I'm kinda not up to much, though. Why?'

Carly abandoned the banksia cones. She looked along the beach, eyes narrowed against the glare and lifting breeze.

'You should go see Curtis at the CES,' she said. 'Ask about the dole or whatever jobs are around. Which won't be many.' She gave a casual shrug. 'That's what you do. Here.'

Johnny had never been on the dole. It was something never talked about at home. It wasn't for people like the Shoebridges. It was for spongers, dope smokers, and useless bastards.

'Are you on it?' Shoey avoided saying the word, pretty sure it would feel like he was offering an insult.

Carly sat, arms wrapped around her legs. She had a light blue windcheater tied around her waist as if she intended to spend the whole day, and perhaps the evening, outside.

'Sometimes.' She lifted a slender angular shoulder. 'No work, no choice, eh? Although sometimes I do stuff on the farm for Malcolm. You could too. Anyway, go see Curtis at the CES. In town.'

Johnny nodded. It was an idea, if not a great one. Welcome to the new, dole-bludging, system-screwing Shoey. Still, it wasn't as if the system hadn't screwed him. Raffling off someone's life had shifted the goalposts considerably. Giving him an assault rifle and ordering him to use it, he figured, had put him in a very different category to nearly every other Australian citizen. In short, he owed the bastards in Canberra nothing, and would never believe what they said again.

'I go see Curtis?' He considered the possibility. 'In Adden Bay?'

'Yep.' Carly looked at the sea. 'He'll help you. He helped me.'

Johnny watched waves trumping waves, criss-crossing, overlapping, and undercutting. Shifting sands. Invisible currents. Changing tides. The way of the world, he thought. Decisions, decisions, decisions. But they were hard things to make. He was out of ammo. No, he had one shot left.

'Curtis helped you,' he said courageously. 'You help me.'

Carly looked at him. 'He's a good person, Curtis. I'm not. I'm a mess.' She shrugged, turned her hands up as if showing him something of no value. 'Dropped outta school. Hung out with the wrong people. Probably was one of 'em. Did the wrong things. Had 'em done to me. I can hardly read or talk, Johnny. I couldn't help anyone. Not myself, anyway, that's for sure.'

Johnny let the words settle, extracted as much meaning as he could before reaching for Carly's left hand. He could feel the bones, fine and strong.

'I think you're beautiful.' He couldn't believe he was saying this; he'd never said it to anyone but it was the truth. 'I'm sorry about what happened to you. You're a good person, Carly. Just talking to you makes me feel better. You're the only one who's done that since I got back. It's a big thing.'

Carly allowed him to hold her hand. Borrow it.

'Really?' She looked at him, unconvinced. 'Because I'm pretty sure no one else around here'd agree. They think I'm just some lazy feral.'

Shoey let his grip slide. 'Well, they're wrong. I mean it.' He smiled and for once it felt okay. 'You're a good person. You are.' Although, he thought, I'm not – even if what I did was done under orders, was my duty, and had been a matter of life and death. Even if it was *demanded* by the country. Even if the Prime Minister had shaken his hand at Nui Dat and said that the battalion was doing a *fine* job – well, it didn't feel like a *fine* job. It felt like twelve months of bloody madness.

The boys would know what he meant. Anyone who fought over there was pretty much carrying the same load. Apart from the dead blokes, because surely they would have no load to carry at all.

'Come into town, Carly.' Johnny felt a spark. 'Show me where to go. I'll buy you a coffee.'

Her hands sought each other. He didn't think he had succeeded in giving her much to go on with.

'No, thanks, Johnny.' She glanced at him and away, down the beach, into a pale misty distance where she might have been able to see something of her future or her past. 'I don't like town. You can't miss the CES. It's got a red and white sign. Open nine till four in the main street.'

Shoey's jaw clamped shut. Anger brimmed in his eyes. Faaaaaark! This was the *first* time since getting home that he'd offered someone something other than a punch in the mouth – and instead, he'd got a smack back. He forced himself to breathe.

'Okay.'

'It's the people in town I don't like.' Carly, this time, looked at him. 'Not you. You're nice. Thoughtful.'

Shoey laughed. It felt like an infectious cough. Thoughtful? Yeah, but not in a good way.

'I'm a head case, Carly.' He touched his temple. 'And if I'm thoughtful, it's generally only about myself.' Or the boys. Or those other dreamed-up bastards, Khan, his two dead mates, and that cheating son of a bitch Son.

Carly looked at him from under perfectly curved eyebrows. Her index fingers created the point of an arrow.

'That's not true.'

He felt her hand, dry and light, on his forearm. Warmth flowed. She was trying to calm him, if he could be calmed. It struck him some people did have the power to help. She did.

'Thanks, mate.' He reached for his smokes. 'I mean it. You do not know how much.' His face felt like twisted leather.

'You'll feel better,' she said. 'I promise. One day. Maybe we both will.'

He nodded slowly, the two of them sitting in silence that seemed to have blown in on the wind.

'Everyone's always got something—' she appeared to study the clumps of black seaweed on the beach that reminded Shoey of dead bodies, '—to get over. That's life, eh?'

Johnny came up with a quick smile, perhaps from his childhood – before things hit the fan, anyway.

'It is.' He lit a smoke, felt it sort his thoughts then lay them down in a quiet hollow. 'Anyway, I'll go see Curtis. And I'd like to see you again, Carly. You know, around. Just to talk.'

She seemed not to have heard. Or what she'd heard wasn't particularly good.

'Oh, sure, maybe,' she said. 'I ain't goin' anywhere.'

Fifteen

The riflemen spread out, infiltrating the bush, the heat holding low to the ground. Johnny, loaded with belts of M60 ammo, moved forward with Barry. To his right he saw Lex, black barrel of his M16 swinging gently, as if the tall guy was a diviner and his weapon a divining rod. A bird twittered then abruptly stopped. Johnny's guts tightened another notch. Charlie had to be close. Closer than close.

Side to side, up and down, Shoey scanned the ground and greenery. It was endless what he had to look for: a wire, a cord, a slit in the ground, a broken stick, snipers in trees, the tiny prongs of a mine, the eyes of camouflaged men, and the muzzles of loaded weapons.

A whispered message was relayed from point.

'Bunker. Hold up. Geddown. Cover everybody.'

Johnny and Barry sank into the leaf litter. With practised care they set up the machinegun, keeping the belts as clear of the ground as possible. Silence assembled itself from the top of the trees down. An acute sense of waiting intensified as the seconds ticked by. Another whispered word.

'Standby.'

'Fire in the hole.'

There was a brief rustling forward then an explosion that jerked the ground. Two more flat, hard bangs followed. Smoke rose. Barry raised his eyebrows then turned back to his weapon. At any second Johnny expected the place to explode as triggers were held on full auto and everybody, VC and Aussies, let loose.

There was nothing.

At a hand signal, the boys rose, separating from the trees and shadows. Within five metres they were absorbed by other trees and other shadows.

'How come,' Lex whispered, jabbing a finger at the bush ahead, 'it's always *their* turn to hide?'

Johnny grinned. He couldn't help it. Suddenly he was smacked in the head by a sound so loud and close it knocked him over.

A mine.

For a moment he stayed down, pinned by the weight of his gear. Smoke rose, a misty blue mushroom. He wondered if he'd been hit, decided he hadn't and knelt, weapon up. Someone shouted.

'*Medic!*'

Someone screamed. The sound climbed into the trees. Men moved incrementally. The black aerial of the radio waggled above a bush. Someone was calling for a dust-off. The screaming went on.

'Be *fucking* careful, Shoe.' Barry pointed. 'We'll go there.'

Johnny nodded. They moved two metres, setting the M60 to cover a trail and a small clearing. Something flickered. Johnny thought of a rabbit. Barry reacted. Vegetation burst into mist. The pounding of the automatic weapon drowned all other noise. No screaming now.

Or if there was, Johnny couldn't hear it.

Khan, Trung, and Thang climbed out of the trench and ran. Fighters fled like wasps. The sky was distant, as if glimpsed through broken glass, patterns changing as the boys twisted and turned along trails they knew were not mined or booby-trapped. A fire team of five had been left to cover their retreat, commanded by a veteran with bullet scars in both legs. Khan was thankful he had not been selected to join them.

He was also thankful for the jungle boots he wore. They were the best footwear he'd ever had, allowing him to run without looking at the ground. His pack, slapping lightly, seemed to have been inflated with guilt. The loss of rice was a serious blow but that was how the gods had seen fit for those bullets to fly, he decided. And that was that.

Behind them he heard explosions. Grenades. The tall bastards were blowing the tunnels. Well, hopefully that would hold them up for a while – that, and the comrades who would fire from the earth then melt away. Now a mine went up. The weight of the explosion was like thunder in a cave. Someone's just got the call from up above, Khan thought, as a thin screaming came through the scrub.

He ran on, leaves tearing at his face as a machinegun added sledgehammer blows. He imagined a fleet of bullets pursuing him.

'Shooting at shadows,' he called to Trung. 'No chance!'

'Yes,' Thang called back. 'But we're the shadows!'

It did not feel good to run. Khan wondered if they shouldn't just turn and blast it out with the Australians. But they were under-manned and under-prepared and now he could hear helicopters. Dust-offs or gunships, he wasn't sure, but the fighters weren't about to hang around to find out. To stop was to die and to die at this point was to lose twice.

He ran on, holding hate for the enemy in one hand, and love of his comrades in the other. These were the weapons, love and hate, not B52s or Cobra gunships, that would win this war. He knew it, his comrades knew it, and the whole country knew it. And because Johnny was capable of imagining Khan and his life, and he had fought the North Vietnamese, he knew it, too.

Shoey's patrol set up a perimeter the size of a public swimming pool. Green men in green grass bent over the three casualties, one a Charlie fighter with a missing kneecap and a bad head wound. Two Aussies had been caught by the mine. Tommy Dean was dead and Patto looked bloody awful.

'Jesus Christ,' Johnny muttered, for no good reason other than he simply had to say something. 'Get that chopper down here.'

He steadied his rifle against a tree. From the corner of his eye he watched purple smoke leak as if from a small volcano. In his chest there was a deepening emptiness as he scanned a chequerboard pattern of green on green with straight shafts of bamboo climbing through it. Snakes and Ladders, Vietnamese-style, he thought. No winners here, only losers.

Behind him, Tommy Dean had been carefully wrapped in plastic, and put to one side. TD, as he was called, from some tough outer suburb of Melbourne, was so permanently gone it was beyond any words that Shoey had. All Johnny could do now was his job: to search the jungle over open sights, and shoot anything that moved. Patto had been hit in the legs and was quietly swearing and crying. The sound of it ground in Johnny's head and stomach.

'Holy shit,' he murmured. 'Madness.'

Thankfully he could hear the dust-off, the blurred whacking getting louder and louder. Fast and low the chopper came in, bubble-headed, iron-coloured, open-sided, slender skids rocking as it hovered over the thrashing grass. A team of blokes converged.

Sleeves rolled, backs bent then up went a small forest of arms, five camouflaged faces turned to the sky. Patto was lifted into the open door, a translucent drip handed over like his passport out. Next the wounded Viet Cong was put aboard and then a long, heavy parcel was taken from the grass, and held carefully aloft. Hands released, hands received, and the Huey rose above the chaos – the feeling of the coffin leaving the church, and the church leaving the clearing.

See yer, Tommy-boy, Shoey thought, some long day down the road.

Johnny could picture the white egg-shaped boulders of the Long Hai Hills as clearly as the tiring Main Force fighters could see them. The North Vietnamese force was now well into the final stage of their mission, Khan looking back at where they had come. The tops of trees and scrub formed a knobbly wedge that spread out into farmland. There were villages to the left and right and the shaggy heads of palm trees drooped as if heat-exhausted.

'Notice something, Khan?' Captain Van pointed generally with his AK. 'No smoke.' He smiled wearily. 'When the Americans are involved, they torch everything. It makes them feel that they're achieving.' He turned back to the trail, the boulders ahead like stacked skulls. 'Thankfully, rocks don't burn. Or they'd have cooked us like chickens years ago.'

Khan walked into the welcome shade of the hot granite slabs. The narrow path, ages old, wended its way, so it looked, into ancient eye sockets. The Long Hais would swallow the soldiers. The rock pile would hold them safe in its heart and belly, and regurgitate them to fight battles with better odds.

'Not a great success, men.' Captain Van stood to one side, watching his fighters file past, ragged, muddy, and loaded like beasts. 'But without rice, we are nothing.' He patted Trung on the shoulder. 'And that, comrade, is the truth.'

Khan thought of Noc, twelve hours dead, and the injured Kien. Thoughts like these only added a steely edge to the hate he'd accumulated in the last year. One day he prayed he would stand in front of the Australians, or Americans, and fire a full magazine into their chests. The idea of them moving through this country whenever and wherever they chose, sleeping under its stars and drinking its water, seemed to squeeze the life out of him. They had to be driven away or killed. He would gladly do it.

'Noc.' Thang said the dead soldier's name as he let Khan pass. 'We will talk about him later. Properly.'

Khan nodded, following the foot-worn trail, trying to remember what it had been like when he was a farmer. He thought of a water buffalo called Big Grandpa, could see him ploughing, could hear his hooves pulling out of the grey sucking mud. But when he tried to picture himself working the plough, the motion of it like a small boat in a choppy sea, he was not there.

I guess, Johnny thought, once you've fought in a war, your other self will pretty much just drift away. And it will be up to you to recreate your new self from the wreckage. Take what is left and panel-beat a new personality. Or call it a day and write yourself off.

As the rain drummed on Shoey's carefully rigged hoochie, a different strain of fear entered his consciousness. It was a gnawing, crawling fear that invaded his sleep. It was a fear populated with small brown men, oily-slick, armed to the teeth, gliding through the forest. Unerringly they moved along trails towards him and the bedded-down patrol, with long knives and automatic rifles.

When he opened his eyes, about every third minute, he could see nothing. All he could hear was falling water. The blackness was complete, centuries old, as complex and other-worldly as the inside of a beehive. Yet Johnny knew, out in the liquid darkness, the North Vietnamese were always positioning to strike.

For a moment he imagined himself home, walking along a dusty road, the sky studded with stars. He would be completely without fear. He would be in the place he was born to be. He would be with Jilly, he would be with Jack, his Blue Heeler, he might be on his way to fish in Ted Collins' new dam, or he might be thinking about taking up Bill Grey's offer to teach him how to shear and make some real money. The feeling of that road and those paddocks, and being with those people – his people – was in his bones. It was a feeling equalled by the knowledge that here he was the wrong person in the wrong place at the wrong time. The only thing right about it was his intention to protect the boys with every last measure of guts and skill he had.

He moved his hand three inches and touched his rifle. And wondered for the thousandth time, how, from a far-flung town in sheep country, he got here. Then he gave up wondering and slept, knowing Barry was on sentry, the one person he trusted absolutely to inhabit the darkness as the enemy did.

Barry Neville Grainger was incapable of letting his mates down. Barry Neville Grainger was capable of limitless killing. Barry Grainger was the perfect soldier; Johnny knew it, just like he knew had never met anyone like Baz before and never would again. The bloke was unmatched.

Khan, Trung, and Thang sat in a dim corner of the cave Johnny had dreamed up, a cave that penetrated deep into the

Long Hais. The boys shared a cigarette, oil lamps throwing a soft light over clusters of soldiers as they recovered from the day. The low murmur and muted movements reminded Khan of the noise of a peaceful barn.

He looked around, seeing weapons, the warmth of wooden stocks married to the deadly efficiency of black gunmetal. And he looked at the men, drawn from the fishing and farming villages of the north, parts of the south, and everywhere in between. This was definitely a peasants' war, he thought. It was the poor fighting the rich for the good of the people, and the party. So be it. Uncle Ho had spoken.

Khan imagined the American bases. He pictured jets, attack helicopters, tanks, artillery, the thousands of big men, the millions of tonnes of equipment weighing down the ground. Even that flag of theirs looked rich. It was not like silk but velvet in bold red, striking white, and deep blue, as if everything in their country was clean, beautiful, and without guilt. The Australian flag, well, it was just some dull old blue thing with some stars and something square stuck in a corner. He couldn't imagine that country or those odd people at all.

'What do you think will happen to Loc?' Trung asked pensively. 'If he is not buried? Will his spirit remain unhappy?'

'The Australians will bury him,' Khan said. 'Not properly. But they will bury him. It's something they do.' It was true. At least the tall bastards did that.

We did, Johnny agreed. Yes, we always did that.

The three North Vietnamese soldiers sat in silence, thinking of Loc while Johnny thought, in general, of the enemy.

'I guess when you die,' Khan spoke quietly to Trung, 'your soul rests, and you exist in the thoughts of your family and friends. As we are doing now. Thinking of him.'

'We'll have our chance to pay them back.' Thang nodded slowly. 'This is where they operate. And this is where we fight.'

'What about Kien?' Trung glanced at the older men. 'Will the Australians execute him? I hear they throw prisoners out of the helicopters.'

Thang shook his head. 'I doubt it. But you can bet you'll never see him again. One way or another, he's for the chop.'

You're right about that, Johnny agreed; but not at our hands. His countrymen from the south might decide he has to go and that'll be that. And with a bit of luck, you fellers might be next.

The Australian patrol moved out, snaking its way into the bush. Shoey had the sense of leaving yesterday in the awful drowned darkness of last night, leaving it in the clearing where Tommy Dean began his long trip home. Looking behind, he hoped never to come back this way but guessed he was heading to places that would be a whole lot worse.

'I just remembered,' Lex whispered, stopping in the steadily rising heat. 'I have a shitload of library books overdue.

Those fines mount up, Johnny. Five cents *per* book *per* day. Non-fiction may be *even* more. I could be up for millions.' He lifted a thumb, presumably in the direction of the Black Rock public library, Johnny guessed. 'I should go back now, John, shouldn't I?'

'Yeah, you should,' Johnny said. 'And don't forget to lock your bike up outside.' For a moment he pictured Lex, the mock-serious idiot on some wide sunlit beach, board loosely pinned under an arm as he checked out the waves, knobbly knees below flowery boardshorts, smiling just for the hell of it. Instead, here he was holding an M16, being paid to kill Viet Cong or be killed by them. 'Or you could simply go throw 'em at the bastards in Canberra.'

With every metre covered, the patrol penetrated further into the Minh Dam Secret Zone. This place, where the Australians ruled by day and D555 by night, was where the two forces would meet head-on. It was inevitable, because that was the plan, and everybody knew it.

Khan and Thang, armed, squatted in the cover of boulders deep in the night-time recesses of Johnny's mind. Around them the dark shoulders of the Long Hai Hills swelled and rose. Thirty metres in front, bare rock met straggly bush. It was a logical assault point for the enemy, although Khan was sure the Australians would not strike.

He knew the tall bastards preferred to fight in daylight, apart from setting night ambushes. Generally they harboured in the dark. Or retreated to their base where there was electric light, strong protection, and beer in blue and green cans. They even watched movies. It seemed a ridiculous way to fight a war. They did not value time as the people did. They were not tireless like the people were. They were mercenaries flown in to fight, with no idea of whom, where, or why they were fighting.

Not quite true, buddy-boy, Johnny thought. We did know something about you, your ideas, and your country. And to prove this, he allowed Khan to take flight in his imagination, to float away from the Long Hais and over the paddy fields, villages, mountains, jungles, and rivers. Johnny allowed Khan to feel the earth pressing the last of its rising warmth into his bare chest like love, to show his Vietnamese enemy that the Australians were not ignorant dogs but accomplished jungle fighters who had some understanding of their enemy. To underestimate the diggers would be a serious mistake.

'I'd kill for a smoke.' Thang rested his wide forehead against the cold barrel of his AK.

Khan chuckled, Johnny seeing that the rice farmer-turned-soldier did at least have a sense of humour.

'You mean we'd be killed *for* smoking.' Khan waved a finger. 'By either side.'

'Yes, it would not be smart.' Thang stretched his stocky legs. 'It would be better to be in bed with a girl somewhere.'

'It would be.' Khan thought of Phuong, who had hold of his heart, and although he didn't know where she was or what she was doing, he did know that she was caught up in the war as surely as him. 'That is the truth.' One day he hoped to see her, and tell her that she was beautiful, intelligent, and brave, his favourite woman in the entire world.

Well, that's a turn-up for the books, Johnny thought. You don't seem *such* a bad bastard. Not that it would've stopped us killing each other back then. And now? Johnny looked at the inlet that was a couple of miles east of the Pacific Highway in southern New South Wales. Of course not. People had sat around a table and signed a piece of paper. What did the President of the US say? An agreement to end the war and bring peace with honour? Johnny shook his head. Still waiting, sport, he thought, still waiting.

Sixteen

Johnny parked in the main street, the old shops crowding respectfully around a two-storey pub with a fancy veranda. He could see the red Commonwealth Employment Service sign. This is a first for the Shoebridges, he thought, walking. Perhaps a change not for the better, but that couldn't be helped.

He went into the small office. A few palm-sized cards were pinned to green boards. A young red-headed man in a shirt and tie sat behind a desk. He was kept company by a pot plant, a photocopier, a rack of pamphlets, and six empty chairs. Shoey could smell dust, tea, and paper.

'Good morning.' The bloke looked at Shoey with a watery blue-eyed intensity. 'What's on your mind, sir?'

A laugh branched across Shoey's chest, more like hysteria than good humour.

'Jesus Christ—' He saw the guy's name, Curtis Stringer, printed on a tag. 'Curtis. You don't wanna know. Unless you really want your day ruined. And don't call me sir. Call me Johnny.'

'Well, Johnny, I'm here to help.' Curtis stood. 'Would you like a cup of tea?' He pointed to a small alcove partially hidden by a curtain. 'The Burko's just boiled. Then we can talk employment.'

'Or unemployment.' Johnny shook the pale freckled hand that was offered. 'As the case may be.'

Curtis nodded sagely. 'I'm familiar with both. Now, tea?'

Johnny felt as if he'd walked into a web. The bloke was a character, obviously. It was also easiest, he decided, to simply go with the flow. Plus, he did appreciate being treated politely.

'Sure. Thanks.' Shoey sat in the chair that he figured was his for the taking. 'Why not? Ta.'

'Why not, indeed?' Curtis's eyes lit up. 'You see? Already we're making progress!'

Johnny sat while Curtis disappeared behind the curtain, the musical tinkling of a teaspoon the only noise in town. The employment officer reappeared, carrying thick gold mugs, mugs that Johnny reckoned were owned by every household in Australia. One was handed across.

'I'm sorry I don't have biscuits.' Curtis put his mug on a coaster featuring the Sydney Harbour Bridge. 'Usually my mother sends some down. Anyway. Next time. So what type of work have you been doing, John?'

Johnny thanked him for the tea and spared a quick thought for Curtis's well-intentioned mother.

'Unfortunately, mate,' Johnny said, 'I've been in Vietnam trying to kill people.' He picked up the hot mug. 'Not very successfully. Unless you count some of my mates who I didn't manage to look after. I'm sorry to be a smartarse, but that's the truth.'

Curtis leant on his forearms, shirtsleeves neatly buttoned at the wrist. His gaze held purpose.

'John,' he said. 'The responsibility for your actions in that place should be shared by everyone in this country. Might I be right in assuming you did not volunteer?'

'I certainly did *bloody* not.' The words ripped up out of Johnny's throat.

Curtis nodded, sipped tea. 'You'll see the statue of the digger down by Memorial Park. Although Adden is not a very progressive place, I hope you'll find the support you deserve here.'

Johnny took a good hard look at Mister Curtis Stringer.

'Curtis,' he said, 'I think I already have. Now, how does this CES thing actually work?'

Curtis held up a form bearing the red CES logo.

'Step One, surprise surprise, is that we have to fill out one of these things.'

'Okay, let's go.' Johnny shifted his chair towards the desk, angled it to one side, aware that everything in the place might also be a little angled off to one side.

'You'll need benefits ASAP.' Curtis uncapped a black ball-point. 'I can expedite that. Basically because there's not a job

I'd judge suitable for a person recovering from long exposure to a high-stress situation. Unless you could see yourself working in an abattoir.' Curtis looked up, pen poised.

A laugh jerked upwards in Shoey's chest. He felt he might have to slap himself.

'Mate, I do not.' Johnny drank tea, trying to get a grip. 'So has anyone told you lately that you're good at your job?'

Curtis stopped. 'God assures me I am doing my best.'

'Well,' Johnny replied, 'he's right. Now, someone told me I have to do an interview. So, can we get on to that quick-smart as I've—'

'Already done.' Curtis sat, pen pinched between two fingers like a dart to be thrown. 'My office will not be run like the Spanish Inquisition. I make a judgement on a person's situation on behalf of the Commonwealth. And that's that.'

Shoey surrendered to Curtis's process, which seemed allied to the slow-motion feel of the old wooden town, the treed hills, and the curling coastline that lassoed the place. He figured he'd stumbled into somewhere weirdly kind of special. He hoped the feeling would last.

During the war, in a clearing, Johnny had walked around the twisted wreckage of an armoured personnel carrier. It had been left far behind, unlike the memories it generated in its failure to protect the soldiers who rode in it. Now it seemed Khan also pictured that same piece of wreckage as it rusted away in the silence of peacetime.

The minds of people, Khan decided, although sometimes more resilient than armoured plating, remained damaged for just as long. He also knew, as Johnny knew, that he would never be happy in the way he had been before the war.

Khan felt that he'd absorbed the deaths of Thang and Trung, and most likely that of Phuong as well. He also held a hundred thousand other stilled hearts and silenced voices somewhere in his soul. Few of the millions from the north were coming back and the reality of that hovered like a black cloud – a cloud as poisonous as the actions of people in high places in countries he knew existed somewhere far over the horizon.

Johnny couldn't argue with Khan on that score. It wasn't as if the Viet Cong rocked up in Bourke Street and opened fire in Myers. Both Khan and Johnny knew the diggers had to travel a bloody long way to get into the fight. So you definitely have us there, Shoey admitted. You definitely do. Now get on with your dinner, if you could call it that.

Johnny pictured Khan eating dinner with his aged parents before leaving the house for an evening walk. The one-armed fisherman followed a winding road that soon plunged into darkness. How peaceful the sky was, Khan thought, now that it was decorated only with stars, and how perfect the river on which floated only ducks, lilies, and lotus. There were no jets, no bombers, no Hueys loaded with Marines or Australians, and no patrol boats on the rivers machinegunning buffalo or people. There was no enemy at all.

Except the ones we carry in our heads, Johnny noted. We certainly *can't* lose them, the real and the imaginary, the living and the dead. Endlessly they move up and down the trails of memory, setting and springing traps, constantly changing shape and form. And they will always be more complex than the soldiers they haunt, he decided, which is why the bastards are so hard to silence.

Khan saw that the country was slowly coming back to itself. Painfully it was settling into its recent history, to begin the long process of healing. He only hoped that one morning he might wake and find himself free of the anger no one felt he had a right to have. Until then, he would simply be Khan, the smiling not-very-good fisherman, the unhappiest and poorest person he knew.

At least you won the war, Johnny reminded him. Although we really don't like to admit that.

Shoey had the key in the car door when a woman built like a forty-four-gallon drum bailed him up.

'You been to Vietnam?' She pinned him with tiny, piercing eyes, her mouth set in a straight red line. 'Someone said you had.'

Johnny opened the door. 'How's that any of your business?' He spoke mildly but felt himself swept towards a spillway that dropped into a pool of white fury.

'I just hope you're happy,' she said. 'With what you did.' She waited for him to reply but he was too busy trying not to spit in her face. *If you were a bloke*, he thought, holding on to the door as if the flood had doubled and he was hanging on for his life, *I would rip your bloody head off.*

The fury he felt was volcanic. There was so much of it. It was a blackened battlefield, an earthen pit, a row of sealed steel coffins. So many people were involved, so many bad places, ugly sights and violent actions, that he stood silent, crushed by the load he had to carry away from that place. And because it was inexplicable, so heavy and involved, he became the fury.

'Leave me—' he punctured the air once with a stiff forefinger, '—alone.' The woman walked away, Johnny watching her go, anger pounding his skull. Then he got into the car, found his cigarettes, which was the first miracle, and got one lit, which was the second. 'Holy sheezus *Christ*.' He sucked in smoke. 'My bloody God.'

He felt like a boxer who'd been flogged in a dirty fight. Set up by a bunch of bastards who'd left town on the first train. Who am I, he wondered? How can I be so hated? Yeah, hated by the Viets, those boys, I'll wear that. But here? Don't people realise how a raffle works? The army? Orders? The government? A war?

'Just drive, idiot.' He knew it was impossible to leave much behind, but he did know he could ditch the old bitch who still glared at him from the footpath, and that'd be a start. 'Just get goin'.'

This he managed, not caring that he was heading out of town on a meaningless road, doubting he could get any more lost than he already was. Then, as the trees grew higher and the hills got steeper, in a ferny hollow he saw a little pub called the Bellbird Hotel. He turned in.

Seventeen

Johnny walked into the empty bar of the hotel, sat on a stool, and looked at sepia photographs of bearded men standing on tree stumps. An upright piano faced the wall, the keys the colour of old horse teeth. Shoey lit a smoke. In the silence, he could feel his heart beating.

The bush beyond the window was tangled and dense. Tree ferns held up open umbrellas of lime green. The leaves of vines shone like keyholes, giving glimpses into locked rooms. Further back, gumtrees speared skywards, bearing scabs of black that testified to bushfires long gone cold. *Leeches in there*, Johnny thought; little baby fellers, not like the big black bastards in Vietnam that left slime as they took blood.

His anger at the woman in town, at himself, had subsided into purposelessness and fatigue. He looked out at the surrounding trees and thought of the boys never coming back from where they never should've gone. Where were the thanks? Where were the apologies, the better-late-than-never justifications? Even the scorecard was hidden. There were only reheated reasons, leaving the blokes who'd survived and the broken families of the dead with memories like anchors stuck in the past. And now, Shoey thought, this *specially* selected crew could haul on those anchors but they would not budge because you can't go forward when your mates keep calling you back.

A large woman in hip-hugging jeans came through a doorway hung with plastic streamers. She reached for beer taps like a crane driver reached for levers.

'Sorry to keep ya, love,' she said. 'What'll ya have?'

'No problem.' Johnny ordered a pot, guessing but not caring it was probably called a middie in New South Wales. He paid and sipped, the dark taste made sharper, flavoured with guilt, by the early hour. 'I like the view.'

The woman gazed at the bush.

'Walk fifty yards in there,' she said, 'and you'd disappear. Tiger country, that. Get lost in a heartbeat.'

Johnny could not see any threat. He saw an opening, the point of a leaf brushing his cheek as he entered. There would be the sponginess of rotted gum leaves and the cool perfume of eucalyptus. Overhead was the light of his childhood and beside him the shade would be welcome as sleep. Tiny birds would decorate tree trunks like ribbons in a kid's hair. No weapon required.

'Nothin' to worry about in there.' He managed a smile to show he wasn't trying to be disagreeable. 'Nothin' to hurt ya.'

'Ya reckon?' The woman wasn't convinced.

In that bush Johnny saw a place to sit and just be. No people, no mines, no traps, no ambush, no well-aimed bullets, no fear twisting your guts . . . just a blank space where it was possible the worst things might leave you alone for a while.

'I'll be back in a tic.' The woman turned away. 'Give us a yell if you need anythin'.'

Shoey thought about what he needed, and imagined the perfect girl, who might be more like Carly than Jilly. But what would he do with a girl that was any good anyway? Something in him had turned to stone. No, not stone. Something seemed to have simply gone bad. He could gently hold a pup but he couldn't properly kiss a girl. What had gone wrong? He was back, safe and sound, wasn't he? The killing was over. He'd committed no crime, kept his part of the bargain, did his duty more or less – but it didn't seem to be making too much of a difference.

'Nah, I'm right.' He nearly laughed. Oh yeah, sport, you're *really* all right.

The woman left the bar, he thought, as if she was glad to be gone. Five minutes later he did the same. In the gravel car park he saw a red phone box boasting an old black telephone that looked to be in working condition. In his pocket he had coins.

Johnny dialled Jilly's number, the phone ringing in some old Carlton cottage that he imagined as being cramped and too close to the street. Probably raining, too, he thought, knowing Melbourne. Miraculously, she answered, her voice distant, breathy and cheerful, the coin dropping through the guts of the phone as if he was playing a poker machine.

Johnny let the line clear then asked how she was. Well, she was fine. How, and where, was he? Johnny felt something catch in his heart, seeing the old, young Johnny Shoebridge in a red Miller shirt and Amco bull denim jeans disappearing around the milkbar corner, with Cam shambling along ten steps behind yelling for Shoey to wait. He wondered if Jilly saw him go.

'New South Wales coast,' he said. 'Don't worry. I'm not runnin' around with a rifle or anything. I'm okay.' He heard her laugh. It was like a little dose of good medicine.

'I'm pleased to hear it. I doubted you'd be out shooting things. You're all right, aren't you?'

'Yeah, I guess.' He wanted to tell her that he loved her because he was pretty sure that he did, he just couldn't find the place where he'd put that love. Maybe he'd just lost it, like a lot of things. Maybe if he sat quietly and thought back through the last couple of years he might find it, like a set of car keys left behind the teabags.

'When are you coming to Melbourne, Johnny?'

Johnny wasn't sure whether that was an invitation or a warning to stay away. Yeah, he knew they had spun out of each other's orbit, but he also knew she wasn't a girl to give up that easily. People thought she was cute, curly-haired, and funny – but she was more than that. She was smart, independent, and determined. She'd grown up and wasn't bound by anyone's ideas. She'd left Taralia perhaps more completely than he had. Or needed it less.

'Come as soon as you want to,' she said. 'I'm not going anywhere. Be careful, John. You know, don't climb any trees or swim too soon after lunch.'

He laughed, surprising himself. 'I won't.' He said goodbye and put the receiver down.

Don't climb any trees. Johnny liked that; something light and funny that only she would say and he would get. As he headed for the ute he pictured her putting on the kettle, fingers to her forehead, worrying as she wandered around some cramped kitchen with mismatched chairs. He also imagined the uni guys she'd know: clever, casual fellers with no blood on their hands, their futures like shiny railway lines that reached to the horizon, whereas *my* future, he thought, is more like a rusted train line that simply circles back to where it started from.

Johnny drove out of the car park and over a dark, scrub-choked creek. Immediately it set him thinking about that guerrilla-fighting bastard Khan, and his AK. Endlessly he'd rise from the low jungle mist, step out of the bamboo, and try to put a bullet into Johnny's head – or come after him hand-to-hand with that effing bayonet. But *why*? The war was over. If only the bastard would *go away*.

'Yeah, *go*,' Johnny muttered, wondering where, now, his enemy *could*.

Jesus! Just *away*. It then occurred to Johnny, in a single shining moment, that if he could imagine Khan being *here* then why couldn't he imagine him actually being somewhere *else*? If he allowed his enemy to embark upon a mission that was not to do with killing, perhaps that might allow the both of them to move a step closer to the end of the war. It might be the only way out, Johnny decided, since his chance of removing Khan from the real world was a chance that was gone forever.

Johnny pictured Khan fishing on a reedy bank, a few simple bamboo rods poking out over the olive-green water. A sparse parade of sampans plied the river, loaded with everything from coconuts to sawn timber to piles of red and green chilli. A rowboat, Johnny saw, was moving downstream, piloted by Son. Johnny imagined a conversation.

'Hey, Khan.' Son feathered an oar in greeting. 'It's not a bad day to be out here.' He changed course with a few deft strokes and allowed the boat to nose into the reeds. The oars stowed, he stepped ashore. 'You know, my friend, I can take you to a better fishing spot. Just near my family's vegetable gardens. There are eels there, too. Let's pick up your gear. If you are interested.'

Johnny saw that Khan couldn't think of a good reason to refuse. Friendship was a hard thing to turn away from, unless you were a complete nutcase. So the good communist Khan and the bad communist Son put everything in the boat, and together headed out into midstream.

'Smoke?' Son pulled out a white pack of American Kent. 'There's tobacco or hash. Take your choice.'

Charlie loved to smoke, Johnny knew that. And American cigarettes were favourites; bloody hard to get over there now, he figured, but available on the black market, like everything else.

Khan took a plain cigarette. There was a wad of bank notes in the box.

'No hash, Khan?' Son shrugged. 'It's good.' He laughed, produced the same lighter he had used last time they met. 'It sells well.'

Khan took a drag. 'Hash gives me too many answers,' he said. 'None of them right.' Son's family, Johnny decided, had been quite wealthy before the war, his father high up in district affairs. This, most likely, had something to do with Son escaping the army. Maybe that's where their fortune had gone, in buying their son's life. It happened everywhere, but in communist Vietnam, Johnny figured, it was a most dangerous thing to do.

Son plucked a bank note from a pocket. It was pale green, well-worn, and possessed a powerful and exotic aura.

'An American dollar bill.' He held it out to Khan. 'Maybe it is from Texas or California.'

Khan held the note in his fingertips, disconcerted by

the unexpected image of a single eye staring out at him. It seemed a rather odd symbol to have come from America, he thought, as he imagined that country, like its soldiers, to simply be big, brash, obvious, and confident. Perhaps it was cursed, this dollar bill. He handed it back.

'One day I will tell you, Son,' Khan said, 'about the battle for the fire base that Thang and Trung died in. Because I have never told anyone and it must be told.'

I'd like to hear that, too, Johnny thought. Since I was there.

Son nodded, rowing towards a small jetty, and a well-kept house. The smell of chickens was strong. Khan could see them strolling and scratching, pecking their way around a large vegetable garden.

'I would be honoured,' Son said. 'Although I am not worthy and I know it.'

'But you have honesty in your dealings with me.' Khan felt this to be true and important and Johnny agreed. 'That is not to be underestimated.'

Son let the boat drift into the jetty. Deftly he stepped past Khan and looped a rope around a crooked pole.

'We will eat,' the trader said. 'Then I will show you where to fish.'

Johnny watched from above, or from across the river, trying to see how and why these men were so different from the Aussies. Sure, he knew they were *somehow*, but he was struggling to see reason enough to have tried to massacre the whole bloody lot of them. Oh, yeah, of course, the government *told* him to because those men were *communists*, although Khan was nothing but a poverty-stricken fisherman, and Son little else but a travelling used-car salesman, except there was not a car in sight.

Johnny tried to imagine killing them and couldn't. The time for that had gone, but neither he nor Khan, although they'd made it home, were free. The road ahead merely continued on from the road behind.

At Son's suggestion, Khan placed his rods on a bend in the river where the water circled in a deep hole before rejoining the main current. Reeds rustled along the bank, like so many crossed swords.

'There are many eels here.' Son sat rather than squatted as Khan did. 'You should set traps. I could help you. Eels sell well.'

'They're your eels.' Khan watched the tips of his rods, hoping to see one twitch. 'Your mother'd chase me away with a broom.'

Son smiled, freed his smokes from his shirt pocket. His eyes remained invisible behind sunglasses. He appeared lazy, but Khan knew he traded far and wide on the waterways and lazy, careless people made no profit in that line of business. Or they ended up dead.

'They are *everybody's* eels now.' Son laughed as he tapped out another cigarette for Khan. 'Still, we could become communist kings of the communist eel trade and distribute our communist eel wealth. You can marry comrade Lien.' He wrist-whipped his lighter into action. 'How would that be?'

Khan nodded his thanks. The American cigarette was rich and smooth. He smoked it without guilt. The spoils of war.

'Lien would be too much for me,' he replied. 'Besides, I don't think she'd like to be queen of the communist eel trade. She might prefer the silk business or something a little less slimy.' Khan laughed; it felt good, like a cleansing puff of fresh mountain air.

'Anyway,' Son said, pocketing his silver lighter, 'it was Phuong you liked, wasn't it, Khan? She liked you, too. I remember.'

Johnny was as surprised as Khan that Son had any idea about this.

'You're amazing, Son.' Khan saw one of his rods quiver. 'What don't you know?'

'I only know,' he said, 'that I am privileged to fish with you. And share in a victory I did not fight for.'

Got that right, Johnny thought. You dodged a bullet in more ways than one there, pal. Not the Lone Ranger, though. Plenty of people in plenty of places pulled that stunt.

'I'll tell you one thing,' Khan said. 'There was a lot of loss involved in winning.'

119

'I know.' Son looked across the river to the flats where rice grew in a hundred thousand fine green tufts. 'I'm a bad penny, as they say. But believe me, brother, I'll help you if I can. You just have to ask.'

Khan grinned at the river trader. 'You don't even get onto the scale of badness, Son. Badness is those bastards ordering other bastards to bomb us from the stars!'

Son took a deep drag. 'True, I'm not that bad. But if I could've ordered someone to bomb them, I would've. They can't imagine it, can they? What it was like. Even I felt the earth shake.'

Khan reached for a rod that dipped. Thinking of the bombing was too much. He let his mind duck under the water where he summoned a big fat silver fish that would quickly be landed. Fishing possessed a kind of holiness, he felt. He had taken it up not only because it was something he could do, he felt it linked his soul to the river, the creatures in it, and drew him away from the poisoned killing grounds of the past.

A good decision then, Johnny thought.

'Those B52s,' Khan said slowly. 'I never saw one. Ghost bombers. They flew too high, near the moon. But perhaps it is better to concentrate on fish rather than Americans and their warplanes.'

Son watched the water. 'Indeed. Fish are friendlier and fishing is more productive.'

Johnny reckoned most Charlie liked to go fishing, as did a lot of Aussies. He imagined Khan's dead young friend,

Trung; could see him as a fibbing, smiling fisherman whose monsters always just got away. And Thang, the strong one, the square-head, he'd be one of those blokes who sat by the water, happy to be drinking with his mates rather than wetting a line. But when the Ho Chi Minh Trail called, Johnny guessed that was the end of their time together on the river. And on earth, as it turned out.

'I wish I could find Phuong for you,' Son added. 'I can generally find what I want, Khan. Somewhere downstream.'

Khan imagined how it might be if Phuong came back. He felt he could love her properly because she had been to the south, and would understand how he had changed. He would not hold back. If she agreed, they could resurrect something from the ruins. Yes, it would be shaped by the war, the awfulness of what had occurred and what they had gone through, but it would also be a great victory; that love could outlast hate, that the state of war was only temporary, that it was possible to regain and share a peacefulness of their own making.

'I wish you could find her, too, Son,' Khan said. 'But even you might find it difficult to row to the stars.'

'I would,' Son said, 'if I could.' He sniffed and grinned, smoking stylishly. 'We might do some planning. Nothing is truly lost until you decide it is. She might not have passed on, Khan.'

True enough, Johnny thought. True enough.

Eighteen

Shoey was on point, living a lifetime in every step. The surrounding bush seemed to possess a ceaseless fluidity. Wherever he wasn't looking melted into tones and textures of liquid green. Wherever he was looking, heart-shaped foliage was imprinted on his brain as sharply as leaves pressed in a book.

He searched the spaces between the trunks. He studied tree stumps and tree tops. He searched for the oddity, the unusual, and the obvious – all the time taking slow steps, putting his feet down as gently as a cat puts down its paws, his rifle at the ready, safety off.

Johnny could feel the space around him through his skin. The fine hairs on his arms stood up. He was aware that he existed in a dimension never before visited, a floating world vibrating with life overlapped by the shimmering shadow of death. Slowly he moved, in a trance of concentration, down a path of his own making.

Ahead, a narrow dirt road curved through a tunnel of thick, whippy growth interspersed with bamboo. Here, reportedly, Charlie had been moving. Johnny stopped and the patrol stopped with him. Fat drops of sweat eased down his legs and back. I don't like this joint, he thought. It is bloody evil. The wall of tangled greenery radiated suppressed violence. He would've liked to burn it, bomb it, back off, and never return, but that was not on the cards. So he willed himself to detect the enemy, knowing if he couldn't, he would have to move through the place.

The skipper came up and they squatted, stone-like in the heavy heat. Never once did Captain McCrae take his eyes off the wall of green.

'Story, mate?'

Johnny moved his head a centimetre. 'Don't like it. Gimme a minute.'

The skipper nodded, settled in next to a tree, SLR levelled. Behind them the men fanned out and sunk down, every weapon and eye trained outward. There was a thrumming to the silence. Shoey attempted to X-ray the mass of canes. Was Charlie in there, flat-out on the forest floor, fingers curled on triggers, taking aim over black sights?

The air was wrong, holding back like a saved breath. The Cong had many degrees of advantage here. Charlie knew the ground, the plants, night, day, friend, foe, spirit, and neutral. He was born of it, died within it, then became it. And he was a cruel, calculating little bastard.

Seconds passed, compounding Johnny's perception that the situation was only getting worse. The place was in a state of paralysis but he sensed a signal for action was an instant away. Less.

'*Three o'clock!*' Barry shouted. 'On the *ground!*'

The M60 opened up. Pressure waves crossed the road. Dust lifted. Vegetation flew. Shoey hit the dirt and cracked off ten shots knee-high. The bush shook, the sky fell. There was wild movement. The noise lifted, pushed to the clouds, auto and semi-autos firing non-stop. A digger sprawled onto the road, a booted foot at a strange angle, an open hand near a dropped weapon.

Where *were* the pricks?

Johnny could see none of them when he absolutely hungered to kill *all* of them. Invisible, they were firing from an impenetrable green blur screened by rolling smoke and rising noise. He emptied his magazine, flicked it out, snapped in another, let go the full twenty. Then possessed by some mad kind of love he found himself crawling like a furious wombat to the downed digger – and with Dave Roberts, they dragged Danny-Boy Jacobs back into the bush by his wrists.

Shoey had never felt fear like it. It filled him, driving out everything except blind strength.

'Fuck me!' Robbo yelled, as they hauled Danny into cover. 'That'll do! Get down!' Roberts hit the deck, twisted to his left, the tendons in his neck standing out like reinforcing rods. '*Medic!*' Then he threw a grenade hard and flat like a cricketer returning to the keeper. 'Cop that!'

Johnny grabbed his weapon, the grenade exploding across the road as if a teacher had smacked a yard ruler on a desk, demanding silence. But the firing went on as if half the world was involved. Shoey clicked out the empty mag, smacked home another, and blasted off half to suppress the bastards if nothing else. Twenty metres away he saw a thin, black-eyed fighter retreating but his AK was coming up, needle-pointed with a silver bayonet.

It looked like that bastard Khan.

Johnny fired twice.

Later, Johnny had pictured the ambush from Khan's side of the road, and was able to access another angle on how this firefight had been. He could see the enemy guerrilla in a depression filled with dry leaves, his oiled weapon resting steady on open palms, as he stared into the bush where the Australian patrol had taken up position. Johnny saw Khan blink. Was that a shirt button, the enemy soldier asked himself? A white finger? A green knee? A black barrel? A shifting shadow? Was anyone *actually* there?

Oh, we're here, all right, Johnny thought. We're here *big-time*.

Khan studied the bush, heard a bird, wished he was one

then banished the thought. He was here to fight and if necessary die – but still his guts squirmed, his skin registering every prickling needle of vegetation. Now he felt what might be a scorpion creeping into the folds of his shirt but he could not move.

Do not sting me, brother scorpion, he prayed. If you are there.

Khan sensed his comrades ranged around him. Each was camouflaged with fresh-plucked leaves attached to their helmets and packs. Each was committed to the moment, this one battle of fifty thousand, to kill or be killed or both. Khan also sensed the imaginary scorpion had departed and was grateful. To strengthen his resolve he allowed the feeling of the earth to heat his belly, the power of it to strengthen his heart, its history of victory to put molten steel into his blood. This is our land, he thought. We are men of this country. Get ready, mercenaries, you're about—

'*Fire!*'

The bush opposite blew outwards. Vegetation above Khan's head was chopped into fragments. Dirt leapt as he fired at weapons firing. Leaves shook and were blown away, then remarkably Khan saw a soldier sprawl onto the track, a large Australian with blond hair. It was so unexpected it was if the man had fallen from the sky.

The enemy had spread. Khan's section was taking heavy fire. He emptied his weapon across the road, remembering to shoot low. Ramming home a fresh magazine, he saw two soldiers drag the wounded man into the bush, the three so suddenly gone he had no chance to shoot.

Captain Van swore as another M60 opened up. Now a grenade exploded to the right, the bush disintegrating, splinters whirling.

'We're out!' Van swept an arm. 'Fire and move! Withdraw! Go!'

Yeah, as bloody *usual*, Johnny thought, but it was with a disgusted admiration he watched Khan and the Charlie fighters evaporate calmly into the bush. Black magic, that was. Vietnamese voodoo. Good tactical soldiering.

The fighters around Khan moved, keeping low. Disciplined and brave, they fired as they backed out along tiny tracks. Then Khan was following, firing from the hip as he gratefully reached a pair of trees. Taking a final look across the road, he saw a prone rifleman with a grease-blackened face, elbow coming up as he levelled his weapon. Khan fired, bullets flicking bamboo fronds, and a year later and three thousand miles away, Johnny was astonished.

Yes, I *did* see the bastard again, he thought. I really did.

Two rounds sizzled inches above Johnny's head. And now, like always, Charlie was gone, probably a mile away in ten seconds. But as spooky as the little bastards were, Johnny held on to the sight of the Main Force fighter as proof the pricks were human – so they could be killed, they could be blown up, they were not ghost men, and that was reassuring.

The firing stopped. Men moved towards men. Urgent words travelled short distances. Orders and instructions were fed through the undergrowth like wires. No one stood. Shoey saw an intravenous drip rise, the clear line unfurling like a snake escaping. A radio squawked, the skipper calling for a chopper as Johnny slotted home a fresh magazine, and searched the bush opposite. To underestimate the enemy would get him, or worse still, someone else, shot in the head.

Charlie had flown. Johnny could imagine the fighters backing down tracks more like burrows, carrying their wounded and dead. They had the toughness of bull ants, he thought. You could jump on them with everything you had and they'd still come up fighting. And they'd leave nothing behind but blood, spent cartridges, and the smell of strange men floating among the blue stink of gunpowder.

Shoey stayed prone, SLR into his shoulder. His mind screamed at him to think about a thousand things but he refused. He shut out everything except his duty as a forward scout and a killer of Viet Cong. He knew he was changed. Maybe it occurred to him there and then. Maybe that's why he mistakenly labelled it as unimportant and temporary.

His brain was hardened. His head was only interested in the business of searching the bush, knowing who was friend, and who should be shot. His old self, a knockabout kid called Johnny Shoebridge, was gone, replaced by a stranger he didn't dislike or disown because this stranger had proven to be reliable where it was deadly – and that was something of immense value, purchased at great expense.

Johnny was rotated off point. With Lex and Barry he prepared to cross the road. The wounded had been choppered out, Shoey watching the Huey lift off, thinking it the most beautiful thing he'd ever seen, vanishing like a dream into wakefulness, leaving him rooted to the spot.

'You know,' Lex said, his M16 held in the crook of his arm as if he was an English lord out shooting pheasant, 'this just seems to be getting more and more dangerous. I'll be bringing a note from home. I have a severe allergy to violence directed at myself. I'm a student of the arts, John. I'd be a lot happier writing about this in a poem than actually doing it. I need a year off. At least.'

Shoey felt a momentary release of pressure, but his head was jammed with his time up-front and centre. He smiled but wherever he looked a merry-go-round of greenery spun. Thousands of decisions made wiped away thousands of memories held. These firefights were tempering his personality like iron. He was changing by the second although he didn't know what he was changing into.

Barry, two metres away, shook his head as if Lex was as foreign to him as the VC.

'That bloody school you went to, Lex, it rooted your mind.'

Lex appeared shocked. Up went his eyebrows. He clamped a free hand to his hip. '*Really, Barry?* Well, amigo, I think you're being bloody ungrateful, you know.' He exhaled at length. 'Just because I told you two boys that forks go on the left? It's something that's puzzled Shoey for years. And now he can confidently go ahead and set a table without a worry in the world.' Lex raised a finger triumphantly. 'And *that's* the benefit of a private school education.'

A column of angry-looking red ants marched past Johnny's boot. He gave them space. A thought struck him like a forearm to the face.

'Just wait till we have to defend one of those fire bases.' He checked his rifle for the tenth time in two minutes. 'That's when the shit'll really hit the fan.'

Lex sniffed hard. 'Not me, sport. I have a piano exam. Grade Two. We're a musical family, Shortbridge. My sister is a gifted xylophonist, despite her extremely large tits. We'll be touring old people's homes up and down the Gold Coast when we get home, John. I'll get you a free ticket.'

'I'm busy.' Johnny grinned. 'But I like the sound of your sister.'

The order to move out lifted the patrol from the under-growth. Shoey, knowing he had no choice, stepped onto the road. Every time he put down a foot he expected to hear a click, and to be engulfed in fire and flying metal. The place reeked of danger. He had the urge to scream or vomit.

The vegetation rose like the hair of a madman. Charlie had had days to booby-trap it, but the patrol moved on and in. This slow-motion pursuit reminded Johnny of the Hare and the Tortoise, yet the Aussies were neither hare nor tortoise, and Charlie was both. He stopped. Something like a badly poached egg hung from a thorny stem; it was the remains of a human eye. Johnny ignored it, searching doubly hard, trying to out-think Charlie's mine-laying strategy of striking when attention was directed elsewhere.

Clear. As far as he could see. Which wasn't nearly far enough.

'God help me,' he whispered, and meant it.

Moving forward, he considered the company's upcoming role as defenders of a proposed fire support base. This base, an artillery battery and HQ, would serve as bait to entice the VC to attack in the open and in numbers – an invitation, Shoey thought, Charlie might just decide to take up.

Bigger battles lay ahead. Things would escalate. No one could stop it. Only the generals welcomed it.

Nineteen

Shoey walked towards the river mouth with his fishing rod and Alvey Junior tackle box given to him by his dad ten years ago. He'd bought some frozen bait on the way back from town, and the bag of pilchards still managed to give off a well-seasoned and old-fashioned smell of sea.

Sitting where he'd first met Carly, he rigged up, feeling like a kid. His dad had taught him to fish; how to tie a half-blood knot, use swivels, and select hooks and sinkers. As he baited up, he pictured himself and his old man on the bare bank of the Rocklands Reservoir. There they were, sitting in aluminium deckchairs, trying to catch redfin with worms.

It was like looking at a photo album in bright sunshine; the never-never land of the past hauled out into the open, with none of the kindliness of shadows to soften anything. Johnny let out a breath and consigned the memory to the too-hard basket. He cast and settled down to wait.

Across the inlet he saw a guy sitting on a driftwood log. The bloke, fishing with a handline, was an Abo, Johnny reckoned; some unidentifiable element of belonging keyed him into the landscape. Johnny lifted a hand but got no response.

'Yeah, good on ya, sport,' he muttered. 'Suit yourself.'

Johnny was aware something in his head had shifted. He gradually got the feeling, like water stealing in over sand flats, that he was adrift in his own country. Perhaps he'd worked so hard at *seeing* Vietnam in an effort to *see* the Viet Cong that he had left himself behind.

He lit a smoke and watched his line, a silver thread from rod tip to river bottom. At the moment, it seemed that this was about all the connection he had to anywhere.

Toughen up, prick, he told himself.

Then, oddly, it occurred to him that the opposite might work better. How about *softening* up? How about that? How about trying to understand what everyone else was saying about the bloody war? Maybe the demonstrators had a point? Maybe him and the boys were bloody savages? And the only way forward was to ask for forgiveness?

Never. He sought forgiveness from no one here, just as he had never expected mercy from anyone over there. It was war. And that it was a war not of his making didn't change anything.

Just thinking about talking to the other side made him feel sick. Besides, talk and listen to bloody who? Uni students? Politicians? That bitch back in town? What did they know about what he'd done, what had happened to him, to his mates, what he'd been ordered to do? Hanging tough was *always* the only way out of this. Johnny looked across the water, seeing the other fisherman was gone.

Had he ever been there? Or was he just another ghost, like Khan and his mates? Shadow men haunting shadow men?

Shoey took a drag. Somehow smoking made it possible to sit and calmly consider the idea that he was three-quarters crazy. That he was a lunatic in search of something but not knowing what, where, or how to find it. From over the water he heard a bird – that single bell-like note he'd heard before, and it came, he thought, like a signal to hold on.

Just in time.

As Johnny sat by the inlet he conjured Khan on his way to visit the fish caged at the jetty. While walking, the one-armed veteran bumped into the good-looking girl, Lien. It was obvious to Johnny and Khan how delicate and beautiful Lien was in her white *ao dai*. She carried a basket of red, blue, and gold sewing things and something like a melody of loveliness rose from her, and a beguiling scent. But it was not a melody or scent intended for the one-armed Khan.

Johnny laughed; you're a bloody idiot, champ, if you can't see that. But he figured Khan could see it, just like he could imagine it, because they both realised when a broken-down soldier stood close to a girl like Lien the more distant she became.

'Good morning, sister Lien.' Khan spoke gently, noting that as he did she became younger, and he older. 'It's a fine day.'

She replied in kind but her words had no weight. Walking away, Khan knew that the sight of him darkened her life. His missing arm and his return from the south marked him as someone on intimate terms with the spirit world. In a brotherly way, he would've liked to tell her that he was not a ghost but only one lucky soldier with a melancholy mind trying to find a future.

Yeah, yeah, Johnny thought. Aren't we all? But he could not ridicule his old enemy because the bastard seemed intent on telling the truth – and the truth was gold, no matter who told it, who you were, or where you came from. So Johnny imagined Khan trying to smile, not because he was happy but because he was desolate. Like Johnny, too often he saw Brutus the bulldozer pushing red dirt over the broken faces of Thang and Trung and twenty others.

For different reasons, neither of them would ever be able to forget it.

You guys shouldn't have taken us on then, Johnny thought. Surely you knew what we had? Who we'd call? What we'd do? Yet still you came. Orders are orders, I guess, Johnny mused. Orders are orders.

He watched as Khan walked out onto the jetty. The sun, pale bronze, infiltrated the water with golden rays. Upstream, mist rose like spirits departing. Downstream the red-tiled roof of Son's house was visible on the bend. Johnny decided that Khan should hate that mongrel Son for dodging the war, although this was not as simple as it sounded.

Did a person have the right to make up his own mind about fighting in a war? Was every order given by unseen men to be obeyed without question? Were the people in charge gods? On whose authority were they acting? And what was it they sought to gain? And besides, on a more human level, Johnny saw that Son was repentant and respectful. And he had said he would try to repay this famous debt to Khan, which would prove interesting if the trader could be trusted – if a debt like that could ever be settled.

Johnny cleaned the flathead he'd caught, throwing the froggy-looking heads and guts into the water. Glancing up, he saw Malcolm striding down the track, his hair flat to his head as if recently combed.

'Gidday.' Johnny stood, aware that he was an unpaying guest on the man's land. 'How ya goin'?'

'Well.' Malcolm nodded, his height made even more impressive as he stood uphill. 'Yourself?'

'Fine. Thanks.' Johnny had to stop himself from saying, *sir*. The man might have been a general, the way he presented himself. 'A nice spot.' He looked around to show his appreciation. Dusk was descending, the night slipping from the bush, darkly sombre. 'Thanks for lettin' me stay 'ere. Appreciate it.'

'You're welcome.' The tall farmer's attention stayed on Johnny. It seemed ownership replaced the need to look elsewhere. 'I was wondering, John, if you might consider doing a bit of work for me. Labouring, really. Blackberry spraying and rock-gathering where the tractor can't go.'

Sounded simple enough, Johnny thought. Do-able, even. And possibly a step in the right direction – whatever that direction might be. He met the man's stare.

'Sure. Right. When?'

'Come up to the house in the morning.' Malcolm pointed up the slope rough-patched with bracken. 'You know the way. Bev will give you lunch. Eight-thirty, if that suits. Good.'

Johnny nodded, watched the farmer go then turned to the inlet. He thought about the Abo he'd seen fishing; had he imagined the resentment coming over the water? The connection to the place? Maybe, maybe not. Feeling exposed, he moved to a handy rock, squatted, and lit a smoke, pondering.

So many people wandered the paths of his memory, piling experience on experience until he felt he was going to suffocate under an avalanche of images, noise, and echoes.

137

No wonder his old self, who really did seem like a good, honest, Disneyland kid, had gone away. The old Johnny Shoebridge had never really liked thinking too much or too deeply, so it was always going to be problematic now that he had no choice, that in attempting to fix his head, he had to think all the bloody time.

Johnny imagined the comfort of having his SLR, fully loaded, across his knees. It wasn't that he wanted to shoot anyone. The last thing he wanted to hear was the head-smack of large-calibre gunfire or feel the mind-numbing sting of bullets whipping past his eyes. No, he would've just liked to have that weapon, the power it had to protect and defend, a trusty companion from the past, a reminder of what had been demanded from him and the price he'd paid.

What could replace it?

Well, he was looking for something, a key, a fact, a person, to help him away from the wreckage of himself and towards some kind of recovery. And perhaps that he *was* looking was the main thing because he reckoned if he gave up, everything would fall in a heap. And that was being polite.

Off a cliff was more like it.

Twenty

Shoey knelt in the milky tropical water, looking towards the beach with only his eyes showing, like a crocodile. He could see two diggers sitting on deckchairs. They wore jungle greens and were armed with M16s that shone like black snakes in the hot sun. The sea was like dishwater. *Germy*, his mum would've called it. Behind him Lex floated on his back and Barry stood belly-deep, tattoos on his arms shining as he sipped from a can of Vic Bitter.

On the beach Aussies and Yanks smoked and drank as Vietnamese women, some in bikinis, some in traditional shirts and trousers, engaged in one sort of business or another. There were trinkets and souvenirs for sale. Food and drinks were set out on mats. Flimsy bars lined the street and unidentifiable music only added to the stinking head-ache Johnny had from drinking the evening before.

'So, Barry,' Lex said. 'How'd you rate the ladies from last night? On a scale of one to ten.'

Barry sipped beer. Didn't look at Lex. Didn't move, didn't blink.

'Five,' he said, never taking his eyes off the beach.

Johnny laughed, knew himself to be one corner of a triangle, the strongest shape of all. He *knew* Lex and he *knew* Barry like he knew no one else on the planet. He'd been with them in action and owed them his life. It didn't matter where they came from or how smart or dumb they were. Or what they said or knew. It only mattered what they did; that they were deadly serious about killing VC who were trying to kill him, or any other Australian. Three lives he had now, Shoey thought, and a share in many others.

'Yeah, they were all right.' Johnny's guilt over paying for the girls was outweighed by the brutal nature of what he was involved in. 'Value for money,' he added, which was what was expected. 'What'd you think, Lex? Any of 'em suit the arty-farty type?'

Lex floated on his back like a long bumpy island, concentrating as if it was his life's work.

'Well, I don't think Mother would be too pleased if I turned up for Christmas dinner with the two or three who didn't seem overly keen on underwear. But they did have the skills, Johnboy, you can't argue with that. Anyway, let's go get a beer.' Lex righted himself, stood. 'I'm in danger of sobering up.'

Johnny wanted the talk to go on. It linked them like lights illuminating the dark place they were in, had come from, and would have to go to. He breathed deep, knowing that whatever happened, for however long he lived, he would never be totally alone.

Johnny wondered what it had been like for the D555 fighters living deep under the granite skulls of the Long Hai Hills. He pictured Khan sitting on his bedding, looking at the rough stone walls. Was he thinking of his chances of survival? Was he thinking of Phuong? Was he thinking of home? Or did he only think about killing the enemy? Did those Viet Cong ever think like Aussies?

Probably not. Charlie lived closer to the earth than the diggers. He was also fighting an invading force, survived on air and dew, and lived with a history of bloody invasion and appalling atrocities. Khan and his comrades knew what it took to drive foreigners out of Vietnam. They'd been doing it for thousands of years, according to Lex, who knew that kind of shit. And there was no reason to think they would stop now.

Johnny decided that Khan, like most Charlie, would look to the spirit world more than the diggers because statistically, that was very well where he was likely to end up. If this happened, Khan would see his sacrifice as necessary, if and when his ancestors demanded it. Johnny also imagined his enemy praying for Phuong, the missing girl, hoping that she may have survived as the flood of fighters inundated the south, the living replacing the dead like new leaves, endlessly.

Who knew what lay ahead for anyone, good guy or bad? Not me, thought Johnny, although he had a fair idea he was never going to be napalmed by Phantoms or carpet-bombed by B-52s, just as Khan would not fall into a pit of spikes or step on a mine. Life in wartime was the ultimate game of chance. The only outcome guaranteed was that you would never want to play the game again.

We are born in bad times. Johnny could imagine Khan saying that because it was true for the Vietnamese. Any time three or four countries turned up to bomb you off the face of the earth you knew it was going to be a rough couple of decades. Johnny could also see that the Charlie battalions viewed themselves very differently to the Aussies: the Australian view was to survive, get home, get back to real life, and try to forget the bloody war – where Charlie accepted his fighting unit as a stepping stone to victory in a fight to the death for his country. And that even if D555 were wiped out, they paved the way for the brothers and sisters that followed. The North Vietnamese would fight to the last man or woman to win and everybody in that country knew it.

Johnny glimpsed Khan watching thoughtfully over his sleeping mates, Thang and Trung. It was clear he loved his friends, his country, and he loved Phuong, as all soldiers needed comrades, a home, and women in some way. Johnny also knew Khan was truly courageous. And in war, no matter whose side you were on, to have courage was the most important thing of all.

How did things *really* end up for the bastard? Johnny thought about this a lot. Did Khan survive? Did he cop it? What did his gods have in store for him? Did they sacrifice him? Did they spare him? How did the universe, finally, treat him?

Shoey, Barry, and Lex climbed up into an open truck for the ride back to Nui Dat. Two armed diggers, as sober as the boys were drunk, sat with weapons pointed skywards. Studiously they ignored the men they were escorting. Johnny simply watched the world go by, the smell so strong it was as if someone was holding used toilet paper to his face. The heat clung like steam and ramshackle houses and ravaged land tumbled in and out of his vision. By the road the people watched the passing truck as if hypnotised.

'Now, you see, Barry—' Lex drew lines through the air with his cigarette, 'what the words *foreign land* mean.'

'Yeah.' Barry glanced at a pile of burning garbage, dismissing what he saw as if he was leaving the country within the hour. 'Shithole.'

Johnny wished he was sober. He could not meet the eyes of the Viets. He wished he was on a ship, a plane, a bloody rowboat out of here. It was worse to be unarmed, wearing a stupid flowery shirt, and no hat. Rattling along in the truck, he felt like a tourist gawping at the people standing in stinking poverty – poverty that was probably only going to get worse, the whole place possibly turning into a slaughterhouse when the Aussies left.

Were the diggers winning hearts and minds, let alone the war? Were they helping or hindering by simply being here?

The answer wasn't obvious. Twenty metres away he saw a roadside concrete house like a bunker. A sick-looking pig stood behind a wooden fence in green mud and a little boy sat on a rock. Johnny saw the kid staring as if he could see the future, and there was nothing there.

'Poor bastards,' he muttered, hoping it might be good karma for somebody that he recognised what he was seeing was wrong. 'God help 'em.'

It'd be a relief, he thought, to be back at camp. He would be with Aussies only and have his weapon. He would also be surrounded by miles of barbed wire and artillery ready to fire.

'If anybody should protest against the war,' Lex said, watching an old woman carrying a towering load of firewood, 'it's the bloody locals. Barry? Your thoughts. Feel free to mention the French occupation. Fifty words or less. In your own time. Normally I'd ask for coloured pictures, but I do believe you don't have your Derwent pencils.'

Barry shook out a smoke and lit up. He didn't look at the people or the wandering dogs or the ragged palm trees. He appeared unmoved by the smell of sewage, rotting vegetables, and burning rubber.

'This place,' he flicked a match, as if he had spread petrol, and was going to torch the joint, 'is rooted.'

One of the armed Australian guards turned his head.

'Jesus, mate,' he said. 'Language. We have National Servicemen on board, soldier. Some have even been to university.'

The boys laughed and Lex appeared to perk up.

'Yes, thank you, sir.' He nodded enthusiastically. 'I myself was studying Arts at Monash University until the government volunteered my services. So if you'd like a short presentation on early European settlement in Australia, I think the chaps might see it has certain similarities with what we're involved in here. It'd only take twenty minutes or so.'

The guard sucked in a breath and shook his head as if hard-pressed for time, or a suitable answer.

'Mate, *personally*, I'd fuckin' *love* to hear it. But someone else might shoot you in the face.'

Barry glanced. 'Gimme yer rifle.'

Johnny had to smile. The situation was so ridiculous that it was funny – not all the time was it funny, and not in every way was it funny. But at the moment it was like being on stage in some sort of long and elaborate practical joke. Eventually, though, when the curtain did come down, everyone would see that what they had been involved in was no laughing matter whatsoever.

The truck rattled on, Johnny with it.

Twenty-one

Johnny moved down the rocky slope spraying blackberries, pumping the hand lever. Something about the work disgusted him. The smell of the chemical mist made his skin crawl. He'd had enough of this shit in Vietnam; inhaled any number of mysterious soups sprayed out of low-flying planes, all in the good cause of denying Charlie cover, and killing his rice.

Suddenly, Johnny Shoebridge didn't want to poison anything. He didn't give a stuff about bloody blackberries ruining decent land. Or the cover they'd give to rabbits. He'd had enough of this liquid pox that clung shining to the soft leaves of the English weeds. He'd knock this slope over and that'd be it. Johnny-boy was over and out. This wasn't the army.

'*What shit!*' Anger rose as he pumped and sprayed. 'What *utter* shit!'

The chemical stink poisoned his thoughts. Just the idea of using it, inhaling the drifting mist, made him sick – and ten minutes later, the slope finished, he walked away from the backpack, the feel of a sweat-soaked shirt more like a memory of the jungle than work just done.

He lit a smoke and gazed at low mountains rising from unbroken bush. No VC in there, sport, he thought. That's the good news. She's nothin' but a bloody garden so cheer up! This, he conceded, was a stupid thought, but the truth held value. He might be half-mental but he *was* safe.

Glancing around, he saw Malcolm striding down the track in the company of a dark-skinned bloke who wore a red-checked shirt and green work pants. Maybe it was the guy who had been fishing on the other side of the river, Johnny wondered, and uncrossed his arms in an effort to look like an obedient employee and not a good-for-nothing hothead.

Malcolm, stopping, allowed his gaze to travel to the discarded pump.

'All done, John?'

'Up to and includin' this section.' Johnny bracketed the gully, a smoke between his fingers. 'But the spray's makin' me crook. I'll have to go on to somethin' else.' Or take off, he guessed. Your call, boss.

Malcolm considered Johnny's response. Or perhaps how it was put.

'It's never affected anyone before.' The tall man spoke slowly. 'I've used it myself. It's off-the-shelf from the supplier.'

Johnny shrugged. Carefully he ground out his Marlboro and dug the butt into the dirt with his heel. He wasn't angry, but he'd taken delivery of a solid block of uncooperation. That poisonous crap he would not use. He said nothing.

'All right.' Malcolm pointed to a rocky corner. 'We'll move on. Perhaps you can give Thomas a hand piling those stones so I can get the tractor in there.'

'No worries.' Johnny was pleased to agree because his next move was to walk away, get his gear, and ride off into the sunset.

The big farmer, he decided, didn't look quite *as* pleased but with a nod he turned back up the hill. Johnny introduced himself to Thomas, a solemn man who shook hands lightly, as if acknowledging Johnny's presence but nothing else. Fair enough, thought Shoey. This is your patch, mate. I know something about that story.

As Johnny carried rocks he brought up the image of the one-armed Khan fishing off the old village jetty. Well, the bastard had to do something to fill in his days, Johnny figured. No disability pensions for the communists, no sir. So it seemed reasonable Khan might be fishing, and keeping an eye on his fish stocks while Johnny kept his mind's eye on him.

So what do you think of the spirit world now, feller, Shoey mused. After the B52s shattered the earth and your people were vaporised? How'd your spirits go with that? Surely that would've blown the theory of any sort of a protective higher power? That the gods were solely on your side?

Not entirely, Johnny decided, on Khan's behalf. It was the North Vietnamese point of view that Trung and Thang had brave, good, and patriotic souls, no matter what the world had dealt to them. And then Khan put forward the theory that if war unleashes evil then might it also prove the existence of good spirits?

Go on, Johnny allowed. Since you're on a roll, I've got the time, and a couple of close mates who deserve a decent life hereafter, if things might be balanced up a bit at this late stage.

Khan tapped cigarette ash. Maybe, he thought, in the next world good might wash away evil like the tide erased footprints?

Could be, sport, Johnny thought, as he put another rock on the pile.

Khan also considered that perhaps the courageous souls of Thang and Trung were helping steer the life of bad brother, Son, in a more worthy direction.

That too sounded reasonable, Johnny decided, just as it was reasonable that one day he would head to Melbourne to see Jilly and find out once and for all if there was anything between them left to salvage.

It was also not beyond Shoey's imagination to consider old enemies might travel along similar roads in order to reach an acceptable peace – or at least an honourable parting of the ways. Incredible things did happen in war, and after. His surviving those two massive battles for the fire-bases proved that.

The pile of rocks increased, like the weight of silence between Johnny and Thomas, until Johnny announced it was time for a smoke. Together they sat by the pile, Thomas not smoking, both looking down on bush that rose and fell like a swelling sea.

'How's it go workin' for Malcolm?' Johnny took a drag. 'He seems like a fair-enough sort of a bloke.'

Thomas nodded, with one hand on a rock as if it was a child's head that he was blessing.

'He's orright.' He did not look at Johnny. 'He said you been to Vietnam. A couple of the black fellers round here went, too.'

Shoey lounged on the grassy ground. It was nice to be close to it. He imagined the springy red worms, the fat white grubs, the soil held together by fine white roots like veins. He'd never had the same feeling in the jungle. The Vietnamese landscape simply didn't offer him the cover he sought. Or the connection that assured him he was fighting for a just cause.

'All the black fellers that I saw over there,' Johnny said, 'were bloody excellent soldiers. Terrific. Naturals. Top blokes.'

Thomas appeared to process this information as he stared down the grassy slope.

'Billy Redpath's still walkin' it off. Can't play footy or nothin'. Drinkin' too much. Smokin' too much. So he's walkin'.'

Johnny thought about that. 'Where's he walkin' to?'

Thomas watched over bush. 'Round here.' He nodded. 'His country.'

Johnny did not find that odd. When you found yourself in the wrong space, or with the wrong people, the bad stuff would come bolting out of the blue hard and fast. Better to be a moving target in a happy land. Well, as good a plan as any.

'I'm walkin' too, mate.' Shoey rested on an elbow, appreciating Thomas's air of difference and indifference. 'Just about as far away from Vietnam as I can get.'

Thomas looked at Johnny. The sun polished the curved bones of his face.

'Billy don't talk. He just walk.'

Johnny took a last drag and felt an idea stir in the compressed smoke in his lungs. At some point he would have to visit Barry's family and Lex's. Not only did this have to be done, he needed and wanted to do it. And soon. Of course it wouldn't be good. It would be bloody terrible, but there was no way around that.

He glanced at Thomas, who stared at the inlet as if the view meant just about everything. No wonder Charlie fought so hard, Johnny thought. You didn't cough up twenty thousand years of history to foreign bastards intent on bombing you back to the Stone Age. You didn't bow to generals who drank duty-free whiskey while they ordered the destruction of an entire country's rice crop. You didn't give in to invaders, full stop.

Shoey blew out smoke. Politicians could look at a map and see where the mountains and rivers were, but that didn't tell them anything about the people. The Vietnamese had never been beaten. You could have found that out in the library. But no, the bigwigs wanted their answers spelled out in blood, and that is exactly what they got. This I know to be true, Shoey thought, because I saw it happen.

'Give my regards to Billy.' Johnny gave Thomas half a salute. 'I mean it.'

Thomas nodded but said nothing.

Twenty-two

Shoey lay eyes-shut on his stretcher in the tent, rifle by his head, listening to the night sounds. There was a murmuring like the sea but it wasn't water. It was the movement of air over a land of paddy, jungle, mountains, rivers, marshes, and bush. It was the gathering of a million whispers in foreign words and it held no comfort or peace.

The Australian base felt like a fully armed pirate ship, he reckoned, in the middle of an enemy ocean. He could feel the massive weight of the guerrilla army out there in the dark. There were hundreds of thousands of the tough skinny strange cruel little men he'd only once or twice seen close up, their faces even more secretive in death.

Day and night, they were heading south down roads, tracks, trails, and waterways. They were living in tunnels and caves and on boats. They were holed up in the hills, villages, and jungle outposts. And they were always planning in that singsong, quack-quack language that no Aussie he'd ever met could understand. There were well-trained battalions. There was village rabble, but their purpose was singular and overwhelming. *Get the invaders out.* This was the whisper that Shoey and rest of the diggers could hear, a whisper that never, ever stopped.

Until he had hit the jungle, Johnny had never felt the magnetic pull of his own country. Now Australia was a dream as bright as a bloody Bristol paint chart. The sun back home was the same simple yellow as Golden Circle pineapple. The people were hardly mysterious. There were no punji stakes set to spear you through the guts. No stolen landmines to blow your legs off. No kid giving you a grenade as an early birthday present. But this place, Viet*nam*, existed in the shadow of shadows as complex as an endlessly shuffled pack of playing cards.

As Shoey drifted through the haunted landscape of a soldier's sleep, he sensed the rustle and sigh of the VC moving. And five seconds after the first mortar rounds hit, he was running blindly through smoke and fire, love and hate, shouting and shooting, caught in the strike zone where armies collided.

Outside the wire, inside the compound of Johnny's mind, Khan hugged the ground. With volcanic intensity the Australian base opened up with artillery, M60 machineguns and semi-automatic rifles. Five seconds later the thumping *whump* of mortar shells kicked Johnny and Khan in the kidneys, as opposing crews went at it punch for punch like fat men fighting. In midair the shells crossed before plummeting dumbly to earth. And there, luckily or unluckily, an explosion might be traded for body parts.

Khan was ordered forward to probe the defences and provide covering fire for the sappers. Stiff with fear he crawled out of the trees. Beside him were four brother fighters. In front, two sappers snaked away across the ground that had been cleared by the Australians.

'This is not good!' Thang hissed, the low belly of the sky slashed with red and green tracer. 'This is hard!'

Khan had no time to reply as an M60 from the base sent fifty rounds scorching a metre over their heads. Now a searchlight joined the battle, relentlessly exploring as grenades like hammer blows exploded on either side of the fence. The sappers were at the wire, cutting carefully, wearing packs loaded with explosives. So far so good; the team was unseen, working in the roaring flashes of the firefight.

A thought touched Khan like a warm hand. Thank goodness Trung was on a scouting mission to an Australian base sixty kilometres away. As a sapper-in-training, tonight, he would've been sprinting with the others towards the artillery batteries. There, he would've found himself within the jaws of a hundred barking weapons that sought to take his head off.

An explosion rocked the ground and a fireball rose. Within a circle of moving light Khan could see men, artillery, and tree stumps. Blackness returned, the gunfire ceaseless as he waited, pressed to the ground, for the sappers to return.

It seemed impossible he would not be hit. Every time he fired, an enemy pinpointed the muzzle blast, and sent back a bullet or three. Metal flew, artillery thundered, and just when Khan *felt* he was to be killed a bugle sounded. The raid was over.

Thang shouted, 'We wait twenty seconds for the saps! All right?'

Khan nodded. A pendulum, like a guillotine blade, swung over the back of his neck as he hugged the ground. Then, spotting a lone figure leap out through the wire, he and Thang turned, to scuttle like crabs for distant cover. The other sapper, they knew, was gone as surely as yesterday.

I knew you were out there, Khan, Johnny thought. Or someone just like you.

Shoey shot at shadows and the brief fiery stab of muzzle blasts. The bush appeared to swarm with fast-moving fireflies. If he hit anyone, he didn't know it, as the enemy remained virtually and intentionally invisible. Lex, beside him, smacked home a fresh magazine and worked a round into the breech.

'They're just stuffin' aroun—'

An explosion ripped the sky, smacking down every other sound for the count of three. A mushroom cloud of light and heat floated away like a hot air balloon.

'Er, maybe not.' Lex ducked into his weapon pit. 'That was the real fuckin' thing. And I don't mean Coca-Cola, John. Or marra-yu-whana. I think that was what some people around here might call a bomb.'

There was screaming and controlled shouting. Two more machineguns opened up in crazy counterpoint to a bugle that sprayed the darkness with notes that rose and fell with no rhyme or reason Johnny could detect.

It was as if a switch had been hit. The firing beyond the wire stuttered, like the last few hailstones on a tin roof in a summer thunderstorm.

'Geddown, you stupid pricks!' Barry yelled, lying prone behind the heavy weapon perched on its black bipod. 'It ain't over, you dumb bastards!'

Lex laughed, his teeth bright in the dark. He shouted back, 'Barry! Is it your birthday, mate? Is that your idea of a speech?'

Johnny stayed in his pit, pretty much stuck in the mud anyway. Reloading, heat from his weapon rising into his face, he listened as the sound of firing eased – only to make way for the sounds of the wounded.

'Better go see what we can do.' Lex stood, coated with mud, the butt of his M16 tucked into his hip. 'The arty boys have copped it. Bring the bandaids.'

Around them men appeared from the ground. The base was like an ant nest stabbed with a stick. Shoey, Barry, and Lex headed towards the artillery battery that had been bombed by sappers. Sandbags had been hurled sideways and a mortar was on its side. Men crouched over men down. Orders and questions cut across the cries of the wounded. The ground seeped fumes. Somewhere a shot was fired.

'Nightmare on a loop.' Lex lit three cigarettes, handing two over. 'Anyway, welcome to Marlboro Country, boys. I hope my horse is all right.'

Johnny watched as the docs and medics went calmly to work.

'This was just a test,' he said vaguely. 'Two thousand would've turned up if they were really fair dinkum.'

'Ding dong.' Lex inhaled long and hard. 'Avon calling. Next week, Aussie pigs, we bring tanks.'

Johnny grinned, and saw Barry shake his head as he scanned the perimeter, his M60 held across his hip. Outside the wire, fires burned eerily as if the country was devouring itself. What did Bazza see out there? He saw the future, Johnny decided – because that was the direction it always came from.

In a solid downpour the boys began rebuilding the artillery position with sandbags. Johnny thought the place had the soft dreamy look of a chalk drawing fading in the rain. But when he found part of a foot, he knew this was no dream but a man-made thing, and that surely someone must take the blame.

Captain Van seemed happy, Khan thought, as the fighters travelled through farmland towards the Long Hais, the haunted hills that dominated Johnny Shoebridge's mindscape. This was despite the loss of two sappers, three other fighters, and twenty wounded, one who'd been shot through the stomach and was about to die.

'The Australians think we are weak.' Van strolled around as the men stopped in a dark village to fill their water bottles. 'They'll soon see that we're not.'

Khan sat slumped against a stone wall. The people of the settlement kept out of sight. A wise decision, he decided. After a firefight the captain was in the mood for anything. Khan had seen him execute two informers with his handgun after an ambush went wrong. Thang lit a hand-rolled cigarette, drew on it, and passed it over.

'The little boss has big plans.' He indicated the small man with a subtle nod. 'Seizing a fire base is one of them. The impressive victory.'

Khan knew this was true because it had to be true. The war could not be won by harassment alone. Van was a man who studied history and applied what he learned ruthlessly. Within weeks the northern battalions would hit the

Australians with force as unexpected in the south as an avalanche. But it wouldn't be a wall of ice and snow but waves of men and weapons that would bury the tall white bastards twice; once when they were overrun and again when their countrymen put their skulls in the ground.

'It will be a glorious battle.' Khan used the word *glorious* instead of *victorious*, because he also knew that not every battle had to be won to win the war. 'One way or another.'

It was about bleeding the enemy into submission. Even if it took a hundred years and five million dead. The French had discovered that at Dien Bien Phu, in a deep valley where they were slaughtered in their thousands. Khan expelled a breath. Even his cheeks felt tired. These battles were like the universe, he thought. They went on forever, raiders falling on Vietnam like meteors, the people fighting back with everything from garden hoes to a handful of Russian MiG jets.

He looked up, hoping to see the silver spread of stars. Instead it began to rain. Someone said comrade Truc had died. Dispirited, Khan rested his forehead against the stock of his AK, and shut his eyes.

The only way out of the fighting was to fight. No mercy, no forgiveness, this dangerous road had to be travelled until a final victory, as bright as the sun, was achieved – but to get there, Khan knew D555, and hundreds of thousands of others, would have to travel many miles through the treacherous dark.

And we were always waiting, Johnny thought, with firepower.

Exhausted, Johnny shut his eyes, and tried to block out the heavy tropical heat. He imagined himself at home, walking beside the Hopkins River a mile out of Taralia. It was winter and the cropped grass between islands of blackberries was powdered with frost. Through slow-rising fog the sun sailed. The quiet was powerful, the feel of open grazing land serene. Gumtrees appeared and disappeared like ghost galleons adrift and Connelly's grey tin woolshed, dripping with dew, waited in misty silence for shearers to arrive from places up north. In his hands Shoey carried his old man's .22 rifle, a Lithgow single-shot.

Johnny saw himself hunting rabbits but it was the grip of the land he sought in his imagination, the state of simply being – there. And for a moment, he was, and slept.

Twenty minutes later he opened his eyes, right hand automatically finding the stock of his SLR. The self-loading rifle he'd used pretty well, and the more he used it, the more the weapon changed him into a profoundly different person. Who that person might turn out to be, he didn't know, but he guessed he'd find out one day. If he ever got out of this place alive.

Thoughts of the Hopkins River receded, as did the fleeting and beautiful idea of becoming a travelling shearer with a ute and a dog. Refuge did not lie in the past or in wishful thinking; refuge depended wholly and solely on fighting for a future. The knowledge of that was terrifying. The big battles were coming and everyone knew it.

Twenty-three

A forested hill shrugged off Malcolm's fences to rise from the shoulders of green paddocks. Shoey decided to climb the thing and pocketed smokes, lighter, and a bar of chocolate. Filling his water bottle from the tank, he felt a familiar sense of excitement. There was even the dark flutter of fear as his body automatically prepared and programmed for patrolling.

War's over, idiot!

Johnny laughed, but it was only a short laugh. What was happening to him was weird and alarming. He was sweating yet he hadn't taken a step. His hands shook as he scanned the paddocks. His nostrils flared as they drew in air. His ears sorted sounds in micro seconds.

No enemy here, ya bloody dingbat!

He banged a fist into his chest.

Snap out of it, ya dopey bastard!

Johnny strode away from the hut, standing straight, barging through blackberry canes that grew on either side of the path. It felt as if he was driving a fully loaded truck with no brakes. The inlet on his left and the farmland on his right overloaded him with input that screamed, *Assess! Assess! Assess!*

Shoey went down on one knee, felt his arms come up as if he was levelling his weapon. Instead his right hand unerringly fished his smokes out of his shirt pocket and he found a flat stump to sit on that butted up to a small bushy bank. Breathing hard, he searched the river and track. Then he looked overhead.

'Nothin',' he muttered. 'Bloody nothin' but blue sky and a nice breeze.' Breeze or no breeze, Shoey was steaming. He sucked in smoke as he forced himself to see that rocks were only rocks and trees just trees. 'That's a bit better, boss.' He felt like a capsized boat righting itself, decks streaming water, until he was presented with pains in his head and an image he could not ignore.

In a jungle clearing there were two rows of bodies wrapped and strapped in green ponchos. Overhead a hammering Huey descended towards his two best mates, and seven others lying in long grass that thrashed like a crowd of hysterical mourners. Men in muddy, bloody green shirts knelt, calling the chopper down, and down it came, black-goggled doorgunners perched over matching M6os.

'Ah, get up,' Johnny muttered, hearing the soothing sound of cattle somewhere far up the valley. 'And get goin'.' So, somehow, he did.

I am nothing but that bloody war, he thought, walking unsteadily. I am nothin' but an old map and a fistful of photos of dead faces. But I am still moving despite the fact that this dreamed-up bastard Khan walks with me – no, he doesn't walk with me, he rises up to fire, with the one intention of getting my head or heart clear in his sights. But I am not powerless in this fight, Johnny reckoned; I will not give in.

In the evening, after eating with his parents, Khan headed down to the jetty. Conversations from the houses came and went like gently swirling water. There was a spike of laughter and a baby cried, but the human presence was less than a whisper on the night.

He had spent so much time in darkness living in the D555 cave system, night patrolling, ambushing, on resupply, or recovering in an underground hospital, he felt the blackness favoured him. It had also frightened him almost to death with what it had hidden. Now Khan sat calmly within it thinking of the broken souls, the dead and the living that the war had tossed aside as it smashed its way across the country.

I'm not *completely* broken, though, he thought. My better self, the pre-war Khan, is looking to the south, suggesting I should follow, to search for what might make me whole. And who knows, Khan mused, I just might venture there.

Well, you probably should, Johnny put in, because I've got a plan to head off in that direction myself. First port of call, all going well, would be an orchard block down on the Murray River where Barry's folks lived. Then, if he hadn't flipped out totally, he'd head on to Melbourne where Lex's family were in Black Rock. And finally to Carlton, where Jilly was studying – and after that, well, who knew and who cared?

Khan looked downstream, and saw a small boat rowed by a man in black. It was Son, a citizen whose soul was also made incomplete by the war, like everyone, but in a different way.

'Son,' Khan called gently across the water. 'You are back.'

'Brother Khan,' Son answered softly as he rowed steadily. 'I am. We must talk.'

After Son secured the boat, they walked to Khan's tiny house. There, as the rain swept in, they shared a bottle of Jack Daniel's whiskey, the downpour drowning out their voices as they talked about the idea of going south.

Movement is good, Johnny thought. In battle or not, movement is good.

Johnny walked quietly through a patch of dry, rocky forest above Malcolm's farm. It was like being in a big old house, he thought, that had been locked up for fifty years. Cobwebs hung off dead saplings. Fallen timber broke at a touch. The air was musty and the dirt powdery, softened by a silky carpet of skeletal leaves. He paused.

The top of the hill was crowned with a few sentinel trees and round boulders that reminded him vaguely of the Long Hais. There was the smell of smoke and Johnny spotted it rising straight up from among the rocks. For a moment he considered turning downhill, but the idea reeked of gutlessness. If he was trespassing it was doubtful that someone would shoot him. So he lit a cigarette, walked out, and saw with surprise it was Carly sitting alone by a small campfire.

The bottle of Jack Daniel's its once fancy black label almost worn off, stood on the old table between Khan and Son. The bourbon had a rich smoky flavour that overwhelmed Khan with what he thought of as 'American-ness'. He and Johnny knew that it was not intended for him to drink. The bottle had been taken from the hands of American ghosts. They were big men, some black, some white, wearing battered flak jackets, who sat in a circle, their close-cropped heads full of thoughts and anger that Khan couldn't guess at. Behind them a flag of a screaming eagle plunged earthward, talons out in an attack never completed.

'I am thankful for the whiskey,' Khan said. 'But I feel I am stealing it from bad spirits.'

Son was silent for a while. 'This bottle came from Saigon airport, I believe.' He smiled, lifted his eyebrows. 'It was liberated from a bar, not taken from a dead man.'

Khan accepted Son's explanation as authentic, although it probably wasn't. The alcohol was warming but it also delivered a vision of the mountains and jungle floating in a swamp of sorrow, anger, and US poison. This vision would only taint the memories of his friends. So he managed to dispel it before it ruined the process of getting pleasantly drunk.

'Khan,' Son said. 'I heard a rumour about a woman called Phuong from our valley. Supposedly she lives in a river village in an area of the south I have visited.' He offered Khan a cigarette from a white and blue pack. 'This Phuong is war-wounded and has not been able to return home. Of course, it might not be the same person. Phuong is not an uncommon name and northern women fighters are no great rarity.'

Khan felt his heart bump hard into his ribs. It was as if the afterworld had momentarily opened a door and Phuong walked out into the light. He saw her smile and his spirit soared. Perhaps, *perhaps*, he thought, it just might be her?

'And my plan,' Son said, topping up Khan's cup, 'is that we go and find her.'

'But what about my fish?' Stupidly, it was all Khan could think to say. 'Who will look after them?'

Son laughed like the true river pirate his grandfather had been.

'My mother. No one will touch them when she's around.'

Khan could feel the allure of distant places. The power of the downstream current was coming through the walls. He sensed the complex ways of water, the righteousness of the idea of this journey, the possibilities of what might be discovered in the south, as did Johnny.

'But I cannot row a boat, brother Son.' Khan held up his empty sleeve with his left hand. 'You have no room for a passenger.'

Son put his cup down. 'You will not be a passenger. You will be my guide. As you have been since you returned from the war.' He put out his hand. 'To the south, my friend. To find sister Phuong.'

Khan gripped Son's hand. 'Yes, Son. I agree. When will we go?'

Son pulled in smoke as if it fuelled his calculations.

'The day after tomorrow. I need to get supplies. If that suits you?'

Khan nodded. It suited him. Why not? He felt feather-light and dream-like, as if he was already afloat on the wide brown river. He studied Son, the pirate, the bad communist, and knew that sometimes the men who you felt might do the least, did the most. The war had taught him that.

We'll see, thought Johnny. We will see.

Twenty-four

Lex lay on his stretcher, examining an American combat knife he had somehow come by. It amazed Shoey just how many different kinds of weapons were floating around the joint. He had seen captured Thompson machineguns, ancient shotguns held together by wire, homemade handguns, German Lugers, English Webley revolvers, Colt .44 Magnums, Swedish SKS rifles, Remington pump-action shotguns, crossbows, heavy machineguns, and submachineguns that looked to be old and German. All of them could kill you, he knew that.

'This fire base we're going to build—' Lex examined the long silver blade, 'will be right in the middle of tiger country. And it'll be our job to be the goats tied to a post. It really does sound like something the RSPCA should take an interest in, John. You know, even farm animals have feelings.'

As usual, Johnny laughed at Lex, and blew a cloud of smoke at the sagging green tent top. For a while he listened to the heavy drumming of the rain. A fine mist filtered down, leaving the taste of canvas on his tongue. Sometimes he simply imagined he was on a Scout camp, everyone mucking around with ropes, pearl-handled pocketknives, smouldering fires and him, at least, puffing on one of his dad's smuggled smokes.

'There'll be tanks, though,' Johnny said. 'There'll be jets and APCs. There'll be gunships and there'll be Spookies. There'll be bloody everything.'

'There'll be bloody us,' Barry put in, crew-cut head hunched between thick shoulders as he studied the wooden floor, hands draped over his knees. 'And two thousand of those other little brown bastards.'

Lex grinned, head on his pillow. He waved the knife like a conductor leading an orchestra.

'Barry-boy,' he said. 'No one on earth could've said it better.'

Barry raised his head, made no comment, looked outside at rain that fell in bright grey sheets as if washing sunlight from the sky. Lex rested the combat knife on the ammo crate that Shoey had barked his shin on about forty times.

'Have you girls heard what they're goin' to call this new base?' He laughed, pinged a fat rubber band from home he wore around his left wrist for good luck. 'Charlie'll shit himself when he hears it. No, it's not Bearcat, Mrs Shoebridge. Or Black Horse or Hellsville, Barry, like the Yanks. It's Fire Base . . . *Leslie*. Named after Captain Rat Tooth's lovely wife.'

Barry spat into the rain. 'His wife's a bloke.'

Johnny wove his fingers together to help him think, as his sister had taught him when he was five. He glanced at his two mates, and felt in the strangest and most powerful of ways, that this leaky green tent was possibly the best place he had ever been.

When it was Khan's turn to view the model of an Australian fire base that had been attacked, unsuccessfully, he dutifully lined up with Thang and Trung and the rest of their section. Captain Van, using a stick, pointed out the strengths and weaknesses of the defences encountered by the two battalions who had been repulsed with minor losses.

'As Uncle Ho tells us,' Van began, 'the battalions made noise from the east, with gongs and bugles, then attacked from the west. Although the fighters entered and killed a number of men, they were driven away. This time, with this new base we are hearing about, our informants will give us better information. And we will have more men and greater mortar and artillery support. The flood will hit the gates and the gates will open.'

Khan studied the model. He noted where the Australian troops had been deployed, the artillery positions, mortar crews, machinegun posts, and Armoured Personnel Carriers. He also saw a tiny model pig tucked in behind a bunker. When he caught Trung's eye, Trung winked.

'The new base,' said Captain Van, 'according to our informants, will be stronger than this old one. But we will attack in our thousands. We will be joined by other battalions at full fighting strength.'

It seemed illogical to Khan that the commanders would take such an obvious bait dropped in on their doorstep. Didn't they know Phantoms flew at a thousand kilometres an hour? That fleets of fifty choppers could bring machinegun and rocket fire like rain? The Americans would love to help the bastard Australians in this kind of battle – which was exactly why, he figured, the base would be built, to call the men from the north in from the mountains and jungles and mow them down like grass.

'Our greatest courage,' Captain Van announced, the words echoing in the darkest reaches of the cave, 'will deliver a great victory. As we speak, two of the finest People's Liberation Army Battalions are on their way to join us. They are young, well trained, and fearless.'

Khan looked at the miniature pig behind the model sandbag walls. He could see its fluted ears and corkscrew tail. It was beautifully made. He could imagine Trung's fine fingers shaping it. Perhaps we are all bred for slaughter, he thought. It seems like the popular opinion.

'Have we *ever* lost a war?' Captain Van asked quietly, studying his men. 'Has any foreign army *ever* beaten us? No. You must see and believe that we know *how* to win.'

Khan did believe because it was true. He knew that a

battle like this could be won. The battalions could smash through the flames and carnage, but the cost would be high – as was the chance of him not making it back to the cave with his friends, to his blanket, sleep, and safety.

Roll the dice.

Again and again.

And eventually, Johnny thought, someone will win. Or perhaps we might all lose. In a war, that can happen. Especially to the people sent to fight it.

Twenty-five

Johnny sat by the fire drinking tea with Carly. He felt a fragile calmness that stood over the exhaustion brought on by the newsreels in his head. Right now there was a flickering film showing the remains of a VC guerrilla fighter in black pyjamas. The man had been run over by a tank, and Johnny and Barry had been detailed to bury him. In ten seconds Johnny remembered the whole awful hour, in colours he wished never to see again, before managing to shove the images down into a black corner.

'You can see a lot from up here.' Carly pointed to the treed coastline edged with pale rock. 'They used to hunt whales from that bay. In rowboats. I'm glad they don't anymore.'

Johnny looked at the dark blue sea. Men like ants pickin' on a big dumb critter. Typical.

'Not a job I'd take if it was offered at the CES.' He was pleased that he was able to make a joke, even if he felt as thin as a tin Chinese whistle, capable of nothing but a single note. 'No way.'

Carly sat with her back against a boulder, hugging her knees.

'Me neither.' She looked at Johnny, released her knees, and put her hand down on old gum leaves as soft as cloth. 'So how you are you feelin' now? You seem better. Calmer. A bit less jumpy.'

Johnny nodded slowly, sipped tea. 'Yeah, maybe. Anyway, I'm gunna go down south in a day or two. I gotta go see the folks of a couple of blokes I was with. Blokes that, ah, got killed. Good blokes.' He felt a burst of hard pain. 'My mates. Best blokes ever.'

Carly knelt, moved, and rested her hands on his shoulders. She kissed him once on the cheek then studied him, not taking her hands away.

'You're a good guy, Johnny.'

Around him the air swirled. The closeness of her, the scent, softness, and toughness of her made him dizzy. Her hands, light, flat, and hard, pinned him. He knew she'd been through the mill. He knew she might never get away from this place, might live a fractured life, had a cloudy future and a violent past, but as injured as she was she was giving him hope. Something he wished he could give back to her.

'Carly,' he said. 'You're a beautiful girl. I can't tell you how good you are. You're gunna have a good life.' Thoughts pressed hard as he imagined how this might go, if he acted now. But if she did let him, or want him, it would be all wrong because his ideas of sex and love had been twisted by the war in ways he didn't understand. One thing he did know was that Carly deserved better than being with the wrong person at the wrong time. 'Thanks.' He touched her arm. 'For everythin', yeah?'

She nodded and moved away. Smiling, she smoothed her dress and sat.

'Yeah. The truth's a good thing,' she said. 'You'll be right, Johnny.'

That he'd ever be right he did not know. What he did know was that the truth came in a thousand forms; perhaps even in the form of an imagined enemy fighter known as Khan who at one time was as real as Johnny himself. He shrugged, feeling as if he was full of scrap metal when all he wanted to be was that pliable young bloke who took it as it came, gave without thinking, and had not carried out orders to kill people.

'So,' he said, 'what are you gunna do for the rest of the arvo?'

Carly looked where three folds of land, blurred by trees, formed two small valleys.

'I'm gunna help my old man get some timber.' She surveyed the forest below as if pinpointing where her father was to work. 'He's cuttin' ironbark for a stockyard.'

'I'll help,' Johnny said, sitting up. 'Shit, yeah. I can use a chainsaw or an axe. I wouldn't want money, Carly.' He simply wanted to do something good and honest, do something to show her something of what he felt, what he was. 'Just give you a hand. Before I go.'

Carly looked at him. He could see she didn't think this was a great idea. Now, skilfully, she tied her hair back, as if other things could be rearranged as easily, just this once.

'Okay.' She knelt, brushing leaf scraps off her hip. 'But we'd better get goin' because Wesley won't wait. Impatient is his middle name.'

Johnny put out the fire as Carly gathered the tea things.

'We go that way.' She pointed downhill.

'South,' Johnny said, as if she'd asked.

After Son had rowed away, Khan sat on the wet jetty. Below, his cages of fish were invisible in the olive-coloured water. For once he thought of the soldiers he had killed and wondered what would happen if he invited their souls to sit with him. He doubted they would, the Australians, unless perhaps he also invited the men they'd killed so it was equal.

Way too soon, feller, Johnny thought. The dead would only want to be with their own. Even I know that.

It occurred to Khan, as it had occurred to Johnny, that he'd hadn't truly hated the enemy all the time, apart from the B-52 crews, in Khan's case. Khan detested them and always would. But he hadn't burned to massacre every enemy soldier, although given the chance, he would

178

have. He grinned. Better just to send the bastards home. That would have suited everyone. He wagged his head in agreement, admitting he was fairly well gone on Jack Daniel's.

No, he mused, it didn't seem hate was involved with every moment of day-to-day fighting. It was more like hate was a big black umbrella over the entire country that everyone fought under. So who were the idiots who put that umbrella up in the first place?

Shiny-faced men far away, as always, in countries, like America, Australia, France, and China.

Which is where we, the people of the countryside, came in, Khan thought. Those with the least power were brought together to create a breaking wave of violence that cost a million lives. But it had gained a victory, it surely had.

'I am as hollow as a drum,' he muttered, lit a cigarette Son had left him, and studied the cloudy sky. The moon rode high, a pale horse without a rider, he thought. Or perhaps it was a seahorse swimming in the waves. A lonely traveller, anyway, in a lonely world. 'Khan is as empty as a bottle of Jack Daniel's,' he added for his own drunken benefit. 'Everything poured out. Nothing is left.'

What I'd like, he thought, is for someone or something beautiful to come into my life. He looked down, his bare feet above the water, three green nylon ropes piercing the surface, anchoring his fish cages. As well as you boys, he corrected himself. As well as you boys!

179

He smoked on, thinking that at least he could still believe in the possibility of beautiful things. That seemed like a miracle of some sort.

Oh, they're out there, all right, Johnny agreed, those things. It's just that they're mighty hard to find for people like us. But we cannot give up the search in case we stumble on something sometime, somewhere, somehow. It could happen. You never know.

Shoey made his way along the trunk of the felled iron-bark, lopping branches with an axe so sharp it scared him. Ten steps behind, Carly cleared away the fallen limbs as her father, Wesley, wielded a chainsaw. Sawdust spurted like blood as the timber-getter dismembered the tree with quick cuts. It was, Johnny thought, like butchering a giant, the crushed undergrowth like the velvet padding of a coffin. An old General Motors truck fitted with a heavy winch stood on the track, and down in the valley, Carly's house sat like a small white Lego block on a couple of open green hectares.

With one final furious smoky blast, the howl of the chain-saw flew off into the trees. Silence settled. Wesley pushed away a branch with a lumpy black boot.

'Cuppa tea, eh?' He spoke like a man who did not like speaking. 'We're gettin' there.'

Shoey wanted to hold his arms out to the forest. It stood over and around him. It swaddled his senses and cooled his mind. He would've liked to wander off down the track by himself, sit on the ground, and have a smoke. Except he was pretty sure Lex and Barry would be waiting around the next corner, grinning like monkeys.

Instead Shoey got up onto the back of the truck with Carly and her dad. There, tea was poured and fruitcake taken from a plastic lunchbox.

'So, John.' Wesley looked at him from under the brim of a smashed felt hat. 'Vietnam, eh?'

Johnny was aware, suddenly, the boys had climbed up onto the truck to sit on either side of him. He could feel their shoulders, hard and warm, as they waited, enjoying this turn of events – that once again he was on trial, about to have his courage tested. Shoey nodded slowly but his knee was jiggling and his hand was shaking.

'Yep.' The word towered over everything else in his life. 'That's right.'

'Welcome home.' Wesley looked away, sipped tea from a chipped white mug, let silence return.

It was as surprising as an uppercut. Barry and Lex, with a laugh and a pat on Johnny's back, jumped down to walk away, lighting smokes as they went. *See, Shoe? Not so bad. Not everyone hates our guts. Elephant stamp, cobber. Gold star. Keep up the good work.*

'Thanks, Wesley,' Shoey said. 'Thanks.'

Khan wobbled his way back to his room as quietly as he could, trying to not wake his parents. For a while he sat by a small oil lamp and drank tea. Then he took his AK-47 from its hiding place in the wall. It was swathed like a metallic baby in a towel and plastic, oily to the touch, the wooden stock worn and scarred. Three magazines, ammunition, and the AKM bayonet he left safely wrapped and hidden in one of the bamboo roof supports.

He tucked the assault rifle into his shoulder and single-handedly swept the darkness. Then he lay it down, staring at it, a thing he had once loved. But he wouldn't take it to the south. Khan doubted he'd find any sort of future at gunpoint again. In fact, he doubted that he'd find any sort of future at all. Yet he would go with Son because Son was a trader, and who knew what things they might find that the war had left behind?

I've gotta say, Khan, Johnny thought, although you'd better keep this a secret from the Australian govern-ment; you're more human than I thought. I also know that although we were both killers, I would like to state here and now that we were not killers at heart and that we did not murder anyone. And even if the world does not care about this, or understand what it means, it is possibly the most important thing of all.

Twenty-six

Shoey's company rested inland forty metres from the slow-moving river, their perimeter set. The heat, saturated with humidity and smelling of mud, pressed down. To Shoey it felt as if he was in the grip of some deadly tropical disease. In an effort to counter it he thought of Ballarat, where he'd visited his sick grandma every two weeks for six long months. He remembered a city of stone buildings soaked by misty rain and a freezing wind blowing old people down the streets like boats with wet sails.

'*Farrrk* me.' Lex leant against his pack, M16 poking up between his knees. 'There was nothin' in the brochure about this bloody weather, Johnson-berry. I've hardly brought the right clothes. Something cotton and white would be good, don't you think, Baz? Cheesecloth, maybe. Or linen. *Jesus.* How bloody hot is it?'

Barry sipped water from his canteen. 'Too fuckin' hot.'

Shoey marvelled at Barry's ability to remain silent. Those were the first words he'd uttered all day, and it was the middle of the afternoon. Lex laughed, snapped back into the moment.

'Baz,' he said, 'Channel Two weatherman. You'd be bloody brilliant.'

Barry's eyes moved but that was about all. 'Wouldn't I?'

Young Pete, the radio guy, crawled over, a cigarette in his mouth scribing circles as he made progress like a three-legged dog.

'Fantastic,' Lex said. 'Here comes Mr Squiggle.'

Johnny reckoned Young Pete looked about ten. Beneath the green and black camo grease, his pixie face glowed pink, and his ears stuck out like the handles on a trophy.

'There's a big Yank patrol comin' up behind,' he said quietly. 'The skipper said don't shoot the bastards. They'll be here in five.'

The boys swapped looks. Heads swivelled. A quiet buzz went through the company. Then along a track the Aussies would never have used, fifty men in helmets and battered flak jackets appeared from the bush. Shoey could hear them clearly, the sound tempting him to crawl away as far and as fast as possible. He knew the skipper would be going nuts. Making noise like that was madness.

'Yo, Aussies.' A tall Marine, holding an M60 tucked casually under a thick arm banded with tattoos, nodded. 'Happenin'?'

'Hopefully,' someone said, 'fuck all.'

Johnny saw the skipper was talking to the American captain, a tall, gangly guy with round glasses. His men, Marines, had slung off massive packs and sunk down on open ground close to the river. They reminded Johnny of beasts settling, except wrists flicked Zippos, and blue smoke drifted.

'You know, Aussie,' a big Marine drawled to Johnny, an ace of spades tucked into the band of his helmet, 'we hear we the big hammer and you the anvil. That's the plan.'

'Don't forget the jets,' Lex said. 'As well as the hammer. Bring as many jets as you've got. And tanks, we'll have a hundred. Bigger the better. And Spooky. We love that thing. It's on our Christmas list. Bring it all.'

The Marine nodded as if he was listening to distant music. His dark skin glistened. His temples shone like mirrors. His eyes looked red and unhealthy.

'We do, friend. We always do.'

Johnny was aware a few of the diggers had slipped a little further back into the bush. Casually they'd hunkered down, holding their weapons. The Marines appeared not to give a stuff about anything. But never did Shoey underestimate them or their firepower. They talked loudly. They languished against their packs and tossed cigarettes and lighters around. But they'd fought up north in battles the Aussies could only imagine. Johnny was glad to see them. But like the skipper, when they moved out, wishing good luck, he felt he sat in a safer place.

'One minute.' The boss knelt, compass in hand, map on the ground. 'That way.' He pointed towards a wall of bush. 'Don't get me wrong,' he added, 'I like those guys. But Jesus Christ, they scare the shit outta me. Right. Let's move.'

The company melted into the scrub. Around them heat and silence settled, and again Shoey felt the fear. It pressed hard and he pushed back, drawing from the boys, the power of his weapon, his innermost self, and the inevitability of the situation. It was like being dragged underwater and having to fight there, endlessly.

In the middle of the night, Khan's D555 battalion exited the caves of the Long Hai Hills. Below, the land blended with the blackness like the shore with the sea. Khan, listening to the sound of hundreds of pairs of sandals and boots, knew he was part of a powerful migration to the west. The slender bag of rice he carried might well be a one-way ticket. He fought the idea. It would not help.

Thang was in front of him and Trung behind. There was no turning back. The informants had done their job. Both sides were setting their traps, and although Khan sensed a lack of cunning in the operation, he knew that the commanders looked over the heads of the men to the higher objective – and that was to win the war and not save souls. It was obvious that death marched with D555. Khan sensed it kept pace, studying the faces, selecting those it would take. Johnny knew how he felt. It was like having an iron hand hovering, ready to bring a samurai sword down hard on his skull.

Khan made sure to look only ahead, concentrating on Thang's powerful shoulders. He did not want to meet death's stare. Forty kilometres away, the brand-new Australian fire base was rising from the raw earth. In one night's time it would be the white-hot centre of fire and fear. It would be a place for the dead, the dying, and the wildly fortunate. And it would be love and hate that would fuel the furnace, because that was what the Vietnamese people fought with.

Khan walked on, knowingly heading for the precipice. And there he would have to jump. You and me both, Johnny agreed. We're in this thing together – as enemies, my friend, as sworn enemies.

Twenty-seven

Shoey set off for Malcolm's place but the closer he got the slower he walked until he stopped. Not yet able to see the house, he could picture the private village surrounded by prime green grazing land. The thought of being given orders was too much. Johnny did not want to work for the big man anymore.

'Bugger it.' He wondered if this was the beginning of the end, if he was now unable to do anything a normal person was supposed to do. He looked around, hoping for something in the landscape that might give him strength, but saw nothing. 'No way,' he murmured. 'Not today.'

Johnny knew, suddenly, that beliefs he'd always held – that work was good, that he was a kind person, that his country and its citizens were fair, and that the attractions of women were endless – were like birds dead at his feet. It wasn't stubbornness. He wasn't simply pissed off with the job, lazy, or annoyed. He was changed.

Working for the big man was just not do-able. Why not? Because it made no sense to Johnny. And why did it not make sense?

No reason. That was the worst bit. No reason at all.

Walk, Johnny told himself. Walk up the bloody hill and get to work. But he knew he wouldn't. Well, he would walk up there to get his dough, and tell Malcolm he was leaving but that was it. So he set off, feeling as if he'd lost the lot but couldn't remember having placed a bet.

'Square one, idiot,' he said. 'That's where you are.'

For a moment he looked down at the inlet. It was time, he decided, to visit Carly, and say goodbye. Then he'd head out on the mission he had set for himself, no matter that it might leave him in a far worse place than he already was. Bad luck. It had to be done.

Son steadied the rowboat as Khan climbed down from the jetty. It was a boat neither Khan nor Johnny had seen before, long and slender, loaded with boxes wrapped in green plastic. The river trader took Khan's bag and stowed it.

'I am like a snail,' Khan said. 'I can carry everything I own on my back.'

'It's good to travel light.' Son flipped the mooring rope off the post, waited for Khan to settle himself then gently pushed the boat out into the current. 'It gives you options.' He grinned as he fitted the oars into rowlocks. 'Like cash.'

The waterway took hold of the wooden craft. Khan was immediately aware of an entrancing and timeless sensation, as if the spirit of the river welcomed him on this journey, would gladly show him the country it flowed through, the country he had walked over and fought for, the country whose stomach he had slept down deep in. He gave himself up to the waterway as he would to sleep and dreaming. What would happen in the south would happen.

Son rowed elegantly, a stroke here, a stroke there, resting with the oars out like slender wings. Mostly he let the river do the work.

'Say goodbye, Khan, to this place.' Son nodded towards the village that huddled in heavy rain, the jetty deserted, standing on bandy legs thrust into olive-green water. 'For a while.'

Khan looked at their village and was moved by its perfect beauty and simplicity. It lay on a plain of rice and rivers, in sight of hump-backed limestone hills caught in low clouds. He wondered if Thang and Trung might wander the hamlet's tight little lanes at night; going where they pleased and taking what they needed without anything being touched. He hoped so, because they deserved to share in the peace hard-won in the south, and brought back to the north by the ragged remains of the victorious peasant army.

To go home after war, Khan thought, was as close as one could get to heaven on earth. He took the cigarette Son offered as the long bends of the river took them further away from his little room and old parents. So why was he leaving?

To find Phuong.

It was a plan as simple as it was impossible. Yet here he was, moving downstream towards her because whether she was alive or dead, it was in the south where she would be.

'Something will happen, Khan.' Son looked like a movie star in a black jacket and tiger-striped combat pants. 'Because something always does.'

You better believe it, boys, Johnny thought. I hope I do.

Malcolm handed Johnny an envelope that he shoved into a back pocket. It wasn't that Shoey didn't like the big man. It was something that shimmered within himself, the colour of a migraine. It was a feeling of hopelessness that made it impossible to see that the work had any value.

Was it the newsreels in his head that had stuffed him?

No, it was the reality they recorded. And the fact he was always remembering the boys whose souls were shot out of them on that one God-awful night. It just wasn't possible to wash away that much blood with soap and water, time, words, work, sleep, or beer.

'What do think you'll do now, John?' Above Malcolm's head, the tangled vines reminded Johnny of a map of the Red River Delta, where he figured that bastard Khan lived. 'Do you have an idea?'

'Say goodbye to Carly.' Shoey pictured her face, some of the loveliness lost but enough left to last a lifetime, if she was lucky. 'Then head south. That's about it.' He had no intention of outlining his plan to a stranger. It was one highly classified operation.

'Best of luck.' Malcolm put out a wide, warped hand. 'Look after yourself.'

'Thanks. You, too.' Johnny meant it. The man might be well-off but he was fair and reasonable. There was a lot to be said for that. Shoey turned and walked away.

Twenty-eight

Shoey's Delta Company made their way through the wire into Fire Support Base Leslie. The smell of turned earth, diesel fuel, and sawn trees swirled as choppers touched down, disgorging men and equipment. Here the boys were met by a small, lightly built major with sleeves perfectly folded and new combat boots. The bloke's face was pink and his grey sideburns were as neat as two five-cent stamps.

'Welcome to the wild frontier, men.' The major stood close to the front rank of soldiers. 'FSB Leslie is now operational. A place of tall tales and true.'

'That's a line from Disneyland,' Lex whispered to Johnny. 'Sunday nights, six-thirty on Seven. I suggest you catch it. The last one I saw was about a giant beaver called Steven. It's unbelievable what those critters get up to when no one's watching.'

'Donald Duck.' Barry shook his head. 'I hate the prick.'

Lex laughed and Shoey shuffled subtly away from potential

trouble. Glancing around he saw groups of men digging in, sandbagging, stringing wire, and preparing mortar sites and artillery batteries – but FSB Leslie, Shoey reckoned, wouldn't exactly terrify Charlie back into the Long Hais. It was no Fort Steel where the Yanks had two thousand Marines on deck and every bit of hardware that flew, fired, bombed, shot, or burnt the hell out of the living and the dead.

'Ever asked yourself, Johnny-boy,' Lex muttered, 'why we don't get helmets or flak jackets? Is that a fashion thing or what?'

Johnny studied the scrub beyond the Australian perimeter. Trees ringed the expanse of open ground like runners about to race, giving him the impression that as soon as he looked away they shuffled forward. Crouching among them, stretching for a thousand kilometres, were as many shadows as the gathering VC battalions would ever need.

What Shoey saw only reinforced his feeling that Charlie was out there, because too many frightened informants had spilled their guts to all be wrong. A wave was building, and it was the enemy who would decide how big it would be, and when it would break. But Shoey knew it would be firepower, guts, and numbers that would decide the outcome – and fear, because he knew fear would question everyone constantly and relentlessly.

It was easy to see how the wrong people got shot. Or why a rifleman snapped or an entire patrol might go mental. He had been one second away from chopping up two kids chasing a chook down a jungle track. The actions triggered by fear could not be calculated or predicted. He simply hoped that when the time came to fight with or through fear, he would do so – because failing to fight was the worst thing he could imagine. And that included dying.

Anyway, orders had been given, and would be obeyed. He and the boys were to dig fighting pits to support an artillery battery. So this is what Shoey went and did, thinking that two years ago he'd been at Taralia High, kicking the footy at lunchtime then walking home with Jilly, holding hands.

Now this.

A model of the new fire support base had been set up in a small clearing. Or this is what Johnny pictured, as that was what the enemy always did. Each section of Khan's battalion encircled it in turn until every fighter had memorised the layout, and their part in the impending attack. The briefing was exact, although Khan knew that in the fury of battle, strategies could collapse in seconds. He walked away, not convinced that they had the numbers or armaments to destroy the place.

'It will be brutal.' Thang spoke quietly as the boys ate a meal of cold rice and fish sauce. 'Yet, with new comrades arriving, we might be able to do it.'

Khan wondered if his face was as drawn as Thang's. Only Trung had the slightest sign of youth blooming in his cheeks.

Even in these most deadly of months the boy kept smiling. Maybe he was an angel?

'Smoke, Khan?' Trung held out a crumpled packet. 'One each.'

Khan grinned, took a smoke while shaking his head ruefully at the wonderful little idiot.

'You're a great man, Trung.' He held up the hand-rolled smoke. 'Perhaps we will share this one and you can keep two for tomorrow. Thank you.'

'Oh, light up.' Thang tapped his top pocket. 'I've got a few. Chopped-up cow shit but better than nothing. We'll get some good cigarettes after the battle. Those Australians smoke like chimneys.'

'The bastards are going to go up in flames.' Trung grinned. 'I heard there will be five battalions of us. Maybe seven. We'll massacre them.'

The boys lit up, Khan hiding a sense of terror. The Australians would have planned their response to any attack. Their back-up would be immense. He also knew there would not be seven northern battalions. Or five. There might be three all-up, if they were lucky. And if things went well, three might be enough. After all, Khan knew the commanders' sole aim was to leave the support base as nothing but a bloody smoking hole full of splintered bones.

'I have to go over in the first wave of sappers,' Trung blurted. 'I'm going to die, aren't I?' He lapsed into silence, looking at the two older men.

Thang put a hand on his shoulder. 'The brave are especially selected and protected. You will do well. And you will make it. I feel that very strongly.'

'We will follow you over.' Khan saw that Trung was crying, tears rolling straight down his round cheeks. 'We will be fighting like crazy. I will come looking for you.' If I can, he thought; if I'm not hit by then.

Trung shook his head, a tear springing away. 'I want to go with you two. I can't go first. It will be awful. Nguyen said there will be a *hundred* M6os. I'm going to die, aren't I?'

Thang gently moved Trung's shoulder back and forth.

'We will be right behind you. This is our land, little brother. We cannot let those bastards steal it. They're going to die tomorrow. And we will help you, I promise on my mother's grave.'

Khan felt himself floating through this conversation, as did Johnny. Time passed unnoticed as he thought of Phuong. Gently he was lifted with a love that spread to Thang and Trung, and widened to include every man of the battalion, even those he knew as pigs and braggers.

'All we have to do is be brave, Trung,' Khan said. 'And attack. The rest is out of our hands.'

Khan could feel the boys had settled into another place. We have already accepted our fate, he thought. All that remains to be seen is if we – if *I* – am brave enough to go and meet it.

'There can't be a *hundred* M60s.' Thang smiled his strong-man smile. 'Those cheap bastard Australians'll be lucky to have two. And they'll be gone in the first five seconds.'

Khan knew if he swapped a single look with Thang, Trung might see what they all knew; that M60s might turn into waves of screaming Phantoms and thundering Cobras – because the Americans seized any opportunity to unleash their air cavalry, a unit whose motto was 'death from above'.

But we, the people, Khan thought, have never been defeated. This was the truth. And we will win; if not tomorrow, on a day that is coming, no matter how high the price.

'When it is our turn to go—' he spoke for his own sake as much as anybody else's, 'we go. That is how it is.'

Into the firestorm.

That's right, buddy-boy, Johnny agreed. You on one side and me on the other – and just maybe this is where we get to meet right in the bloody middle.

Twenty-nine

Carly's house was visible between the straight trunks of gum-trees. A big yellow dog chained near the back door rose up to bark, and blue smoke drifted from a thin chimney. Taking a deep breath, Johnny continued down the driveway. A Marlboro for you after this, matey, he promised, his unease mounting as he walked out in the open. Was he watched? It felt like it; he wouldn't have been surprised if the barking of the dog brought someone out of the house, or from the bush, with a rifle. The place, he felt, had potential for sudden violence.

'Hey, Buster.' He called softly to the dog that watched him with golden, calculating eyes. 'Good boy.' He figured it'd go him if he got too close. It was that type of dog and that type of house. 'Settle, mate. You're right. Take it easy, cobber.'

Johnny knocked on a torn screen door. Tall gums, some burnt, encircled the couple of hectares. A crippled barbed wire fence had given up keeping anything or anyone out years ago, but it was not fences, Johnny thought, that would stop strangers from entering this place. He knew he could not live here; there were too many themes from too many days and nights gone by. Something was off-centre, secretive, and lawless. Here, he reckoned when the sun went down, he'd start looking around and he wouldn't stop until he left the joint running.

Johnny heard footsteps, light and steady. A key ground in a lock. Carly opened the door, barefoot, in jeans and a white polo shirt. She didn't smile but he didn't expect her to. Behind her a pump-action shotgun rested in a wooden rack. He'd bet it was loaded and that she'd know how to use it.

'Johnny.' She pushed open the screen door. 'Come in.'

He saw her face clearly. It told a story of a hard life that she did not see getting easier. And he saw he was not helping. She had a history that was not for sharing and he knew too much of it already. It was time to cut and run, perhaps to save them both.

'Nah, I won't.' Shoey managed a smile. 'I just came to say, well, see ya, Carly. And thanks. For everything.'

He understood she'd taken a risk even talking to him. In this place, strangers, especially those whose motives were unclear, were not welcome. And his motives were not just unclear, they were unknown, especially to him.

'Thanks.' He felt like a swimmer struggling. 'And thank Curtis. And your dad. They're good people.' He could see her courage. She had let the locals know he was to be left alone. She blamed no one for her past, present, or future.

She was, he thought, tough and heroic. 'See yer.' He knew he wouldn't because he would never be back this way again, and he doubted she'd ever leave.

'You're welcome.' Her choice of words surprised him. 'Don't get stuck, Johnny.' For a moment her face was open and unguarded, golden almost, because he was about to simplify everything by walking out of her life. 'It's no good for anyone.'

He knew he loved her in some way. The trouble was he just couldn't feel it, find it, explain it, or tell her.

'Take care, eh?' He looked straight at her. 'Bye, Carly. See ya.' Now that it was clear he was moving away from the house, the dog showed no great interest.

Carly nodded, her hair glowing in a panel of pale sunlight that filtered through the distant trees. 'Yeah. See ya, Johnny. You take care, too.'

He nodded in return and left.

Johnny imagined the bastard Khan in the rowboat, moving downstream, with Son. The muddy banks of the river were like striped walls of green and yellow. There were palms like fountains, their fronds brushing the hot blue sky. Shoey figured he knew something of what Khan might be thinking, because they had been soldiers, and had done what they had done.

The war has gone, Khan thought, like an earthquake. But the fractures ran through the country from end to end and would do so for a hundred years. Surviving it was like riding a flooding river. It was up to each person to work out how to stay afloat, as no flood ever cared if a swimmer drowned or not. Well, he was going forward *on* the river with madman Son. The beauty of their adventure stirred his heart.

'What do you deal in most, Son?' Khan asked. 'Cigarettes? Whiskey? American dollars? Girls' underwear? AKs? What are you after?'

Son rested the oars, his face shaded by an old cowboy hat that worried Khan. Surely he should not be wearing it? That would be a serious offence to the party.

'My share of freedom.' Son tipped the brim of his hat. 'But you will be granted that before I am. Because you fought in the war and I dodged it. And I will have to spend the rest of my life dodging it.'

'You seem pretty free to me.' Khan pointed at nothing in particular, smiled, felt lightened. 'This is about as free as you can get, I think.'

'In a way.' Son dipped the oars, water dripping off the blades in fine silver streams. 'I am an unworthy dog, but a dog who has selected his own somewhat *dangerous* way of life.' He grinned, looked upstream over Khan's shoulder. 'Perhaps that just makes me try harder, Khan, being as I am, outside the, ah, system. Anyway, I am at your service. Everything I have is yours. So, you see, maybe I am not the worst communist in the world.'

Maybe you're not, Johnny thought. And you are, at least, aware of the big issues.

'I don't want things, Son,' Khan said. 'To be in this boat is enough. It is a gift.'

Son shook his head, pretending sadness when in fact Khan and Johnny thought he seemed highly amused.

'Spoken like dear old Uncle Ho himself, comrade.' Son, holding the oars aloft, flexed his muscles, and grinned cheerfully. 'But on the subject of our wonderful communist system and honoured leader, we might have to be a little flexible in our *dealings* with our brothers and sisters downstream. Not all these people have embraced the *entire* Marxist-Leninist philosophy.' He laughed, shipped the oars, and reached for his cigarettes. 'Yet. Probably never.'

'The Americans thought they did,' Khan said. 'They had a bomb and a bullet for everyone.' He took a cigarette. 'I owe you.' He held up the smoke. 'You can have a fish when we get home. A little one. So this woman Phuong you've heard of, Son. She could be anyone, of course.'

Son shrugged and resumed rowing slowly for a few moments, cigarette in the white trap of his teeth.

'Well, there are thousands of war survivors wandering around, as you know,' he said. 'But the river people say she'd served in a northern battalion and was extremely brave. So I put two and two together and ended up with Son and Khan in a boat.'

Khan accepted Son's explanation. As the brown river

twisted and turned, and clouds rolled to the horizon like tanks, he thought of Trung and Thang. The boys would've loved this trip. They would have considered it heroic and right to try to find Phuong and return her home. They also would have simply liked being in the boat, the three of them together, as they had been. Khan knew he must not let them down by giving up or doubting the goodness of the expedition.

'We'll stop in a river village I know,' Son added. 'I have an arrangement with them.'

Lightning sizzled and a mauve streak forked three ways through the clouds. One second later thunder boomed and Khan fell to his knees, his head pulled tight into his shoulders as if expecting a punch. The first strike of a storm always shocked his system. Son looked at him solemnly.

'Khan,' he said, holding out a helping hand, 'I can see you have suffered for bastards like me. I apologise.'

It was Khan's turn to laugh. This was not the easiest thing to do when his heart was galloping like a horse and he was down on extremely wet knees.

'It's not to be worried about.' Seizing Son's hand Khan got up, brushing off flakes of paint, feeling like a crumpled coat being put on a shelf as he sat. 'I'm fine. And despite what you think, you didn't start the war.'

'No,' Son said. 'But you ended it. You saw it through.'

He has a point, Johnny agreed, that cannot be overlooked.

Thirty

Fire Support Base Leslie had an unfinished feel that reminded Shoey of a working bee at a bush footy ground; no job quite completed at the end of the day. Groups of soldiers laboured at strengthening mortar and rifle positions and wiring parties toiled shirtless at the perimeter. Yet the place seemed open to attack from every angle.

The sun, Johnny saw, was slinking slowly into the trees like a deserter as the Vietnamese night circled, waiting to lay down its thick black blanket. Fear spiked. The bush around the base seemed closer than when he'd last looked. All chopper flights in and out had stopped. What was here was what they had. Shoey wasn't persuaded the place was as secure as Fort Knox.

'Does the term *sitting duck* ring any bells for you, Shoebitch?' Lex asked as they pounded their short-handled shovels into the dense earth. A couple of metres away their rifles leant against one of the mortars they were to defend. 'How about Peking Duck? Or Duck l'Agent Orange?'

'Sitting bloody duck.' Shoey straightened, dog tags bouncing across his sweating chest. 'Decoys. That's what we are.'

'Fuck ducks.' Barry kept digging.

The boys worked on. Shoey saw bent bare backs, white, brown, and freckled, wherever he looked. Weapons – SLRs and M16s – stood close to every hand. Sandbagged artillery batteries gave him some sense of security, but not a lot. Thirty metres away he saw an M60 sited in not the best-protected position. Silently he wished the crew good luck.

Johnny took a moment to sip water, savouring it like wine as he thought of Taralia. To the east of town the low hills were bathed in the last coppery rays of the day. The sound of an Adelaide-bound passenger train was like a missed invitation. Cockatoos flew, a flickering white flock, and an eighteen-wheeler truck shifted determinedly through the gears on Staley's Cutting. Then Johnny looked across the fire base, through the wire, to the bulldozed killing ground. In his veins he could feel his life flowing thick and sweet, like honey.

'Lex, you ever read that book *Robinson Crusoe*?' It was one of the only books Johnny had ever finished; a present for his tenth birthday. 'One bloke on one island. Bloody perfect, that'd be.'

Lex stopped digging and reached for his smokes. Barry didn't stop working but slowed down, listening.

'You know, if the boy scouts were running this outfit,' Lex

said thoughtfully, tossing cigarettes left and right, 'at least there'd be sausages on bread. And we'd be going home at half-past eight. Picked up at the gate by your mum, Baz.'

'*Such* a poofter.' Barry speared his entrenching tool into the dirt and picked up the loose cigarette. He lit up and tossed his lighter to Lex. 'You should be in the navy.'

Lex laughed, sitting on the edge of his hole, lighting up.

'Barrington,' he said, 'I'd prefer to be in the Australian Ballet rather than this bloody cowboy outfit.'

Johnny managed to grin although he felt closer to crying. Bring on the bloody *jets*, he thought. Fifty of them. Five hundred! Scare the bastards away; who cares if we don't kill them?

'Me, too,' Johnny said. 'I don't mind dancing. And there'd be girls. Lots of 'em. Skinny moles but that's no problem.' He looked around. The night was about to enfold Fire Base Leslie and draw it in close. Then at some dark hour, the place would explode.

Johnny marvelled at how Khan's entire battalion moved silently through his mind towards the Australian base. He watched as line after line of Main Force fighters willingly entered what would be an inescapable tunnel of terror.

'I am *so* hungry!' Trung whispered to Khan. 'I dream of a chicken the size of a pig!'

'Better than a pig the size of chicken,' Khan replied, trying to keep Trung's mind off the battle ahead. 'How about a grilled pig the size of a roasted elephant?'

Trung grinned and Khan felt as if he had been knifed. The fading light filtered through the branches, gilding the faces of the men. But it seemed to him that darkness walked with the columns, perhaps ally, perhaps enemy. In the distance, through the trees, he figured he could make out the end of the world.

It was where the bush met the cleared ground around the Australian wire. Arrogantly the enemy had dug into Vietnamese earth and were preparing to defend it as if it was their own.

'This time tomorrow,' Trung said, 'we'll be heading home to the Long Hais, victorious. To that roast elephant.'

Khan nodded, gripped his assault rifle, and prayed that it might be so. The commanders had decided that this base had to be obliterated. Strategies were in place. Orders had been given. There would be no backing out. They would attack tonight, and attack again, if necessary.

The hundreds of fighters slowed as each section was told to halt, prepare, rest, and wait. To Khan the soldiers sinking to the ground looked like crops of wheat felled by a sweeping scythe. He squatted, touched the earth, and felt its energy. This was his country. The country of his people. And that does make a difference, Johnny thought. In the most serious of ways. I can see that now.

'Ah,' said Thang, his AK held muzzle-up. 'We are here.' He raised his eyebrows, making it clear to Khan what he meant.

Khan nodded as he slipped off his pack and rested his weapon. Yes, it was the point of no return. But, he thought, we've actually been at that point ever since leaving home. We just didn't realise.

No one did, Johnny agreed. We all got into this, digger or Charlie, thinking there'd be an end to it but maybe there never will be; not for the people who were there.

Thirty-one

Johnny sat on the step of Malcolm's hut, lit a Marlboro, and looked at the inlet. The place was so still he felt like he could breathe in the quiet. For a while he smoked then suddenly the smoke tasted flat and useless. It was about time, he thought, to stop thinking and start doing.

'Get up, sport.' He dropped the cigarette butt and ground it out. 'And get goin'.'

There was no choice in what to do next so he started the ute, pumped the accelerator once then drove away from the hut, and Carly, knowing the difference between leaving and arriving was that now he had a destination. Sure, it was a destination where he doubted there'd be any light or joy, but he was going anyway. Not big a drive, either. First stop was a couple of hundred miles away at the most.

He'd be there late afternoon.

The stump of Khan's arm throbbed as he lay on the sleeping mat in a river village that was unknown to him. He often wondered where it had gone, his arm, after the woman doctor had cut it off. Burnt? Buried? Tossed into the jungle? Who knew? He thought of his lost hand and felt grief like that for a lost friend. A hand was such a wonderful thing. He had never realised how incredible hands were until his right one was gone. There would be no healing, that was for sure.

Yes, healing was always going to be a problem, Johnny agreed. It would be a slow process for all concerned; that's if they didn't run out of time first, because he had the feeling he himself was holding a good hundred years' worth of damage at least.

On the other side of the hut Son slept, but Khan was wakeful. He felt as if he was still in the rowboat. It was not an unpleasant sensation because travelling on a river meant you were steadily heading towards something, somewhere, or someone. He lay listening to the rain. There was an openness to the country now, no matter how dark the night, and wild the storm.

The enemy was gone – from Vietnam anyway, if not his head. It was time to cope with the past, a process like wading a vast river. One slip and you were swept away, dragged into deep water, held under, maybe forever. He listened to the thunder rolling. It is no longer the sound of American B-52 bombers or Phantoms, he assured himself. Or perhaps it was, those bastard crews cursed to bomb the spirit world in ghost planes now and for always.

'It is only thunder,' he whispered, into the crook of his arm. 'Calm down.' Then, before he slept, his last thought was of Phuong, and it made him smile. He was on his way to her, wherever she was, no matter what may have happened to her.

That's the way, champ, Johnny thought. We might be enemies but I can no longer deny that you are a human, and you love this girl. In fact, I wish you luck in finding her, although she was also an enemy of mine, and I would've killed her if I could have. But that was before they signed the piece of paper and brought all that to an end. So get on your way, we'll see what happens, and what it might mean for the both of us.

I can't be any fairer than that, Johnny decided. I cannot.

Thirty-two

Shoey could see it when the Fire Support blokes looked at each other. It was there in the tilt of the head, raised eyebrows, proffered smokes, a shared waterbottle, a nod, and the lightest of slaps on the arm.

'See yers later, boys,' a digger said, heading to a forward mortar position carrying a box of hand grenades. 'I hope.'

'You will, prick.' Barry didn't watch the soldier go; Shoey saw he stared at the perimeter where the last of the daylight did its best to play tricks with the shadows and trees.

'Ever thought of writing Christmas cards, Baz?' Lex knelt over his stripped-down M16. He held a square of stained white rag. Johnny could smell gun oil, a good honest garage smell tainted with death. 'That was really nice.'

Shoey looked at his own rifle. She was ready to go, leaning against a sandbag. In his pockets and pack he had twenty spare mags. On a shelf cut into the side of his foxhole fifteen more were wrapped in plastic. The land pressed. He could feel the enemy, a thousand cobras in a circular woodpile. His fear was incalculable.

'Hey, cheer up, Shoehorn!' Lex locked his rifle back together with the precision of a magician closing the show. 'Why the long face? Look at that lovely hole you've dug. I can see you've spent some time out in the garden. I bet you love getting in among the geraniums. Probably with no clothes on.'

Johnny looked at Lex. Blond hair, blue eyes, jutting shoulders, bony elbows, holding his M16 like a cowboy hippy; suddenly it felt like he was looking at a saint. Then wherever Shoey looked he saw the blokes were all the same. They carried a glow, a holiness, and he knew this place had become *the* place.

'Yeah. Well. Mmm.' He smiled, although it hurt. 'She'll be right, dig.' He spat. 'Look after yerself. You too, Baz.'

Lex leant his rifle carefully, its muzzle covered with a sock.

'Well, I'm relying on you boys for breakfast in bed. I've set the alarm for seven-thirty. Barry, you can squeeze the orange juice. Jonathan, you can do French toast.' Lex held up a finger. 'No Vietnamese spring rolls, I don't think. They're more of a brunch thing.'

Barry tossed smokes. 'Fuckin' pansies.' He sighed, lit up then went back to his M60, the machinegun giving off a dull gleam that spoke of pride, preparedness, and deadliness.

Johnny listened for choppers, hoping there might be one

last desperate supply drop before dark. He'd salute any man, weapon, box of ammo, roll of wire, or extra bloody ray gun but there was nothing. Colour, he saw, was evaporating from the sky as if it was being sucked into outer space. The clock was ticking.

The battalion rose and Khan found he could hardly breathe. Around him was a sea of tiny sounds as the fighting force moved into final positions. There was no clanking of advancing tanks. No planes roaring overhead. No booming of heavy artillery. There was only the sound of rubber-soled sandals, the brushing of cotton and leaves, and the occasional metallic click of small arms being shouldered.

But I heard you coming, Johnny thought, because those trails that you came in on are trails that I travelled in my nightmares.

Thang tapped Khan's elbow and gave him the thumbs-up. Khan understood. Their world had shrunk. Time was limited, filled with love for comrades and country, and commitment to battle. Now he was gliding through the trees, advancing until again they lay down within easy running distance of the open ground.

Darkness arrived like a falling axe. The fire base was swallowed whole but Khan could feel it bristled low down, tensed like a furious dog. Still, the Australians had barely had one full day to secure the ground. There would be weaknesses, and now that D555 had been joined by two battalions of extremely young but fanatical-looking fighters, Khan felt it might truly be obliterated.

Bugles sounded through the trees, their tinny braying bouncing in all directions. This, he knew, was intended to unsettle the Australians. It unsettled him too but it also comforted, as if he lay in the middle of a protective net ten kilometres square. He hoped the bush was filled with thousands and thousands of fighters – and when they attacked it would be with a flash of fire like an atomic bomb.

Tiny lights flared, moved, and blinked. This was another tactic to work on the minds of the men inside the wire. It seemed even the rocks changed places, as if they too were part of the assault force. Nothing was what it seemed except Khan's fear. Everything possessed a fluidity magnified by the night. The countryside ebbed and flowed with fighters. Shadows moved through shadows in Johnny's head, the horror real because it was not imagined but remembered.

Sections of Main Force men slipped forward, running to the flanks. Hundreds of others crawled out onto the open ground to lie like fighters already dead. The silent army was about to throw itself at the enemy base that stood like a boulder in a river – a boulder, Khan thought, that might exist only for a fleeting moment of history. He'd soon see.

Oh, you'll see all right, Johnny thought; whether or not you'll live to remember what you see is a whole other thing.

Thirty-three

Johnny pushed the old ute through mile after mile of parched paddocks until he glimpsed the Murray River. It was a strangely dark and sombre waterway, slow-flowing between trees like the passage of time. In his head he held thoughts that were olive-green and brown: army shirts, dried blood, whipping leaves, camouflaged choppers, bodies wrapped in ponchos, and a patchwork of rice seen from the air. Here he was seeing only tones of grey and brown, moisture sucked away by the long days of a relentless summer.

The dryness agreed with him. It suited his thinness, his narrow purpose. He was nothing but a rusty nail being driven into hard wood, to fix something in place, however un-tradesman-like. He did not know how he was going to deliver his message to Barry's folks, but deliver it he would. At a white service station at a crossroad he filled up with Caltex. Paying, he asked directions to the Graingers' fruit block.

The woman, small and pale, took his ten-dollar note and put it slowly in the till. She glanced at his green shirt then set to work on his face.

'Did you know Barry, love? In the army?'

Shoey could see the thread this woman held, as fine as cotton, as strong as wire. Barry was known here; his family, their way of doing things. They came in for petrol, bread, and milk, and had done so for decades. Barry had stood right here in a cut-off red Wrangler shirt buying Coke and smokes. This image, this truth, unleashed a flash of grief that almost brought Johnny to his knees. He blinked.

'Yeah, I did,' he said. 'We were mates. In Vietnam.' That was all he had but it was rock solid.

The woman pointed to the west. Carefully she gave Johnny directions that included a red shed, a left turn, and a mile of driving. Then she walked out from behind the counter, as if to get a better look at him. In a short-sleeved blue dress, dark hair going grey, she reminded him a bit of his mother.

'D'you want a cuppa tea, love?' She put a cool hand on his forearm but Johnny felt it burn. 'Before you drive out? Or you can eat with us, if you like. We've got a nice little spare room, too. You could see the Graingers in the morning when you're fresh. You'd be most welcome.'

Johnny had to bolt. He could feel his eyes darting like a pair of cornered rabbits. If he lost it here, he might never get it back. He had not factored this in.

'No, thanks, I'm fine, really. Thanks very much.' He backed out, hand up. The pull of his ute drew him like steel to a magnet. 'Thanks. But I'd better go.'

The woman nodded. Perhaps she'd glimpsed a sliver of his panic. 'Godspeed, love.' She followed him, a step or two behind, concern so obvious she walked as if on automatic. 'You need anything, you come straight back. Drive safe. You know where you're goin', don't yer? You know where we are.'

Johnny nodded five times then thankfully, eventually, drove away. The directions he'd been given were gone but the road was like a runway and the fence posts like old friends. So he drove the way he found himself heading, clueless.

'Jesus Christ,' he said softly, reaching for his smokes, seeing a red shed and a dirt road. 'I call time-out, boys.'

He turned off the bitumen, stopped on gravel, and got out. With a dying wattle and a piece of road kill for company, he smoked in stillness so complete it was as if he was the only human being within a hundred miles.

I cannot tell Barry's people everything, he thought. My job is to look after that stuff and tend it like a garden. Then it has to be locked up behind a high stone wall where eventually something will grow over it. Hopefully bloody flowers and not cancer.

Son had traded whiskey for a parachute and cigarettes for an American Ka-Bar knife. The knife he handed to Khan as they drifted away from the village. I can see, Johnny mused, that you guys love that quality US gear. It's just a pity we decided to fight over it, and not simply sell it to you cheap, because that would have saved a lot of trouble.

'The Yanks make good things,' Son said.

Khan hefted the knife. Its handle was stained. There was a silver mark on the blade that might have been made by a glancing bullet. It was indeed a good thing but he was tempted to drop it into the river.

'Also the most awful things in the world.' He slid the knife into its sheath. 'Then we have to pick up after them like spoiled children.'

'Keep the knife, Khan.' Son dipped an oar. 'Use it as a letter opener.' He laughed. 'Or to free a princess from her tower.'

Khan did not really want the knife. Johnny did not blame him. Memories were the most powerful souvenirs from a war. Memories and scars. Enough was enough.

Thirty-four

Wherever Shoey's eyes lingered, things seemed to crawl. In the trees there was an oceanic blackness where lights blinked and bugles blasted strange, sour notes. If anyone had asked him how he felt he could not have told them. The night gripped the earth with claws and there was a seething that reached to the stars. No one was going anywhere. It was way too late for that.

'Our little brown friends are gathering,' Lex said. 'How'd I get here again? I can remember jumping on the Number 16 down St Kilda Road, but after Luna Park, and having fairy floss, John, it's all a blank.'

'Raffle.' Barry's voice, from his sandbagged position, was muffled. 'Winner.'

'Oh, yeah!' Lex's face appeared over the wide lip of his hole. 'I'd forgotten about that, Barry-boy! I was hoping it'd be a Yammy dirtbike but this is far more exciting!'

'*Fuck*.' The word shivered in Shoey's lungs. 'What time is it?' He prayed daylight might be a remote possibility.

'I make it three thirty-thr—' Lex's voice was blown away as the night lit up. Rockets and mortars exploded and the ground jumped. From twenty places M60s opened fire, turning the air into supersonic highways as streams of red and green tracer crossed paths. 'Holy shit!'

Shoey looked out of his shell scrape. He could see nothing but flashes and hear nothing but firing. Then, over the explosions, he heard yelling. It could have come from a thousand throats and probably did. A human stampede was crossing the cleared ground. Charlie was running headlong for the wire like a demented football crowd.

Straining to see, Shoey fired off five rounds then another five at distant movement. The kicking of the SLR banished his nervousness but not his fear. He was fighting for his life and would kill anyone in any way possible.

'*Target, target*,' he intoned, scanning the jolting, flaring, dying darkness. '*Target*.' He saw men running like birds flying. VC. In they swooped.

He gave them everything.

Johnny imagined the enemy sappers about to attack. Khan could see them, crouched shoulder to shoulder, ready to run. There were seven, bare-chested, carrying satchel bombs, homemade Bangalore torpedos, cutting tools, short-handled entrenching tools, and grenades. Four had AKs slung across their backs. Khan knew Trung was among them, away from him now, beyond his meagre abilities to help and protect.

Since nightfall the three battalions had prepared to attack in waves and from multiple directions. Khan and Thang were to go over after the initial rocket and mortar barrage, behind the sappers. Along with hundreds of others, they were to pour through the cut wire and into the base. Once inside it was kill, destroy, and capture weapons. He put a hand on Thang's shoulder. They looked at each other, gripped hands.

'Together, brother,' Thang whispered. 'Together.'

As Khan nodded the bush erupted. Rockets, machine-guns, and mortars smashed into the base. The air leapt into life, convulsing with explosions, light, and shockwaves. And into this the sappers disappeared. To Khan it felt as if Trung was lost in a raging sea – except this was no sea but a designated killing field. There would be no rescue.

Flares lit the open ground. Main Force fighters ran firing and falling, some getting up to go again. Khan and Thang had left the trees, to find themselves in the false and deadly white dawn as they pounded across the cleared ground. Every square inch of air, it seemed, was whipped by flying metal.

Khan sprinted, following Trung's sappers. Still he held on to the idea of finding his friend inside the wire. More soldiers appeared. These were the youngsters from other battalions, boys and girls, their faces set with the sole intention to attack or die. Khan had never seen anything like it. It was as if the earth was tilted sharply towards the holes in the wire. Everyone was being funnelled into a furnace that glowed incandescent, heating up until perhaps the whole place might go up in one massive fireball.

The attacking force reached the wire. Where a section had been blown they crossed easily, Khan praying no mines had been placed. It would have made simple sense to sow the ground here like a vegetable garden and turn it into a slaughterhouse. But the fighters swept on, their objective a mortar crew to be destroyed.

Khan could see the mortars. They appeared well defended by riflemen and an M60. Suddenly he was clear-headed. There was no choice. Forget the odds. Forget the defenders. Forget the future and the past. Forget everyone and forget everything, just run and fire.

With Thang, and many others, he did.

I saw you coming, Johnny thought. And if it wasn't you, Khan, it was someone like you, which was good enough – because we were sent to this place to kill people like each other, and that's exactly what we did.

Thirty-five

The driveway of the Graingers' orchard was two hundred yards, long and ruler-straight. Shoey drove up it under an overcast sky, seeing faded green blinds hanging over the farmhouse windows like old eye patches. A red Monaro sat under a tree and washing hung on a line propped by a stick like a bone. Shoey parked in front of a shed as a black labrador trotted over, tail wagging, eyes shining. It was Barry's dog, Champ; he recognised it from a photo that had dropped out of Barry's gear as it was being sorted.

'Bloody hell,' Johnny muttered, the dog trampling happily on his feet as he got out. 'Good boy. Siddown, bud.' He headed for the back door, which opened before he arrived.

A short, square-shouldered man with grey hair, wearing a grey shirt and grey trousers, appeared. A thin woman followed in his wake. She was looking worriedly at Shoey as if he might be bringing bad news. Well, Johnny thought, it sure as hell ain't good news – even if it was news as old as the hills.

'G'day.' Shoey felt like he was turning up for a funeral. The silence was tangible and so was the sorrow. He recognised its dark filament as being permanent, personalised, and immoveable. Death never ended for the living. 'I'm Johnny Shoebridge.' He stopped. 'I was with Barry. Over there.'

Barry's father took two steps forward and shook Johnny's hand with strength.

'I'm Ron Grainger.' The fruit grower's face was worn, tough, and sun-beaten. It was a face Johnny had seen on every country street just about every day of his life. 'And this is Estelle. Barry's mum. We're real pleased to see ya, John.'

Estelle Grainger's face was like her husband's, worn by work, except her eyes were lost on some boundless continent of sadness. She nodded, tried out a fluttery smile. Ron Grainger put a heavy hand on Shoey's shoulder.

'Thanks for comin', mate. You're real welcome. Come inside.'

'This is Barry's dog.' Estelle Grainger spoke suddenly, as if to get it over and done with. 'Champ. We got him when Barry was thirteen. For his birthday.'

All Johnny could do was nod. He had the feeling he was caught in a terrible, terrible slow-motion landslide.

'He's a good dog.' He looked into the dog's shining black eyes. 'A ripper.'

Barry's mum nodded, as if Johnny had said something important.

'He is. We love him.' She turned away, as if she had already said too much.

Ron Grainger indicated Johnny should go inside. He appeared to brush away his wife's words but Johnny guessed he hadn't at all. At the door, Johnny toed off his Volleys, glad he'd managed to put on clean black socks.

'Barry wasn't much for writing.' Ron Grainger's forehead was lined with furrows like a potato field. 'He was probably pretty quiet over there, I expect.'

Johnny stood in a sparse kitchen. He could smell meat cooking. Two old tin saucepans sat on a gas stove and he was cheered a bit by a calendar on a hook featuring poplar trees like golden flames. The dog's claws clicked merrily on the lino as it headed to a worn green mat and threw itself down. Johnny turned to Ron and Estelle Grainger and took a breath. On your blocks. Get set. Go.

'Barry,' he said, 'and Lex, our other mate, were the best and bravest blokes I ever met. By far and bar none.'

This brought a sudden silence. Estelle Grainger freed a small white handkerchief from a sleeve and dabbed at the corners of her eyes. She turned to a bench and put an electric kettle on. It was a Burko, Shoey saw, the same one his mum had.

'He was a quiet boy but a good boy.' Estelle Grainger took down two mugs and a patterned china cup. 'No trouble at all. I'm sure Lex was lovely, too. Barry sent us a photo. Of you three.'

'Barry looked after his mates.' Johnny sat at the table when Ron Grainger sat. 'He looked after everybody. All the time. He was solid as a rock.' He saw Barry's old man nodding, processing the words. 'I can't tell yers how good he was. Real good. *Fuc*-bloody brave.'

'He *was* good,' Estelle Grainger added. 'Some people didn't see it. But he was. He always made sure the animals were fed and did his jobs.'

Barry's father looked at the hand that he'd rested on the table. Shoey saw it was gnarled and lined, recording the passing of every hard winter and hot summer, every good and bad month, week, year, and decade.

'He was suited for the army,' Ron said. 'Some blokes just are. Did you join or were you called up, John?'

'Conscripted.' Johnny answered as if the word could be shrugged off but it charged him down like a wounded buffalo. There was nothing he could add.

'What did your mum and dad think?' Estelle Grainger brought over tea, fruitcake, and milk and sugar on a tray. 'I think it's a terrible thing to do to our young boys. In this country. Of all places. Silly.'

Shoey could only nod. He felt like a dog with a bee in its ear.

'My mum wasn't happy. And my old man's passed away. But he would've said go, I guess.'

'I can't tell you how much it means to see you.' Barry's mother spoke quickly. 'Dan McCrae came, too.' She sat. 'The captain. He was lovely. Drove all the way down from Sydney. He said lovely things about Barry. He seemed to like him a lot.'

Shoey found himself smiling. He didn't know why exactly. Or where it came from; still, it felt like he was crying. And that he was teetering on the edge of a cliff, just managing to hold on. Well, the bloody *good* old skipper, he thought. Put him up another three notches on the league ladder.

'Yeah, Macca's a top bloke.' Shoey looked at Barry's mother. 'Barry was funny. He was tough and funny. But boy, he had guts.' He saw that Estelle Grainger nodded, looking sadder by the second, as if she knew having too much courage might only make it more difficult for a soldier to get home. 'The boys liked him. A lot. We needed him.' It was more than that but Johnny couldn't say it.

He couldn't tell anyone what it was like when the bodies wrapped in ponchos were lifted into a Huey. Then the Huey went and the dead boys were gone.

'We'll go and see Luke.' Ron Grainger put down his mug and stood. 'Barry's little brother. If that's okay with you, John. He's on the tractor out in the fruit.' He put a hand on his wife's narrow back. 'Then we'll come back, love, for a beer and somethin' to eat. I think we need it.'

Johnny went outside. Ron waited while he pulled on his Volleys as Champ happily headbutted his knees.

'You know, John,' Barry's old man said as they walked across the grey yard, 'the hardest thing about this whole bloody mess is that I get the feelin' it was all for nothin'. That it was just a fuckin' joke put together by a bunch of clowns to prove a point. I'll never forgive the bastards. And I fought in the second one. So. Well. That's me.'

To Johnny it was as if he was staring down from a chopper hurtling over a landscape of deep uncertainty. Vietnam was a strange country that would always be strange. Its history was so tangled only the Viets could understand it. The Aussie politicians didn't have a hope – not that that stopped them from taking a wild guess.

'I just pray somethin' good comes out of it.' Ron gazed into the upraised limbs of fruit trees. Somewhere a tractor growled. 'For someone, somewhere. I just don't know what it could be.'

Johnny hadn't taken three steps when he realised that finding something good for Barry's father was one of the most important things he'd ever do.

'Well, one good thing, Ron,' he said, 'is that I met Barry. He showed what the best blokes do. What they are. I'll never forget him.' He reached for his smokes. 'He was a ripper. I can't tell you how brave he was. He saved blokes. He saved our bloody lives. I wouldn't be here if it wasn't for him. That's the truth, Ron. Him and Lex were the best blokes in the world.'

Ron Grainger nodded, as if Shoey was still talking, and he was still listening.

'If you could just tell young Luke that,' he said, looking for the hidden tractor growling away in the orchard, or perhaps just looking away, 'I'll owe you for the rest of my life.'

To Johnny, answering Ron Grainger felt as if he was answering Danny McRae, or any one of the boys asking a favour.

'No worries,' he said. 'Not a problem.'

The roaring of the red tractor died in the rows of fruit trees. Luke, a wiry kid in a dark blue work shirt, climbed down onto hard grey ground, pulling at the tail of a plaited bush belt. He looked at Johnny.

'How ya goin'?'

Johnny nodded. 'Yeah, good, mate. How are you?'

'Fine.'

The kid didn't look much like Barry, but there was something about him that suggested a shy rural toughness. Ron Grainger did the introductions then walked away. Johnny took out his smokes, offered one to Luke that was knocked back then lit his own.

'You gotta know, Luke—' Johnny sucked in smoke, 'and you probably already do, that Barry was a ripping bloke.'

Luke nodded, his choppy blond hair the brightest thing in the orchard as the sun sank towards a flat horizon. The place didn't exactly make Johnny feel great: it had the feel of places he'd been before, where the geometry of evenly spaced trees and shadows didn't suggest regulation and order but gunfire and carnage.

'I can't tell you everything we did exactly, over there—' Johnny could see Luke understood this, 'but when we needed Baz most, when things were at their bloody worst, he didn't flinch.' Johnny took a steadying drag. 'He went at it, Luke, hard. He had an M60 machinegun. That was his weapon. You can see what I mean, can't yer? That we were in some pretty big blues. Barry saved a lot of blokes. It was life and death and I am not jokin'. I wouldn't be standing here if it wasn't for him.'

Luke crossed his arms and studied the few flat limp weeds that dotted the place. Johnny toed one up out of the ground. Capeweed.

'He was a good feller,' Luke said quietly. 'He looked after me. You know. At school. Playin' footy. In town. Wherever.'

'He looked after everyone.' Johnny felt the truth of what he was saying heavy in his blood. 'Before he looked after himself.' He put a hand on Luke's shoulder, felt springy young bones. 'I hope I'll catch up with him one day.' Johnny looked at the tractor, its belly crusted with clay and dirty oil, a hard-working beast that would just keep on going. 'Anyway, mate, I'll see yer before I take off.' Johnny nodded and Luke dipped his head in return. 'Finish ya work, Luke. Good on ya.' Johnny, feeling like a teacher or a coach, someone old, anyway, watched Barry's little brother walk away before heading back through the trees.

Behind him the tractor grunted into life, as if the world had started turning again on the power of its old diesel motor. Another box ticked, Johnny thought as he crushed his cigarette, making sure it was dead and buried. How many left to go, he didn't know.

The ground on both sides of the river, as Johnny had seen and Khan was seeing now, had been blasted for kilometres. It was a sick-looking wasteland of shredded trees and cratered soil that had crusted in the sun like a flyblown wound. The one-armed fighter could smell foul water and there was a remote, foreign stillness to the place. It was as if the bombing had claimed the ground from Vietnam and now it was just another piece of American war trash.

'I'm glad I wasn't here that day,' Khan said.

The devastation was superhuman. It occurred to Khan that the bombing was done with something worse than hate; it was done with sheer disregard. The enemy never really knew or cared where the bombs would fall because there'd never be any accounting or going back. Khan could feel the staggering impersonality of it. So could Johnny, to an extent.

'I need a smoke, Son,' Khan said, 'if you might have one for an old retired fighter. This place makes me sick.'

Son shipped the oars and came up with a red and white packet from a black bag.

'Marlboro Red, my friend.' Son flicked his lighter, the flame barely visible in the sun. 'America's finest.'

Khan looked across the wasteland. A line of people dressed in black searched slowly for something. Bamboo shoots to eat, he thought. Or human bones for burial. It was, he decided, either a pitiful sight or a sign of victory. The people had risen from the ashes or had returned to them, proving that explosions and firestorms could only do so much damage for so long. Bamboo should appear on our flag, Khan thought; eventually it overcame all, and everything, to survive and thrive.

'What d'you think those people are looking for, Son?' he asked.

'What everyone is looking for.' Son drew on his cigarette then started to gently row. 'A way forward.'

Amen to that, sport, Johnny thought. Amen.

Thirty-six

Shoey, his head engulfed in the shockwaves of massed weaponry, fired at fighters who ran at the gunpits and machineguns. Tracer fire, in magically coloured streams, sailed into and out of the base as rockets, mortar, and artillery thundered. On both sides men went down and the only meaningful measure of time Johnny had was that he was still alive.

The air was filled with the stink and heat of weapons. The recoil of his rifle punched his shoulder as he aimed and fired endlessly. Over and over he sighted on slews of sprinting people in green and black who appeared and disappeared. Then, horrifically, they swarmed into the mortar pit like crazed spiders. Ten of them threw themselves at the firing weapons, screaming and shooting, two instantly blasted backwards, one cartwheeling sideways, another dropping like a plank, the others firing like madmen.

Shoey emptied a magazine. He reloaded then fired again. A metre away, Lex's M16 roared. Barry was standing, unloading a belt into the gun pit as if he was hosing a fire until Johnny saw him fall forward, flat on his face, never letting go of his weapon. Then Lex's rifle stopped and Johnny knew exactly what that meant.

He ceased to think and became nothing but killing rage. A young enemy sapper, shirtless, sprinted towards the pit with grenades on a pole. Johnny gave him three rounds, flesh flicking from his chest. Swinging his weapon around, he shot a crawling fighter in the top of the head. Then he cracked off the rest of the magazine at fighters who were backing off, wounding another. Reloading, he felt as if he'd never get enough breath or bullets.

In a brief lull he jumped into Lex's shell scrape and picked him up under the arms. It was the heaviest weight he'd ever felt, and when a stream of thick hot blood poured over his hands all he could do was gently lower his friend to the ground, and know that here was something else he would never get over. And now, suddenly, although just a little bit too fucking late in Shoey's humble opinion, he heard the gunships.

In they swept, a fleet of flying monsters, mini-guns roaring, rockets piercing the trees. And further away the hallowed, hellish Spooky circled lazily, spewing a bright roaring rain of a hundred thousand rounds on the VC – a sound suddenly insignificant as the worldwide howl of four Phantoms, tailpipes skyrocket red, destroyed the jungle with fifty tons of bombs in fifty seconds. And the battle was over, the VC withdrawing, for now.

Johnny stood, stepped over a couple of dead Main Force fighters, jumped down into the mortar pit and found Barry. Kneeling, he touched his friend's face but what he felt only reinforced what he knew; that everything was breaking down and would stay that way forever.

'Give us a bloody hand, mate!' a medic yelled at Shoey. 'Over here. *Quick*.'

Shoey leapt across, crouching by a digger heaving for breath. It was Jimmy the Smoke, the only guy in Delta Company who didn't smoke. Johnny saw the soldier's eyes were wide open, as if he was staring at a place just up the road that frightened the hell out of him.

'Stay with us, Jimmy,' the medic chanted as he rigged an IV unit. 'This don't look too bad. You'll be right. Back in bloody Bondi in a couple of weeks. No sweat. Just stay with us, mate. We gotcha.'

As Johnny held the IV pouch arm-high, he realised he'd been praying since the first rocket hit. For one mad metallic moment, he wondered if God had sent the jets. And that thought, he decided, made about as much sense as anything else he could come up with.

The Australians defending the mortar pits reminded Khan of fish in a trap. He fired into them and at them. He did not know if he hit anybody. He did not know how he could miss or how he was not killed. Men went down, others reared up as he staggered on, half-blinded by muzzle blasts and half-stunned by concussion.

It was a whirlpool of violence that Khan expected would suck him down and rip him apart at any moment. Amazed he was alive, he fought on, until an unseen arm dragged him backwards. The tide had turned. American machines filled the sky and Australian troops poured in to reinforce positions. The battle was lost.

Khan leapt from the pit to join the retreat. Stopping once, he managed to lift a fighter with no face, and staggered to the wire. Across the cleared ground the bush blazed like a burning city while overhead the sky shuddered. And Khan, seeing that evil thing, Spooky, knew that the spirits of his best friends, Thang and Trung, and many others, were leaving the battlefield. Their duty was done. Now they sought a world that would welcome them to lie down and rest, but he could not, and staggered on, carrying his dying comrade towards the trees.

Johnny, given the chance, would have stopped him with a well-aimed bullet. And that, he reckoned, would've have put an end to this imagining before it started. But he hadn't killed Khan and he knew that it was impossible to kill a ghost of his own creation – although he prayed it might be possible, some day, one day, to lay one to rest.

Thirty-seven

Shoey could not stay at Barry's place. In a way he wanted to but in the end he couldn't. The pain was obvious and too great, like a bad burn, hurting whichever way he turned. It was palpable among the fruit trees and in the yard. It was present in the kitchen and at the table, tethering the family. And Johnny had the feeling that Barry, standing a few rows back in the orchard, arms crossed and faintly amused, was watching as Johnny attempted to extricate himself from a situation that was tightening like a snare.

It was Ron Grainger who released him. Barry's father held up a hand and settled everybody down, knowing that staying was for family only – as it was the family who would endure the birthdays, the mounting anniversaries, the demise of the dog, unwelcome government letters, and the awful visits to the cemetery where it seemed a bitter wind always blew.

'Thank you, John,' was all Barry's mum said, but she said it half a dozen times. 'Thank you so much. Please come back and see us.'

Johnny promised that he would, shook Luke's hand then drove away over dry dirt under a luminous sky. At the letter-box he stopped, left a single sad honk of the horn hanging, then turned for the highway. Smoke filled the cabin as he lit up, the glow of the Marlboro reminding him of the tailpipe of a Phantom as it halved the sky. But when he looked up all he could see were stars.

'Thank God,' he muttered, and found himself thinking of Khan on his river journey with that other bastard Son. 'We're all going somewhere, I guess,' he added, as he drove into a flat grey town where a barred gun-shop window was the brightest thing in the place. 'Even to a dump like this.'

Along the river Khan and Son asked if anyone might know of a woman called Phuong, a northern Main Force fighter who had settled in the district. The locals, fishermen and farmers, would look at the long-haired Son in his silver sun-glasses. Then their eyes would slide to one-armed Khan, who listened more than he spoke, adding a degree of respectabil-ity to the pair. Or this is how Johnny figured things might go.

In a fishing village, Son and Khan were led to a reed hut that stood on a mud bank. With a window on either side of the small entrance, it reminded Khan of a skull sitting on an old plate.

'Inside is a woman from the north,' said the village chief. 'An important man from the party instructed us to look after her. Maybe she is this Phuong you are looking for. If so, you can—'

Khan and Son exchanged looks. The chief gestured with a hand as scaly and twisted as a chicken's foot.

'Go in.'

Son stepped back and Khan walked forward. Johnny watched from above. At the door Khan raised his hand to knock.

'No need for that.' The chief did not explain.

Khan knocked anyway, softly. To enter the hut he had to duck. Inside the heat was thick and there was a sweet smell that soon became sour and sickly. Seeing in the dim light was like trying to peer into a dank pool. A woman lay on a bed, dressed, staring at the thatched ceiling. For a moment Khan thought she was dead until he saw her chest rise. He greeted her quietly.

The woman did not stir, although he saw that she blinked. It was not Phuong. On a small table beside the bed there was a plastic bowl, a scatter of petals floating in clean water. A worn cotton cloth was folded beside it.

'I see you, sister.' Khan knelt, taking up a hand that was cold and limp. 'I pray that you are peaceful. The war has finished. You are safe.' He studied her for a moment before replacing her hand by her side. Then he dampened the cloth and carefully ran it over her face, thinking that this person had become silence itself. 'Imagine a cool clearing in the early morning,' he murmured. 'The dew is on the grass. The sun is on your face. The day is beautiful and you are free. There is no danger. Only birds and flowers. And this one day will go on forever.'

Khan rinsed the cloth and draped it over the side of the bowl. He told the woman he would pray for her and left the hut. Once outside, breathing deeply, he felt he had re-entered the world, that he had stepped away from some bombardment, torture session, or catastrophic ambush that the woman had survived, leaving her true self behind.

'It is not Phuong.' He addressed no one in particular then turned to the village chief. 'Thank you for caring for this person. She is not well, obviously.'

The man accepted Khan's thanks, inclining his head politely as they stood in the bright heat.

'The war has thrown up a thousand complications and contradictions for us,' the chief said. 'She is just one frag-ment. This village has suffered at the hands of many.' He looked at Khan. 'Now, all we want is to live quietly. Thank you for visiting.'

Son offered the head man a cigarette as they walked to the pontoon where the boat was tied. The chief smoked it as he watched them row away. Khan and Son remained quiet until rounding a bend in the river.

'I am sorry, Khan,' Son said.

To Khan the sound of the dipping oars was soothing. He watched the slow swirl of the river and wondered about the nature of whirlpools and eddies.

'Be sorry for that woman,' he said. 'But be thankful she was not sister Phuong.'

Son nodded, rowing slowly and surely. 'Well, friend, the search goes on.'

You can say that again, Johnny thought; and it occurred to him, the emotion arriving without force or fanfare, that he wasn't able to hate all North Vietnamese anymore – and that he wished his enemy luck in his search for this woman, Phuong, because to return for those who are missing, or lost in action, was a most honourable thing to do.

Thirty-eight

The Huey lifted off, rising fast, blades thwacking like the heaviest of heartbeats. Johnny watched it, black-bellied in the grey sky, him way below like one green ant among many on a swarming brown nest. One hundred metres away the roaring of Brutus the bulldozer took over as it pushed dead VC, bloodied arms flapping, into a mass grave. This was the image that Johnny held as he walked around the fire base over the next four days. A whole other mindful of horrors he hoped he would never recall – but random, rolling images refused to be subdued.

Fast and bloody they flashed behind his eyelids. There were pictures of the dead and dying. There were pictures of the broken faces of the loved and the hated – and although Johnny refused to watch, he experienced this merry-go-round of autopsy continually.

'End of the fuckin' earth,' said a digger called Graeme, as he and Johnny stacked sandbags. 'Quite frankly, I'd rather be in Iceland.'

'Jesus,' said Johnny. 'I reckon.' He drank water that had a weird, heavenly taste. 'Gaol. I'd take that.'

But he kept on working, smoking and talking, knowing there was a good chance he would have to fight through something like it again, or worse. And now it was sunset. He looked towards the blackened bush. Skeletal trees proclaimed the area as a memorial forest for the dead. And in that wasteland, he knew living battalions assembled with nothing but killing on their minds.

Was that bastard Khan from the bamboo grove out there, Johnny wondered? Or all three of those guys he'd shot at in the rice ten months ago? One way or another, he had no doubt they were.

It was in this destroyed forest, where the young fighters had screamed their burning lungs out, that Khan prepared for the next battle. On the fourth night, an hour after midnight, the bugles signalled for the broken battalions to form up, and the mad lights again began to flicker like angry spirits. The men and women, in silence, waited for the order to attack.

Johnny, sensing a deep murmur beyond the wire, lifted his weapon.

'The butcher shop,' he whispered, 'is now open for business.'

Thirty-nine

The grim, unknown little town, with a few bright lights, had managed to stop Johnny's ute on the false promise of a hot coffee and a decent hamburger. But no shop was open; it was only the gun store that was lit up like a high-security gaol. Nice-lookin' toys, he thought, checking out the 'scoped rifles locked in soldierly racks – but toys certainly powerful enough to blow your head off, if that was what you wanted.

Johnny stared into darkness that was purple-tinged and smelled of distant bushfire. How good, he thought, would it be to see the reddening tips of two cigarettes in the shadows across the street, and know it was Lex and Baz waiting for him. *Surprise, surprise, Johnny-boy, we were just havin' you on! We're all right! We're okay! Get your arse over here!* That'd be some reunion, all right – but there was no one, of course. What there was, he saw, sited a short way back from the street, was a small RSL hall made of biscuit-yellow bricks, its foyer lit by sick neon light. Parked out the front was a Second World War field gun aimed at the sky.

Well, I'm a returned soldier, Johnny thought. Perhaps the bastards might serve me a beer and a steak. And who knows, someone in there might even be cheerful. He put out his cigarette, locked the car, and crossed the road. A flag of no colour, he saw, hung limp from a metal pole.

In the foyer, Shoey took a quick look at the photographs of young blokes in old uniforms and leathery war memorabilia. Respects paid, he went into the lounge. Empty round brown tables reflected harsh light. Three middle-aged men sat on stools, contemplating sudsy-looking beers. Shoey approached the bar. It seemed silence had followed him in.

'Gidday.' He spoke generally as he took a fiver from his wallet. 'Warm night.'

One bloke nodded but no one spoke. As far as Shoey could see there were no bar staff, only a doorway that might have led to a secret passageway. He waited, thinking, I can play this game all night, you bastards.

'Vietnam, mate?' The closest drinker turned, a short man with fat hands and hair like varnished hay. 'Or are yer just buyin' the shirts at the army disposals?'

Shoey ran his fingertips along the crease he'd put in the pink note. Suddenly everything about the place was wrong. He knew it for sure, like he should've known it five minutes ago when he laid eyes on the mustard-coloured, badly lit, cheaply built biscuit box. Too late, cobber, he thought, but I will give these smart bastards nothing.

'Yeah, that's right.' His pulse rose as he named his battalion; one number and three letters he carried soul-deep. 'Been back for a couple of months.'

The drinkers exchanged looks. The hay-haired bloke rotated a degree or two in Shoey's direction.

'Couldn't really call it a war, could yer? A few little brown blokes armed with second-hand Chinese shit sticks. A skirmish, mate. By our standards. Just say boo and they all woulda buggered off.'

The drinkers chuckled noiselessly. In unison they hoisted their beers, looked wise. The biggest bloke placed a box of matches on his cigarettes as if playing draughts.

'Put salt on their tails,' he said, giving the ceiling his undivided attention. 'Belt 'em with a cricket bat. Save the ammo.'

The ground opened up, Shoey seeing the core of the earth, the blood-soaked pit, and the boys. The drinkers sensed a change.

'Ah, you're right, mate,' said the bloke with yellow hair. 'Terry'll be back in a sec. You'll like the beer. Just put on a new keg.'

Johnny swayed in a red mist. His right knee shook. His fists he disguised as open hands. His vision was down a short tunnel and these three blokes were the only things in it.

'I wouldn't drink with you dickheads,' he said quietly, 'for all the fuckin' tea in China.' He stepped back, hands up, still open, gesturing. 'Come on. I'll show yers a fuckin' war if yers want one. Right here. Right now.' He was ready to go like never before. 'Come on. One of yers. All of yers, I couldn't give a fuck.'

The biggest drinker turned slowly. Everything about him was large and worn. He looked at Johnny as if he was a pest to be flicked.

'Piss off, son. Before you get hurt.'

Johnny laughed. He saw nothing to fear. This bloke'd go down despite what he thought of himself. Johnny did not care how it might end. They could kill him – but he'd do some damage first.

'Outside, ya fat mongrel.' Johnny pointed to the exit. 'I'll be there.' He shouldered through one glass door, kicked open the next, and took the steps three at a time. On a concrete strip he paced up and down like a mad bull. 'Come on! Get out 'ere, you fat *gutless* bastards!'

He gave it three minutes. He gave it five. Then he spat, laughed like a madman, and walked back to his ute. Beneath his feet the bitumen slid like a river and overhead an angry orange moon lit the sky.

'I fuckin' *win*.' He got into his car and started it. And I don't even know the name of this stinking hole, he thought. *Good*.

Johnny pulled out and accelerated, feeling as if he trailed fury like a meteor trailed fire. At his point he knew only two things: one, he was heading south to Melbourne to see Lex's family, and two, he would try to find Jilly. Beyond that, the future, as far as he could see, had no meaning at all.

A bare-chested boy, his ribs like stripes, ran along the river-bank calling out to Khan and Son. He easily kept pace with the boat, jumping over roots, dodging around trees, sure-footed on the slopes of mud. Son shipped the oars and watched with amusement, as did Johnny, because he'd seen fifty little guys like this, up for anything.

'He's a determined little frog,' Son said.

Khan could see the kid was grinning, slowing to a trot, figuring that his request had been heard. Now, with the ease of an otter, the boy made his skidding way down to the water's edge where he cupped his hands around his mouth.

'Hullo, kind misters! I have a message!' He waded into the river that was paler than his knees. 'You are looking for someone, yes? A lost sister from the war?'

Hope spiked. Khan looked at the messenger and pressed it down. There were broken-down sisters and brothers from the war just about everywhere. He himself was one, and certainly no wonderful rarity.

'This young crab might be a river pirate like you, Son,' Khan said. 'By the looks of things.'

'I prefer to call myself a river *trader*.' Son sounded a little offended. 'A person who pursues opportunities for mutual gain. Shall we go and talk to the little cricket?'

'Why not?' Khan needed a break from the boat. His backside was sore and the heat of the day was implacable. The sun baked his head through his green battle hat. The shade on the shore beckoned. 'He's been sent by someone.'

Son steered the rowboat into the bank. The waterway was wide and open, the vegetation lush and green. The place seemed to offer possibilities, Khan thought. The boy waited keenly.

'Word travels up and down rivers like the wind,' Son said. 'Don't get your hopes up, Khan. These people will skin you alive for a buck. The war has only made them poorer.' He nosed the rowboat gently into mud, Khan stepping ashore with the mooring rope.

The boy stood hatless in the harsh sunshine. Khan guessed he was about eight or nine. On his left side he had a birthmark shaped like an apple. The heat of the day hummed.

'Who is this person you are so keen to tell us about, my friend?' Khan held the slack rope. 'How did you know we are looking for a woman from the war, anyhow? Are you magic?'

The kid grinned, his body spattered with mud rapidly puckering into pale freckles of dirt. His hair shone as if he wore a silver helmet.

'Oh, *everybody* knows you are looking for a war lady. And this one ended up in our village after a very bad battle. What did you say this comrade's name was? Please?'

'I didn't say,' said Khan. 'You tell me.'

The boy looked at Khan triumphantly. 'We think her name is perhaps Phuong. But no one knows for sure. You will see why when you visit her.'

'Interesting,' said Son. 'So it is possible for us to meet with this person?'

The boy nodded vigorously. 'It would be my pleasure to take you. She looks after the chickens and pigs and fetches water. Please follow me.' He pointed downstream. 'There's a jetty you would be most welcome to use.'

Khan saw that Son was enjoying the show.

'All right, friend.' Son inclined his head politely. 'If you could guide us that would be good. From the bank. I don't think your mother would like you to jump in a boat with two old river rats like us.'

'Of course I can guide you, sir!' The boy headed for the high ground. 'Follow me. It is only a short way. And if you could remember, misters, that it was me who told you about this gentle lady soldier.'

Khan and Son swapped looks. The heat of the day was mounting. The blue sky was like a weight poised to drop.

'I would never forget an important fact like that,' Son said. 'But this person might not be the one we're looking for.'

The boy stopped at the top of the bank. 'Yes, that's true, mister.' The kid beamed with startlingly white teeth. 'But she might *just* be!'

He's got you there, Johnny thought. You'd better go check out this woman to prove to yourself that you have not lost hope, because to lose hope is to lose everything.

Forty

Another battalion had been airlifted in to FSB Leslie. Shoey was acutely aware of the extra men, energy, and weapons. The freshly turned ground bristled with dug-in pits with logs for head cover and sandbagged positions spiked with nests of M6os. Two Centurion tanks, like a sullen tag team of heavyweight wrestlers, sat camouflaged in their respective corners. Their massive steel barrels, as thick as logs, were aimed directly across the killing grounds that lay open but unseen in the dark.

Barely able to speak, Johnny kept working, and when he looked to the wire he felt a savage determination that muscled in beside his fear. He wanted to kill the people out there. As many as possible.

Since midnight, lights had flickered in the burnt bush and bugles had sounded like crazed birds. The night vibrated as if myriad snakes and ants moved forward, laying up whenever he was looking, advancing when he wasn't.

'Splintex,' a dark-headed rifleman called Noel murmured from his hole. 'We have shitloads of beautiful Splintex.'

'And tanks,' another rifleman added, a sunburned giant from Longreach who Shoey had had a few beers with in Vung Tau. 'Fifty tons each. You bloody beaut.'

'White phosphorous,' someone else added, as if quoting from a shopping list. 'That shit burns underwater.'

Johnny treasured the words that talked up firepower and mass destruction. He prayed they had the weapons to keep the VC on their side of the wire; that when Charlie rose up, the Centurions and the artillery batteries would simply knock them down with waves of Splintex that would shred anything, trees included, in their path.

Other fire bases would add long-range artillery support, and on distant airstrips helicopter gunships sat like giant hawks. Then there were the Phantoms, ready to unleash what the enemy did not have. And he and the boys would be here to do whatever killing they could.

Shoey settled into his pit, a bleak-eyed rifleman staring at the blackness, cigarette butts scattered around his boots.

'Come on, you dirty bastards,' he whispered. 'Let's get this over and done with.'

The Main Force battalions, reinforced by fresh troops, began their advance through the landscape of Johnny's head. To

Khan it appeared the ground was rippling towards the fire base. Hundreds of fighters slowly began the surge that would accelerate into a headlong charge at the Australians, dug in like a plague of beetles.

Khan ordered himself forward. It was the hardest thing he had ever done, moving within the strike force through a fog of fear. Four nights ago, the Australians had been under-prepared. Tonight he knew they were poised to bring hell down from the sky and the hills.

Somehow he put his fear aside. It was the only way he could hit the wire; to accept he was a feather on the winds of war. If he was to die then he would do so knowing he had done his duty. Yet he felt a deep anguish like lost love. He loved his life and the people in it. He also knew he was being manipulated by others, but his minor role was of prime importance. When the rockets, machineguns, and mortars opened up, his courage to attack would prove to the land, the gods, his ancestors, and the enemy, he was here to kill.

It started, Shoey felt, like a mass exhalation of breath. Swiftly it lifted into a storm that rose into a hurricane, the sheer force of the attack pressing like thumbs into his eyes. Then the camouflaged Centurions, a pair of monster cheats, lit up the night with five-metre flashes of fire as they sent shell after shell of Splintex over the wire.

The killing grounds and bush beyond were swept with a hundred thousand flying scalpels. Now the M60s waded in, supporting artillery from distant fire bases began to pound the attackers, and over it all parachute flares floated and star shells drifted as Johnny fired at the ghostly green running figures, every shot piercing his old self until that boy from the bush was gone for good.

And when shrapnel slashed his arms Johnny kept on firing, felling one fighter, dropping another to his knees, shooting him again before finding other targets, stopping only to slam home fresh magazines, praying that whoever he was aiming at he was killing. Whatever wounds he had, physical or mental, he figured he would deal with later. If he survived.

Khan left the trees and was through the wire, almost at a mortar position when he was grabbed by the right arm by a lion, punched in the side by a heavyweight boxer, and flung backwards. This was something that Johnny had not predicted, the Vietnamese fighter on his knees, the earth sliding as the magnesium-white sky pressed. A seismic panic shook the injured Khan. What had happened to him? Where was his AK?

With his left hand he felt downwards from his right shoulder, fingers encountering a mass of splintery pulp and stringy tendons. Somehow his elbow was gone, the arm hanging like the torn sleeve of a wet shirt. Pain flared like a petrol fire. Then he was hit again in the side, a single smashing blow that threw him over onto his face.

'Oh, mother,' he moaned into the dirt. 'Help me.'

A comrade appeared so suddenly it was if he had swooped from the sky. Khan did not recognise him but, looking into his face, felt he had known him all his life.

'Oh, brother,' Khan said. 'My arm. My side.'

The man examined Khan's wounds. His hands moved like that of a musician. His eyes held a deep glow.

'Lie still, friend. Hold your arm like you are.' Taking a tattered field dressing from a plastic bag, he tied and taped it in place. Then he strapped something to Khan's side and secured it tightly. 'You will have to go back, if you can,' he said. 'There'll be people waiting.' He handed Khan his rifle. 'Don't lose this. Make tracks, comrade. You have done your duty. Your battle is over.'

Khan gripped his weapon and stood, swaying, remaining upright with help. Beneath his boots the ground see-sawed as bullets whispered past his head. The unknown fighter turned him around, and pushed him lightly.

'That way, friend. See you soon.'

Khan stumbled away, pain riding on his back with the weight of a bear – a bear that had sunk its teeth into the shattered bones of his right arm and torn holes in his side that he could put his hand in.

'I need help,' he murmured then fell, to lie on the ground like a grain of wheat, his rifle under his hip, the point of the bayonet piercing his good arm.

Maybe I'll die now, he thought. It feels like it.

Unfortunately it's not your time yet, Johnny decided. Someone had to survive that battle, that night, that war, and carry away those memories. You couldn't just leave it all up to me. So keep breathing, sport, although I'm not sure this is a development that will help me a hell of a lot in the long run.

Forty-one

Johnny left the motel, giving it one backward glance as he turned out onto the Hume Highway. Already he was missing the security of the small pine-panelled room, the potholed bed, and the midget fridge that had muttered to him all night. He was also missing the woman in the office who'd called him love, the bloke who'd called him John-Boy, and told him to drive safe.

It was like this country couple thought he was normal. They couldn't see his madly running mind, his lost friends, and the enemy Khan who stalked him day and night. If they had, they would have attempted to understand because they were parents, everyday people – but too late. Johnny Shoebridge was on his way to meet Lex's family, find Jill, then . . .

Slow drive or fast drive?

Johnny put his foot down, although he figured he might simply be accelerating towards a very sudden and serious dead-end. This, he guessed, he had known for months.

'Ah, do yer worst,' he muttered, trees falling behind as if dropped by a hurricane. 'See if I fuckin' care.'

It was a rather strange village, Khan decided, as he and Son introduced themselves to the head man. They were given food and tea by women who seemed sunny but vague. Many of the residents appeared to use a kind of sign language, the place held still by a pervasive silence. Khan shared a look with Son as they followed the chief out behind the houses.

'You need to see this, friends,' the man said. 'To understand us a little more.'

Through a tangle of bush, bamboo, and rank grass was the biggest bomb crater Khan, or Johnny, had ever seen.

'It removed the graveyard and temple,' the head man said, whose knobbly knee joints seemed to have been inherited by the kid on the river. 'A thousand years of ancestry gone in one second flat. The sound deafened three-quarters of the village. It killed thousands of fish. Maybe it was two bombs together, who knows? I was five hundred metres upstream, but the concussion knocked me backwards.'

For a while the men looked into the crater, where creepers meekly attempted to hide the damage. I can believe this did happen, Johnny thought – to a thousand villages, because the bombing went on day and night for years.

'When we had recovered somewhat,' the chief appeared entranced by the hole, 'we found a woman wandering. She was a fighter but had no weapon or papers. And since she cannot hear or talk, we don't know who she is. Only that she is a simple lost soul.'

'The boy said her name was Phuong.' Khan spoke slowly.

The head man nodded, his face hidden in the shadow afforded by his wide hat.

'That was probably a name young Ng heard from people chattering on the river. In truth, no one knows what her name is. We call her Li. But Ng put two and two together.' The old man gave Khan and Son a gummy pink smile. 'He is a smart little fellow. He will be chief one day. And get this crater filled in.'

'May we meet with this Li? Or Phuong?' Son produced a packet of Marlboros and offered them. 'She might be the woman from our village Khan seeks.' He snapped his lighter into action. 'We have travelled a long way, as you can appreciate.'

The village chief drew in smoke. 'Of course. It would be my pleasure. She is happy here. Like a good child. You will see. Follow me. Then we shall have a drink.'

Khan and Son followed the chief back into the village. The crater, although out of sight, existed as a malign and forceful presence.

'You first, Khan.' Son indicated that Khan should step forward.

The head man stopped outside a well-built hut. Khan could hear the sifting or shifting of rice from within the dim interior. Inside, he could see two women kneeling, working, and one who sat cross-legged, smiling.

'After you, uncle,' Son said cheerfully to the chief. 'We would not like to alarm the ladies with our outstanding handsomeness without warning.'

The chief cackled and limped through the narrow doorway. Khan followed and saw immediately that Phuong was not there. For a moment his gaze rested on a young woman who was undoubtedly beautiful, Johnny feeling, against his will almost, a certain empathy with his enemy.

Khan, he thought, this beautiful one, like beautiful ones everywhere, ain't written into your stars. Your past and present self requires another type of woman; a special woman, a wise woman who might well be one in a million, and is more than just a looker. Otherwise it is not going to work for you, for *us*, either in the real world or the imagined world, and believe me, sport, those two places are not that far apart at all.

Forty-two

Shoey sat slumped in his bunker, rifle across his knees. Its muzzle, still warm, was pointed at the gun slit that now showed a horizontal metre of fragile dove-grey light. Thirsty and half-deafened, he was surrounded by hundreds of empty brass cartridges, unable to register anything except that the battle was over, and he and the boys were alive. His shirt felt like cardboard, stiffened with dried blood back and front.

In the distance there was some sporadic small arms fire but it hardly registered. Perhaps it was each side farewelling the other. Or making a half-hearted promise to return. As Johnny moved his cuts broke open but the desire to sleep overrode everything. He needed to immerse himself, for many reasons, in blankness very soon.

'The rabbits win,' someone said.

Shoey heard the metallic click-click of an empty magazine being ejected, and a fresh one inserted.

'Thank Christ for a well-dug hole and a well-made tank,' someone added.

Johnny lit up then tossed smokes to whoever wanted one. A few were taken, lighters ground into action.

'You blokes are all right.' He didn't know if he'd spoken out loud and didn't care. He had come to the end of something, although he knew he was not safe, or due to go home or take leave. 'I could go a long chopper ride,' he added. 'To anywhere a long way away from here.'

There was a general stirring in the gun pits but no one showed any great inclination to leave their temporary protection. It was like the final morning of a camping trip, Shoey thought. Plenty to do but no one was rushing to get up and do it. Especially when a stray Charlie might be out there, keen to add a final point to a losing scorecard.

So the boys sat, talked, and threw a bit of rubbish out of the holes and when eventually the all-clear was sounded they emerged into the early morning to walk around the silent, smoking mess. The battle was over and they had won it; secured their futures at least for the next ten minutes, although Johnny knew he was stuck in the past with Lex and Barry, without a clue as to how he might escape.

What had he done that made the bullets bend around him? Or render him invisible to Charlie firing point-blank? It was a question he knew he would spend the rest of his life considering and always coming up short.

'Holy shit.' He looked across the base. 'What a mess.'

It was nothing like a fort but merely a piece of flat, bombed-out, scrubby ground reinforced with men and weapons stuck in the middle of a foreign country. Bodies, dressed in black and green, lay around like drunken sleepers needing to be woken. 'We're gunna be busy.'

Johnny knew the Aussies were nothing but a bunch of blow-ins. And when they left, the locals, whichever side they were on, would simply move back in. Or they wouldn't, because they never wanted this bit of trash scrub in the first place. He also knew the boys had fought fantastically. That's what he would take away, the greatness of the men – even if it might not be known to anyone who wasn't present, because already the reality of the place was changing. The sky, now a shining early-morning blue, was being bullied by choppers dropping in and lifting off, the ground alive with new troops with clean shirts and shaved faces. Johnny reckoned it was like watching an army of willing slaves getting down to work.

Men moved out, alive, wounded, and dead. Fresh troops took their places, tasked with securing the base for as long as it was considered useful. Quietly they settled into positions and went to work on strengthening them. And the owners of the raw, terrible memories of the last four nights were already locking them down into a place that they prayed not to revisit.

Johnny tossed empty ammo boxes into a heap, knowing sleep was not yet a possibility. He also knew that the type of sleep he needed was never going to arrive. For a moment he looked to the wire, and wondered about the men he'd just fought. Like wounded dogs, he thought, they would've crawled off into the bush to heal or die. Suffer, he thought. Suffer. You knew what we had and still you tried it.

'Determined little bastards,' said a private called Roughy, looking where Johnny was looking. 'Never seen anything like it, really.' He blew dirt out of the back sight of his M16. 'Never want to again, either. Just quietly.'

The Main Force battalions dragged themselves away through the scarred country of Johnny's mindscape. As they travelled the dead were buried and the wounded were carried, walked, or were dispatched to village clinics or underground hospitals. At various junctions the forces split, to complete their dangerous journeys to distant bases, every fighter knowing they could be attacked from the air, or savaged by ground patrols tracking them like wolves.

Khan could walk only slowly, his smashed arm in a clean sling, his side taped with boiled bandages already showing blood. A small, head-injured fighter carried his AK for him. Overhead, branches imprinted shapes and textures on a sky that was changing from grey to blue, and warming up fast.

'Soon we will be safe,' the small man said to Khan. 'Keep walking, comrade. You are doing well. Not far now.'

Even with morphine, Khan felt as if he was wading deeper into a lake of pain and fever. But it was not possible to stop.

'Thank you, brother. I hope I can keep going.'

Khan knew there would be no rest until he reached a field hospital or the Long Hais. It would be unforgivable if his comrades suffered another blow on his behalf. The only reason for stopping would be to fight, pass out, or die. He trudged on, his mind jellied with pain but stalled around the truth that life could be worse than he thought possible, and people more ruthless.

By now he guessed his best friends would lie in a hole gouged by the Australians, their bodies painfully twisted as if they would writhe forever. Hopefully, the locals would exhume and bury them properly. The boys deserved that, at the very least: to lie peacefully, put to rest with care and prayers.

'If we are winning the war,' Khan murmured, 'I'd hate to see what losing must look like.'

Shoey guessed Khan's thoughts to be true, or true enough. He had seen Charlie smashed senseless but there was no sign of a white flag and there never would be. Their spirit reached him, entered his life, and demanded his respect – which he grudgingly gave. Otherwise he doubted he would ever find a path leading to any sort of an acceptable resolution. Declaring peace was a long and painful process. Being at peace might prove to be the most difficult journey of all.

Shoey was hauled into the chopper. Gratefully, half-stunned, he sat behind the door gunner, welcoming the buffeting breeze as the Huey lifted and went, nose down like a hunting dog on the run. Skimming broken trees, the aircraft accelerated then rose, banking hard, the fire base spiralling away like a flicked card.

'My bloody *shout*,' said a rifleman called Marco, who reminded Shoey of the freckle-faced kid on *Mad* magazine. 'Thank *Christ* we're outta that hole. Good luck to the bastards in it.'

Johnny rested his head against vibrating metal, feeling himself bathed in the khaki-green glow of the men around him and the blessedness of the wide-open sky. Below, the country tilted as the pilot strove for altitude, the closest thing to heaven Johnny had ever experienced.

'A-bloody-men,' someone said, 'to that.'

Khan could see the Long Hai Hills in the distance, pale and low, like a winter cloud. Then he found he was no longer walking with the battalion. Instead he was led down a tiny track by a village man, and a tall, silent woman dressed in black.

'What's going on?' he asked. 'Where is my AK?' He plunged around. 'My rifle? Where is it?'

'I have it, brother,' the village man said. 'Relax. We will look after you.'

The woman's hand was on his shoulder. 'Don't worry. We are close now. But please keep quiet.'

Khan accepted this. 'Of course, sister. I'm sorry.'

Ten minutes later he was taken into a village house, to watch as a wooden chest was pushed aside to reveal a trapdoor built into the dirt floor.

'You will be looked after.' The woman in black spoke crisply. 'There is a doctor, medicine, and an operating theatre. Brother Tan will help you down the ladder.'

Slowly Khan descended into the tunnel. Daylight faded, the smell of dirt filled his nose as he was enveloped by air thick and warm. Into the earth I go, he thought. Again.

You're one lucky bastard, Khan, Shoey thought, that I knew there were hospitals in those tunnels and medical people to help. Otherwise you might have died in the bush of gangrene – not that it would've worried me in the least, at the time.

Forty-three

Johnny hit Melbourne at lunchtime and was lost by one o'clock. By two o'clock he'd asked for directions three times and by four he had arrived in Black Rock. At a service station on the Nepean Highway he put a few bucks worth of juice in the ute then spent ten minutes in the grimy bathroom, the floor littered with used paper towel, sprucing himself up in a dirty mirror.

'Rough,' he muttered, sticking a comb in his back pocket. 'Enough.'

He walked out with clean teeth, a smooth face, and no plan but to find Lex's place and knock on the door. Standing by the ute, he buttoned up his last clean shirt, and slid a new pack of smokes into his left chest pocket. I have my doubts about this, he thought. Ten times over.

But still he went.

The beautiful young woman in the granary was not the one who might be called Phuong. She was the chief's eldest daughter and did not look at Khan, although she did seem shyly interested in Son. The woman supposedly called Phuong was older, heavier, and unremarkable apart from a permanent saintly smile. At first Khan found this disturbing but soon saw it as a blessing. This simple person appeared happy. And that was certainly unusual for anyone who had been anywhere in the vicinity of a B-52 bomb strike. True, Johnny agreed. That is one nail you hit on the head.

'Good morning.' Khan bowed to the women. 'You are working and we do not mean to disturb you. My friend Son and I are looking for a woman from our village who fought in the war. But this sister—' he inclined his head towards the smiling woman who ground something, perhaps lemongrass, in a small bowl, 'is not that woman. Please go on with your work. Thank you for caring for her.'

After leaving the granary, Khan was surprised to find that it was the simple woman's smile he remembered rather than the beautiful woman who had robbed him of his breath.

'The sister you call Li . . .' Khan spoke to the chief, who was happily smoking another of Son's cigarettes, working his leathery cheeks hard. 'She is happy. Thank you.'

The head man nodded. 'It's a miraculous tragedy, I guess.'

Khan nodded. 'Yes, you are right. A miracle and a tragedy.'

Son lit up. 'The war is over,' he said. 'Thank goodness.'

'Not for a while yet.' The village elder poked his cigarette towards the jungle that surrounded them like a hedge. 'When that hole's gone we might be getting close. Until then, if you fall in it, you'll still break your neck.'

There's always a chance of falling in a hole, Shoey thought. Or falling by the wayside or off a cliff; all could do you in, the only difference being that one way took a fair bit longer than the others.

The house Shoey pulled up at was a low white weatherboard with a white picket fence. It was set in a busy garden of small trees, flowerbeds, and a circle of lawn featuring a birdbath. The sound of a piano reached out through an open window, drawing Johnny on up a curved stone path. As he walked he thought about Lex living here as a kid, a high school surfie, a lazy uni prick, a reluctant army conscript, and finally he could think no further except that it seemed impossible this neat suburban house, and the family who lived in it, could ever be connected to that distant ugly war – but it was, in the worst of ways.

'Breathe, Shoey-boy, breathe,' he murmured, and did so deeply, smelling the cool scent of well-watered plants. 'A smoke as soon as you get this done.'

Johnny knocked, standing on a patio sprinkled with damp white petals that reminded him of paper swans his sister used to fold up out of drawing paper. The piano stopped and footsteps started, heading to the door somewhat indirectly. A shadow passed glass and a key was turned. At first all Shoey saw was a slender arm, bare legs, white sandals, and light green carpet. Then he saw a blonde girl, blue-eyed, maybe nineteen years old, in a white sun frock patterned with dark blue birds.

'Hey,' he said, realising she was definitely what his mother would've described as *lovely*. 'Ah, I hope I've got the right house. I'm looking for the, er, Lexingtons.'

The girl was lightly tanned and freckled. She had long hair that brushed her arms and was, Johnny decided, certainly attractive in a gentle, lyrical, musical way.

'Yes, you've got the right house.' She smiled, perhaps a little puzzled. 'I'm Francesca.'

It was the right place. Johnny's throat tightened.

'I'm Johnny Shoebridge.' He spoke as if he was quite sure this was the case, and that he knew exactly who he was, and what he was doing here on her doorstep. 'I knew Lex. We were mates. In the, er – over there. In Vietnam.'

For a long moment the girl searched his face. For what, Johnny didn't know, but as she was Lex's sister and Lex was his best mate, he waited and would've waited for hours until she was finished.

'You're Johnny Shoebridge?'

He inclined his head. 'I am. Yeah.' He managed to skim up a fleeting grin. 'I believe. Yes. At last sighting.'

'You've driven all the way down from the country to here?' The girl blinked, tears building in dark eyelashes until they spilled. And still she held the door, staring at him. 'That's wonderful. Thank you so much for coming. I'm so glad to see you.'

'Well. Good.' Johnny managed a smile and managed not to reach for his smokes. Just. He didn't know what to make of the silences, the words spoken, or whether his presence had created a kind of happiness or only more devastation. 'I wanted to see you. You and your family. Your mum and dad. Tell you things. About Lex. How good he was. What a great bloke. How it kinda was. That sort of thing.' Did he know how it was? Yes, he did; it was beyond bloody terrible but Lex was far away and above all that stuff now.

Francesca Lexington stepped forward and hugged Johnny, pressing her wet cheek to his shoulder. Johnny felt something steady and settle. He put his arms around her. She understood something and so did he. She knew where he'd been and what he'd been through. Or she understood because she knew the truth – and the truth marooned them, each on some lost lonely island of their own.

Francesca stepped back. She brushed her hair away from her face then opened the door about as wide as it would go. Across a hallway Johnny saw a lounge room with comfortable-looking speckled white chairs, a grey couch, and a gold clock on a white mantelpiece where there were framed photos he knew he did not want to look at.

'Come in, Johnny.' Francesca smiled. She was a truly attractive girl. 'Mum'll be home soon. She's just around the corner at school. She's a music teacher. I'll make coffee. Or tea, of course.'

Johnny went in. The house was quiet and smelled of flowers. There were small watercolour paintings, some of beaches and boat sheds, on every wall. Lex's sister stopped in the doorway of a bright kitchen with a black and white lino floor. The blinds were white and there were clean plates in a dish rack. Again Francesca smiled at Johnny, Johnny smiled at her, and somehow it made it all seem just a whole lot worse.

Khan existed in a world of murmuring shadows and dark, sweating walls. People came and went, silhouetted, like messengers from another world. His arm had been removed and the wound in his side cleaned and closed. Slowly he was recovering, with the help of antibiotics liberated from a doctor's surgery down south.

'We are worms,' a fellow patient said, a fighter who had lost both ears, his blistered face yellow in the weak light. 'Very lucky worms.'

'That's true.' Khan thought of Trung and Thang. 'There are worse holes to be in, that's for sure.' He looked at the ceiling and the hand-sawn timber supports. 'So what happens to us next?'

The burned fighter's glance slowly climbed the ladder that led to the upper levels of the tunnel system.

'That's the question, brother,' he said. 'That is the question.'

It's quite possible you get the hell bombed out of you, Johnny thought, because there's nothing we liked more than turning your underground refuges into cities of the dead with a few tons of high-powered explosive.

Johnny drove away from Lex's house as he'd driven away from Barry's, feeling as if he'd escaped but promising to return. He also knew that when he did return, it was because he'd agreed to shoulder a two-way responsibility of love for the rest of his life. Just like that bastard Khan, he thought, because we are probably more alike than anybody cares to admit – which is a thought I may just keep to myself, for the sake of national security.

Johnny stopped at an intersection jammed with Holdens, Fords, and Valiants. Left, right, or straight ahead? He had no idea.

'Not lost,' he muttered. 'But close.'

Forty-four

Heat hovered over the jungle like an iron lid as Shoey and the Delta boys laboured up a steep ruined slope. The bombed-out hill reminded him of an exploded cake. Smashed trees leant like broken candles, the churned dirt chocolate-brown. An air of tension hovered. Constantly the skipper was on the radio as he scanned the patchy country below. The sound of a light plane, unseen, buzzed like a mosquito that would not leave.

'Somethin's cookin'.' Young Pete stopped to wipe his glasses. 'Just hope it ain't us. Rice-a-Riso with little Pete for puddin'.'

Word was passed along to take cover on the brow of the hill. M6os were to be deployed. There was to be no smoking or brew-ups. Johnny ploughed on through the mud. His shirt was plastered to his back. A smell of decay held close to the ground. Insects hummed. A corporal pointed to a log that oozed sap like blood, Shoey and Pete settling behind it, resting their rifles. The sound of the Cessna Bird Dog had been replaced by an ominous, distant, heavy-duty rumble.

'See that little village down there?' The skipper pointed. Johnny could see a cluster of thatched houses set among trees. A muddy water buffalo stood in a muddy pen. 'Intel confirms a bunker system. It's about to get a belting from the space cowboys from Steelhorse.'

The rumble intensified. Like everyone else, Shoey looked to the east. In seconds, a pair of Phantoms, arrow-like, passed low over the hill, thundering, obliterating every other sound. Continuing on, they released black sticks that tumbled harmlessly towards the ground. For a few seconds nothing happened. Then the hill shook and a fireball engulfed the huts and jungle. The boys cheered.

Clouds of oily black smoke shot through with bright orange fire climbed lazily. The Phantoms circled, untouchable.

'More.' Pete inclined his head. 'Look.'

Two more fighter-bombers circled, set themselves then completed bombing-runs and again the broken, smoking ground bucked and jolted. More noise. More fire. More smoke. More cheers.

'Cop that.' Johnny felt a sinister sense of elation, a measure of revenge that would never be enough. 'Our mates are bigger than yours.' He watched the Phantoms climb away. 'Good luck down there, Charlie. You're gunna need it.'

Khan sensed the jets. Or maybe he heard them. Or felt them through the bedrock. Or perhaps the terror preceded the bombs on a shockwave of Johnny's intent. The raid was beyond belief. Perhaps people screamed but there was nothing Khan could hear within a noise so great it tossed him into a wall. Sections of the ceiling gave way. Supports fell across the beds and the air disappeared. Then – nothing.

Now – something.

Khan was elsewhere. Framed in the broken sky was the armour-plated belly of a gunship. He could see mini-guns spitting and all he could do was lie like a grub in an open nest. With his face hidden in the crook of his elbow he waited until time re-established itself, and the crushing noise miraculously lifted. He looked up, wondering if he might be the last Vietnamese alive on earth. Or already dead.

Nearly gotcha, Shoey thought. Again, you're lucky I know how these things work; that not everyone who should die, does. And that you have as much right to live as me, if the truth be told, which is what I am here for – because I have no time for lies or liars.

Forty-five

Shoey peered hard through a wet windscreen as he tried to navigate the rainy Carlton streets. Was it Cardigan Place, Street, Road, or Lane that he was looking for? At every intersection, people crossed the road as riskily as rabbits, and trams passed through his peripheral vision like green whales. The place was awash. There were sheets of water wherever he looked.

'Holy *hell*,' he muttered, swinging around corners, caught in evening peak hour like a leaf in a stream. 'This is bloody madness.'

He gave it another ten minutes before pulling over into a tight parking space between two trees. Killing the motor, he sat, letting the windscreen fog up and the world go by. All he could see were brick cottages with verandas cluttered with bicycles, loaded washing lines, and broken couches. Girls passed wearing duffel coats and black stockings, the sight of them stirring him enough to pull the keys out of the ignition. If he was going to find Jilly then he'd better get to a phone box and make the call.

Without any great confidence, Johnny set off towards a wide road that thumped with traffic. Within fifty yards he saw there were more cafes than in the whole of Taralia, but not one public phone. The place was filled with damp students and lorded over by Italians and Greeks wearing tight daks and gold chains. In his army shirt, a southerly wind riffling his crew cut, Johnny felt gawky, way out of place, and aware that he was creating an undercurrent of silent disapproval. He decided to take a break and selected a café big enough where he hoped he might go unnoticed.

'Coffee, *signore*?' A short bloke tucked in behind a red coffee machine lifted a stubbly chin. 'Best in Lygon Street.'

Johnny ran the tape measure over the guy and was given the once-over in return.

'Yeah, why not?' He needed a moment to think. 'Where do I sit?'

The guy laughed, cupping a stainless steel jug in hairy hands.

'As close to the best-lookin' girl you can get.' He flicked loose a handle and bashed out coffee grounds as if he was using a hammer. 'Bloody hell, mate. Where you been?'

'Deep in the jungle,' Johnny said easily. 'Deep in the jungle.' He spotted a table. 'I'll be over there.' He dragged out his wallet. The man ignored it.

'Pay later, *signore*. Pay later.'

Shoey sat at a small table. Five minutes later a girl with sooty eye make-up delivered him a creamy-looking coffee that, with two sugars added, he enjoyed. Poking a couple of fingers down beside his smokes, searching for Jilly's number, he came up with nothing but sand. I am now, he figured, even more stuffed than I was ten minutes ago.

As it got dark, Johnny ordered spaghetti and a carafe of the red wine everyone else was drinking. The pasta was rich, hot, and strange but it hit the spot. The wine he judged as shithouse but downed it anyway. Then he ordered more wine, accepting the fact that finding Jill, Jill's street, house, or phone number was impossible at this time.

So he sat and let the night slow-fall around him. A dark-haired girl, more of a kid, he thought, turned to him from another table.

'Are you in the army, mate?'

Because Johnny had been drinking a lot, and the girl was young and sounded curious rather than angry, he presented her with a grin.

'I was.' He filled his glass with wine the colour of blood. 'I was in the Foreign Legion.'

This kept her quiet and, Shoey decided, was about as close to the truth as she was ever going to get.

283

Khan and Son were back on the river. For a while they travelled in silence, a few sampans gliding past on the wide brown waterway.

'We are not out of luck.' Son's face was shaded by a traditional woven hat that he wore as if to please or amuse Khan. 'It is our turn for a change in fortune.'

Khan thought about the nature of luck. Was he lucky? Was Son lucky? Was the smiling girl luckier than the unconscious woman upstream? Who was lucky and who was not?

'We are not *un*-lucky, Son,' Khan said. 'Are we?'

'No.' Son took the boat out into midstream. 'We are rowing our own boat, Khan, and that is great. Now, my friend, there's a village in the marshes where another wounded woman, supposedly from the north, supposedly called Phuong, lives. The place is strange and dangerous but I'm known there.' Son smiled. 'Perhaps they do not consider me a bad communist, Khan. Perhaps I do not see them as one thing or another, either, but only as people.'

'They're not the enemy, anyway,' Khan said, feeling quite within his rights to make this statement. 'The country is now united.'

Son put in a few slow, thoughtful strokes. 'Well, they aren't the enemy anymore. So the story goes.'

There are enemies everywhere, boys, Johnny thought. Just as there are friends and allies. Of course, this can change depending on who you run into and when, how you view yesterday, and what you hope for tomorrow.

Forty-six

Johnny, fairly drunk, wove through a wet and windy grid of Carlton streets, hoping to stumble upon Cardigan Place or Street or whatever it was called. In an effort to orientate himself, to think straight, he took shelter in the narrow tiled doorway of a small hardware shop. In the window was an amateurish display of bamboo rakes, folded overalls, gumboots, camping chairs, plastic cases of Stanley screwdrivers, and an arrangement of red Victorinox Swiss pocketknives, blades open.

'Ah,' Johnny said, sitting on the step, folding his arms, 'just what I don't need. A knife.'

For a while he watched cars pushing on up the road and listened to the sounds of a soaked city. There was hardly anyone around. For a bloody big place, he thought, everyone seemed to go to bed mighty early.

'Newsflash, folks!' he yelled into the dark. 'We lost the war! Charlie got the chocolates!' Fumbling, he lit a smoke, and took a drag. 'Your taxes at work! God save America!' His head, he felt, was either completely full or totally empty, he couldn't work out which. 'No one fuckin' cares anyway,' he muttered. 'I don't.'

The cracks were starting to widen now. They were opening up wherever he looked. He was by himself, walking point in tiger country with no map, no weapon, no back-up, no escape route, and no plan – and it did not get much worse than that.

In the shade of the only tree in the marsh village, Khan saw a woman in white. She sat with her back to him and her head covered.

'On your way, friend.' Gently Son pushed Khan forward with fingers in the middle of his back. 'I will wait here. Take my best wishes and highest hopes.'

Khan went forward over the bare ground. 'Sister Phuong.' He spoke gently from a polite distance. 'My name is Khan and I am looking for a friend from the north—'

The woman turned and Khan stopped, seeing that she had been shockingly burned. Her face appeared to have melted, the flesh healed in sagging pink pools. He could also see that she was blind, and that the burns extended down her throat until they were hidden by the white silk of her *ao dai*. Her hands were twisted and most of her fingers were missing. Napalm, he thought. No, worse than that. White phosphorous.

'Khan?' She focused on the source of the voice. 'Khan, did you say?' Her voice was a croaking whisper. 'From Lang Song in the north?'

'Yes.' Khan found he had sunk to his knees. This woman was Phuong. Yes, she was injured beyond belief but it *was* her, his great friend, his love, his comrade-in-arms, living in this strange, strange place. Carefully he took hold of one of her hands. 'It is me, Khan. Yes.'

Phuong turned over his hand. With a single finger she traced the hard skin of his palm.

'I am not the Phuong you used to know.' She raised her ruined face. 'I think that's obvious.'

'Yes, I see,' Khan answered. 'I am not the same Khan, either. No one is the same and no place is the same. But Son and I will take you home. If you would like to come.'

Phuong did not relinquish Khan's hand. 'The people here have been very kind. I owe them, and many others, my life. But I would very much like to go home with you and Son.' She stopped talking, as if to listen to a breath of wind that moved through the marsh grasses. 'And to see Trung and Thang. That would be beautiful.'

'Yes, it would be.' Khan felt himself lifted, just for a moment. 'It would be the most perfect thing I can imagine.'

Johnny felt this was true. Things like this did happen. People who were lost were found, especially if others had not ever given up looking for them. It happened and so it should. And he was sure it had.

Forty-seven

The 727 accelerated for take-off, a rapid rumbling in Shoey's stomach that was suddenly replaced by a shifting weightlessness as the world dropped away. The big jet banked determinedly to the south and the boys cheered. Young Pete threw himself across a grinning soldier to shout at a sunlit window.

'Sayonara, Charlie! See yers later, suckers! We are *goin'* home!'

Khan was helped from the trapdoor into the early morning by the new doctor who had glowing golden skin. She handed him his AK, complete with bayonet. The weapon had been cleaned, oiled, and loaded.

'Good luck, Khan.' Her fingertips rested softly on his arm. 'You have a long journey in front of you. Please accept our thanks for your sacrifices on behalf of the people. You know which way to go, don't you?'

'Yes, I do, doctor. Thank you.' The cool air caressed Khan's face. It made him smile. The clearing was green, loosely bordered by tall bamboo, as restful on his eyes as if he was looking at a pool of rainwater. 'Thank you.' He bowed and smiled. The small pack he carried felt good on his back. His AK he cradled like a sleeping baby. 'I shall go north, sister. And home.'

I wish you luck, Johnny thought, you one-armed wreck, because the fighting is over and although your story might not be exactly true, it is true enough. And at this point, as we get older, perhaps we can hope that how things should be might actually be how things are.

Johnny sat in the shadowed doorway and lit his last cigarette. A grey drizzle drifted, adding a sense of desolation to the darkness, diluting the lights until they seemed to shine only in puddles. The place was not silent but it was quiet.

'Well,' he murmured, sensing that the old buildings opposite offered fellowship for those whom the world was rapidly passing by. 'Here I am. Like a shag on a rock. Except I can't fly.'

The cigarette he was smoking felt like a fuse and his head a box of dynamite. He didn't know what would happen when he finished it or where he would go. All he hoped was that he didn't scare the women who occasionally walked past, because scaring anyone was the last thing in the world he wanted to do.

'I'm harmless,' he murmured. 'To everybody but me.'

He looked at the stuff in the window, the place so badly lit it was as if no one expected or cared whether anything would ever be bought or sold. For long seconds he gazed at the pale tines of the bamboo rakes, a weight suddenly falling on him as the silver blades of the red pocketknives began to spin, and he found himself right back in the bloody middle of the second fire base battle, watching a terrible silent movie, a retreating Main Force fighter clear in the sights of his SLR.

In slow-motion, in the light of a magnesium flare, Johnny remembered firing twice, saw the fighter's arm burst at the elbow and a fistful of flesh fly from his side. In the white air an AK spun, bayonet glinting, a Russian AKM bayonet, and Johnny knew – he *absolutely* knew that he had not dreamed or imagined this – that the fighter he'd shot was the real, true-to-life, enemy bastard Khan.

Johnny remembered the man kneeling, right arm hanging, elbow blown apart, blood pouring from his side as if from a split hose. He remembered sighting on the fighter's bowed head but he had pulled the shot, deliberately fired low and wide, knowing he'd made the decision not to kill a wounded man, and that *was* how it had been.

That was how it had been.

Yes, that was how it had been.

'*Farrrk.*' Johnny slumped into the corner and sucked hard on his smoke. 'I *spared* you, you prick.' He smiled widely at the dark. 'I *did*. You don't own me, sport. I *spared* you.' He took the last hot drag of his last Marlboro and flicked the butt. 'We're even. I'm okay. I'm all right. I *spared* you.' Tears of happiness, or relief, or both, spilled over his fingers, leaving him gulping like a kid in the corner of a cubbyhouse in Taralia a long time ago. 'I did not dream that.' Johnny shook his head in stunned wonder. 'I did not dream that.' His voice tailed away to a whisper. 'That is true.'

Maybe he woke up. Maybe he'd never been asleep. Maybe he'd been away. Maybe he hadn't moved, but Johnny was somewhat surprised to find he was still in the draughty doorway of a small hardware shop in Carlton, in Melbourne, it was still raining, and it was probably the same night. Without a single thought in his head he watched a girl in a duffel coat the colour of Indian ink draw level on the footpath. She stopped, holding the hood to the sides of her face with pale hands.

'Is that you, Johnny Shoebridge?'

It was the second time for the day, he realised, that he'd been asked this rather difficult question.

'Yeah, it's me, Jilly.' He stood, hoping with each step taken that when he got to the footpath she'd be real, and she was. Between them, instantly, was some kind of fine musical humming. 'That was good work, kid.' For once he couldn't help but smile. 'How'd you—'

Jilly let her hood fall back, misty rain sifting down through the silver light of the street to dampen her nose and cheeks. Then she laughed, eyes shining, and circled his wrist with firm wet fingers.

'I saw your stupid ute.' She shrugged as if she was not at all surprised that this had happened. 'So I went looking. And here you are. Bingo.'

Johnny could only agree. Everything about her that he had loved was there and strengthened.

'Yep. Here I am. Bingo.' He found himself holding her, and knew he had made it across a certain line. 'You did well, mate. Real well. Even in the rain and dark.'

'Even in the rain and dark.' She laughed, and it was as if the two of them were grade-sixers again, folk dancing under the old white flagpole at Taralia State. 'So. Coming back to my house? It's just up there.' She pointed to silver tram tracks that crested a rise. 'It's got an open fire and a tin roof. I'm sure you'll like it.'

'I'm sure I will.' He took hold of her hand and brought it forward and up. 'Lead the way.'

And away, together, they walked.

About the author

David Metzenthen lives in and loves Melbourne. He was an advertising copywriter and a builder's labourer before turning to fiction. He tries to surf, fly-fish, and is a keen environmentalist. The natural world is where he likes to spend his time, and he endeavours to write books that are thoughtful and well-crafted. David is married to Fiona, has two children, two parrots, and a great Irish Terrier dog.